Project Pardus

Elizabeth F. Shearly

Also By Elizabeth F. Shearly

PROJECT PARDUS

ELIZABETH F. SHEARLY

Content Notes

Explicit sex scenes, liberal use of obscenities, parental emotional abuse of adult child, burns, alien genocide, off-page torture, confinement.

Please see the book's web page at www.elizabethshearly.ca for detailed content notes.

Chapter 1

Zando recrossed his ankles on the edge of the display of dull warning lights and went back to scrolling on his screen. Only one more hour till the end of his shift. So much for exciting new horizons. Out his tiny viewport, the distant stars barely even flickered. But something flickered beside his heel.

A little red light blinked steadily. *Weird.* He dropped his feet off the console and leaned forward in his chair. Prox alarm? But where was the alarm part? Plus, this was a space station. The prox alarm was a vestige from the spaceship days—

Lights blinked on faster than he could identify them, and then they were gone. Not that the lights blinked out. The *station* blinked out.

I ran over the numbers again. Still nothing. Not no trend or nothing conclusive. Nothing. The space station had been there, on course for its colony location, and then it was gone. No, *gone* implied that it went somewhere. It was replaced by a patch of space with nothing in it. But even that would have been suspicious. Space is full of junk. No, this was...a perfectly normal patch of junk-filled space containing no trace of anything remarkable at all. If this project going to make my career, I needed *something*.

Lancaster ducked under the curved bulkhead into my lab/office. "Hey Carolina. Tell me you have something for me," he said.

"I do not," I said. "Nothing new anyway. There was a station there, and now there isn't."

Lancaster grimaced. "Okay, we can still hang on here."

"What does that mean?"

"The council wants to pass this project to Miller. Thinks it's outside of our capacity."

The Council for Humanity's Universal Scientific Interests, or CHUSI—I bet someone was proud of that acronym—was designed to provide funding for all of humanity's scientific research projects. But they had become the arbiters of which projects lived and which died a painful death from lack of funding.

And they were going to take this one. What a waste of the favour I'd called in at CHUSI to get a hold of it. Miller's department would bury anything they found under stacks of *Top Secret* stamps so deep they'd reach us here in the Oort Cloud all the way from their offices on Luna.

"What do you need from me?" I said. "How long do we have?"

"Zero," said Lancaster.

"Zero what?"

"Anything. I'm on my way to the meeting where they're going to order the data transfer."

Shit. No, no, maybe..."Ordering the data transfer is one thing. Transferring the data is something else. If I'm not here when you get back, you can't have me transfer anything. Besides, primary data gathering at the site of the anomaly will be required to ascertain its source, supervisor."

"Good, fine, take the—" A lightbulb seemed to click on in Lancaster's brain and then immediately go out.

It hit me a second later. Our clunky old research vessel was gone on a long-term voyage. To keep this project, I would have to be on my way by the time he came out of his hearing.

"I'll take one of the hoppers." It's wouldn't be *fun* to cram into a ship that tiny for days, but it would get me there.

Lancaster was already shaking his head. "They're all away." He rubbed the bridge of his nose, knocking his glasses askew. "Take *Lepton*."

"And what crew? Your cruiser is fancy, but she doesn't fly herself, and I have to sleep."

"Get Yarrow to go with you. Look, Carolina, I have to go. There's no time to fight about it," said Lancaster.

"Yes, go. I'll handle it." Handle telling my ex that we were going on a weeks-long voyage alone together? But losing this project to Miller was not an option. Space stations don't just disappear. If I didn't get a paper out of this, I might never get another project. My parents wouldn't tap their CHUSI buddy for me again.

Lancaster ducked back out, and the door shut with a whoosh, along with the air leaving my lungs.

All evidence pointed to...nothing. Lepton wasn't equipped with the proper instruments to sweep the former location of Pardus Station, so going into the field would only buy us time rather than turn up any more useful data. But the on-board server was top-notch, and

I could continue my research effectively from there, so time might be good enough.

I'd run by my quarters and grab my stuff—but I had to get Yarrow on board with this plan first. Without him, I wasn't going anywhere.

Yarrow liked to keep his door open, so I knocked on the frame.

"There's a reason I keep it open, Carolina. The set of vibrations from a knock are irritating."

"Sorry," I said.

Yarrow fixed his blue eyes on me, his blue skin mottling in suspicion. He crossed one set of arms over his chest, his other set still typing.

"Please proceed. I'm not currently processing this information, simply recording it."

The typing was distracting but, apparently, only to me.

"Lancaster wants us to take *Lepton* into the field."

"Presumably, this pertains to your research. I'm happy to assist. When do we cast off?"

"Now," I said. "Or as soon as the data transfer to the ship's server is finished."

Yarrow stopped typing and swivelled his chair to face me. His antennae waved in the air. "Two things. Tell me about them."

This was part of the reason we broke up. He knew I was worried, and he wouldn't leave well enough alone until he got to the bottom of it. Since speed was of the essence this time, I just dumped it on him. He'd asked for it. "Lancaster is being told, as we speak, to order all my data transferred to Miller." *Where I'll never see it again.* "You and I are about to spend several days alone on a spaceship, and we just broke up like two weeks ago."

"And that makes you anxious?"

"It doesn't make you anxious?"

Yarrow shrugged. "I don't believe we view relationships in the same way. I will do my utmost to quell your anxiety. I'll meet you at *Lepton*'s gate."

How many times had I wished I had those pheromone antennae so I could sense Yarrow's emotions? However many it was, add once more. Okay. We were colleagues, and I could act professional.

I nodded. "Let me know if you want me to sign any requisitions."

"Of course."

"Any alimentation requests?"

"Duplicating yours should be sufficient," said Yarrow. That's all he'd ever told me about his sustenance requirements, no matter how much I insisted I wanted to make something special for him.

"Right," I said. No time for angst. Time for getting all the paperwork sorted out, laying in the provisions, checking the data transfer, and—shit—letting my parents know I was heading out for a while.

I typed out the requisition request for a probe—in case the lab manager was feeling generous—on the way back to my quarters and tossed my duffle on my bed as I punched the button to call my parents.

My mom picked up on the fourth ring and kept glancing at something behind the camera as I told her what was up.

"That's great, sweetie. Sounds like your career is humming along," she said as soon as I paused for breath.

"Yeah, this project is high profile," I said.

My dad stooped into the video frame. "Hi, honey! Finally going into the field, eh?"

"Yes, really soon. It was a little last minute—"

"Great! Good thing we got you a real project. Don't want to be stuck as an assistant the rest of your life."

"Yes, I really appreciate your help with CHUSI—" I broke off as they talked to each other too quietly for me to hear.

"Sorry, honey, we have to go," said my mom. "We're meeting some friends for lunch, and we have to get ready."

"Okay, sounds like fun!" I said, forcing a smile.

"See you when you get back," said my dad.

My wave at the camera was half hearted, but damned if they would notice. My screen flicked off.

Did I need to tell anyone else? My colleagues would find out through the grapevine. I turned over a couple names in my mind, but not hearing from me for a few weeks wouldn't worry anyone. The Oort Research Centre wasn't exactly heavily populated, but it wasn't isolated by any means. Not like Pardus Station, out there in deep space, on its slow trajectory across the Orion Arm. Former trajectory, I should say.

Out between way stations, there were genuinely no witnesses. The only reason anyone noticed that the sprawling station had disappeared was that a cruiser had been scheduled to resupply it on its way by. Last contact had been weeks before, so we didn't even have a firm timeline on the disappearance. The cruiser had taken some readings and sent them to us here at Oort, since our focus was on interstellar vacuum research. The data had trickled down to my desk through a series of rejections from busier folks with enough clout to delegate. I doubted very much that they'd even glanced at the data; we'd all assumed Pardus Station's trajectory had been altered. I'd been the one to establish the station's disappearance, and I'd secured the funding to look into it. My background in ship wakes had served me well in proving that the station hadn't altered course. A couple days ago, I'd submitted an interim report outlining my findings, and already Miller and the council had pounced. But this one was mine, and I intended to take full advantage of it.

I crammed my clothes into my duffle and headed for *Lepton*.

Yarrow was already waiting for me when I got to the gate. He leaned on the scratched bulkhead, antennae brushing the ceiling, and my footsteps echoed on the metal plating as I paced the few steps along the hallway.

Sophia and Salaam emerged from the hatch.

"Supplies laid in. You're all fuelled up," said Sophia.

"The preignition checks are all done, and your probe is in place. She's shipshape for you, Carolina," said Salaam.

"Thanks for doing this," I said. "Lancaster would have cried at the thought of anyone else prepping his baby."

"No problem," said Salaam.

I held out my wrist, and Sofia slid on a payment fob. "I've approved you to expense some supplies, but don't go overboard."

Once they were gone, Yarrow and I stared at each other. It was going to be this awkward the whole time, wasn't it? But it was either take Yarrow, who could literally pilot in his sleep, or don't go at all and lose the project. Of course, he seemed to know exactly what I was thinking. When I turned to him, he raised the ridges above his eyes, a gesture he'd picked up from humans.

I nodded, resettled my duffle bag on my shoulder, and brushed by him through the hatch. How did he keep his jumpsuit so soft? Not appropriate co-worker thoughts.

I caressed the walnut trim on the smooth white bulkhead as I passed the living area. I'd been on this ship once before, along with Lancaster's other post-docs, just so he could show it off. I detoured into the main cabin to dump my bag—on the real bed—and double-checked the supplies in the galley. It's not that I didn't trust Sophia, but if my life depended on something, I should know for sure that it was in order.

When I climbed the narrow staircase to the bridge at the stern of the ship, Yarrow already sat at the controls.

"I have completed the preflight checklist," he said.

"And the fuel levels?"

"Full. We can stop tomorrow and replenish our fuel tanks should be more than adequate for the voyage."

"Then let's set in our course and get detached," I said and buckled into the co-pilot's chair.

"If you'd like to take us out—"

I waved him away. "No thanks. I'll take a shift later."

"As you wish."

Chapter 2

It used to impress Miller that CHUSI met in a real boardroom, not a virtual one. Their supplicants, of course, called in. This one was from the Oort Research Centre, and they'd got their hands on some data that could prove...volatile. Academic types always thought they were the exception, that he wouldn't be able to confiscate their precious work. But he was good at his job.

The harried-looking guy on the screen was still talking. "Unfortunately, the researcher in question, Dr. Carolina Dawn, is currently on a voyage to expand the dataset."

Why did they always run? He beckoned his "protection" and headed for his ship.

E verything went smoothly until we got to the way station.

I was setting up a few more analyses on the base data when Yarrow's message that we were about to pull in to refuel popped up over my chart. I waved away his communication. Maybe a different distribution would make some kind of trend apparent? But then, no distribution or statistical wizardry could ever fix the dearth of actual data. I drummed my fingers on the edge of the desk and wriggled in my chair.

Finally, I retreated to the galley for a snack. Maybe we should top up our rations as well, just in case. The way station might even have something Yarrow would like. That was up to him, though. It wasn't my responsibility to surprise him with a nice meal. Not that it had ever been my responsibility per se...

The comms clicked on.

"Carolina, please confer with me on the bridge," said Yarrow.

What could he possibly need my help with? Docking with a way station was hardly rocket science, and Yarrow was an experienced pilot, way more experienced than I was. We had never talked much about his life before joining our research team, but he'd been nothing but capable in the time I'd known him. We'd taken a vacation once out to the asteroid belt...

I shook away the memories and stepped lightly up to the bridge.

"They requested you specifically," said Yarrow.

"What could a way station need to talk to the captain for?" I said.

"Not the captain. You," said Yarrow.

I frowned and dropped into the co-pilot's seat, then popped a headset over my ears. "Dawn here," I said.

"Ms. Dawn," crackled the voice through my headphones, "please dock at gate three. Don't bother trying to initiate a chase, as we are fully aware of the capabilities of your ship, and it would be futile."

My heart pounded, and I whipped the headset off. "Who in the hell are you talking to, Yarrow?"

"I hailed docking control, and they passed me over to these…officials."

I tapped my fingers near the controls. "They didn't say what they want? Or even who they are?" They must be from CHUSI. What could be worth chasing us down for? "Slow down, but try to seem like you're complying."

"You're considering not complying?" said Yarrow, his antennae waving wildly.

I popped the headset back on and didn't answer him. "Who do I have the pleasure of speaking with?" I said.

"I'm a CHUSI representative. You have been ordered to destroy all copies of the data currently residing on your ship. Dr. Lancaster claimed it was impossible to retrieve you." I could practically hear the official's eye roll.

"We actually weren't planning to stop," I said.

"Yes, you were," said the official. "Your crew member hailed docking control. Ms. Dawn, please just—"

There was a babble in the background, and Yarrow stared at me and waved at the controls. Should we run? What was this data worth to us? If this was a council representative, they couldn't actually detain us, though they could enforce the order to wipe the data. Nothing was stopping us from going to gather more, though; that would require some kind of permit that they could never have cleared by now.

The official came back on, but I interrupted him.

"Gate three. We'll come in now," I said.

"Thank you, Ms. Dawn," said the official. "I'll let Dr. Lancaster know that you're on your way back with his ship."

I didn't answer. No point in correcting him, getting into another argument, and maybe not being allowed to detach once they'd wiped my data.

Yarrow piloted us into gate three, as requested. Before I'd even opened the hatch, there was Miller, peering through the viewport. He was shorter than I thought he'd be, only a few inches taller than I was. If he tried to board Lepton, I'd physically bar his way.

I smacked the latch pad. It clicked over, and the heavy door swung slowly inward.

"Good choice, not trying to run," he said when the hatch was open wide enough.

His security team stood behind him, but the two of them made no move toward the ship. So much for barring their way.

"You think I'd go against the council?" I said.

"Lancaster jettisoned this data in a desperate attempt to keep control of your discovery. You brainiac Oort Centre geniuses should have figured out it wouldn't buy you much time."

"Do you want a copy, or should I just erase the server and provide you proof?"

"Just erase it. We already have what we need. I'll be taking over the Pardus investigation, as I'm sure you've surmised."

I pulled out my screen, connected to the ship's server, and sighed as I tapped to erase the data. I held out my screen for Miller to verify, and he scanned it and nodded.

"Good working with you, Dawn. I wish all my jobs were this easy," he said.

He stuck his hands in his pockets and strode away, whistling something vaguely familiar. His security detail followed. I sighed again, and Yarrow emerged from the galley where he'd been sitting on the edge of one of the bench seats.

"Shall we resupply so we can depart?"

"Yes, please. I need to take my mind off all the top-secret information the council is sitting on. I don't think they even have anyone look at any of it." An absolute travesty. So many breakthroughs going un-broken-through. I tucked my screen into my pocket and headed for the hatch.

"They would prefer that the underlying discoveries not come to light." Yarrow followed me out and shut the hatch.

I nodded as I hooked up the fuel supply. "They didn't seem to care about that dataset until I realized that Pardus was actually gone, not just off track."

"A physical object disappearing completely is unheard of."

"And it'll stay that way unless we find out what actually happened."

The way station was busy, and we didn't need much, so we just wandered the main concourse while Lepton refueled—and let Miller's ship get nice and far away.

We found a bench facing a nice big viewport and sat on either end. I used to sit in his lap and now we could barely share the same air.

"Please explain why you let them wipe all the data you and Lancaster schemed to keep." Yarrow's voice was flat, and I couldn't get a read on him.

"We currently have permission to go to Pardus Station and gather more data," I said. "The readings from the cruiser were insufficient anyway. I already performed all relevant analyses on that dataset. If we'd refused to comply, that would have given them an excuse to revoke that permission. Since we didn't make any waves, they're assuming that we'll turn around and go back to the research centre. That will give us enough time to get some distance from them before they realize we're not going to stop."

"Once they do realize we intend to conduct more research—"

"They'll wait for us to come back to seize our data again, I know." I stood and leaned on the rail beneath the viewport. "Maybe by then we'll have some answers. The server on Lancaster's baby can do all the analysis we need. That's part of the reason he wanted us to take it."

"You still won't get credit for anything you discover," said Yarrow. "If you wanted this project to make your career..."

I did want this project to make my career, but Yarrow was right. Even if I cracked the biggest discovery of the decade, if the council wanted it buried, it would be buried, and all signs pointed to a *Top Secret* label and a locked drive for anything we found. Maybe that was the real reason I wanted to keep going. What could they possibly want to keep so quiet? The dataset I'd been working on, the one they'd made me erase, had been devoid of...anything. Let alone anything incriminating or groundbreaking. Pardus was there, and then it wasn't, with no indication of what had happened to it. For all we knew, its disappearance was a rare natural phenomenon. But with the way the council was trying to cover it up, I doubted it.

"I'm curious," I said. "Aren't you?"

Yarrow smiled, a rare common expression between us. "I didn't say I don't agree with your actions."

I grinned back. "Okay then, let's go collect some more data."

Docking control didn't bother us as we left, and the way station quickly dwindled to a speck. Yarrow stayed on watch, but with no more analysis to do, I wandered down to my desk and poked around the literature for ship disappearances. When that came up empty, I resorted to reading on my screen.

Yarrow clattered down the stairs for dinner, and I punched the Reconstitute button on his food and sat down to eat mine. He slid in across from me while his meal cooked, spread one pair of hands on the table, and leaned on the elbows of his other arms.

"I'll take a shift before I go to bed, if you want a break," I said.

"That would be much appreciated," he said. "As is the meal." He gestured to the reconstitution apparatus, which beeped. He brought his food back to the table and bent over it.

"How long do you think until they come after us?" I said.

"You believe they will? It would be far more expedient to allow us to gather the data and then appropriate it upon our return."

I grunted in assent. That would be more expedient. Which meant we might have quite a bit of time, though I wasn't naive enough to think they wouldn't be monitoring our progress while they "allowed" us to continue our research. My research. Yarrow was the pilot on this little expedition. The crew.

"Thanks for coming with me, Yarrow," I said. "This little stunt will follow you around for a while as well."

He shrugged. "It's not my first time defying the authorities."

I looked askance at Yarrow, my upstanding, rule-abiding ex-boyfriend. "You'll have to tell me about it sometime."

He glanced up and shook his head. "It's not relevant."

Still not relevant. If I ever spoke of my childhood, nudging Yarrow to do the same, he always told me that it wasn't relevant, same as now. Part of me was waiting for the day that it became relevant, and yet...from the way he said it, maybe it would be better if that day never came.

When Yarrow disappeared into his cabin for his break, I wandered up to the bridge and slouched into the co-pilot's seat, swapping to my control scheme, and pulled my screen back out. The words kept blurring in front of my eyes, and stared into space. Nothing that I knew of could make a whole station disappear, along with all of its inhabitants. There had been no distress call; at least, no call had been received. None of the lifeboats had launched, or if they had, they hadn't been found. It almost made more sense for Pardus Station to have been a figment of our collective imagination, implanted but never really present, than to have had it vanish in an instant.

Something flickered across the windshield, a small dark object, moving fast. I blinked. I hadn't imagined it. I scanned the dashboard: Self-clean, Auto-dock, Light gravity, Noise cancel... None of these luxury functions would provide me with evidence of an outside object at close proximity. Too bad this sleek ship didn't have the research instruments that our usual vessel did. What I wouldn't give for those always-on data feeds. The probe we had on board could only be launched once, so not worth launching here in the middle of nowhere for a hunch of mine.

I could run a few standard scans, so I checked the environs for particles and waves, plus took a sample of the surrounding vacuum and ran a spectral analysis on it. All totally normal, nothing out of the ordinary. Just like the empty space where Pardus Station had disappeared. Just like every other corner of empty space in the vast known universe.

Maybe it had been my imagination? Either way, I couldn't rewind my brain, and that was the only instrument on board that had registered any kind of anomaly. Yarrow came up for the night shift twenty minutes later.

"I ran a few scans because I thought I saw something fly past," I told him as I reset the controls. We liked different configurations, so setting them to the default was just courteous.

"Any idea what kind of something?"

"Not like any space junk I've seen. Plus, I didn't find anything on the scans, no hull impacts. It was moving strangely, almost..." *alive.* I couldn't say that aloud. Of the thousands of alien species, not one could survive in vacuum without some kind of protective apparatus.

"I'll keep an eye out," said Yarrow and nodded.

I relaxed. I'd been bracing myself for him to make fun of me or tell me it was all in my head. I should have known that Yarrow would take me seriously; he had ever since he'd joined our research team, and it was part of the reason we'd been together in the first place.

"Thanks," I said, though what exactly was I thanking him for?

"Sleep well," he said as he fiddled with the controls and restored his configuration.

"You too," I said over my shoulder as I descended to the main deck. The way my brain was tossing around the memory of something flashing past the windshield, I probably wouldn't sleep at all. What exactly made the thing seem alive? I'd had the feeling it had been watching me. Feelings were not empirical evidence. Feelings left no data behind. No one could replicate a feeling.

Turns out, I did sleep, because when I woke up and checked the charts twice from bed, we had arrived. Yup, this was it. The location—former location—of Pardus Station.

I rolled out of the real bed I'd just spent the entire voyage unconscious in, and went through my morning routine on autopilot. We'd launch the probe, grab its data, start running the analysis, then head back to the research centre. We'd have to stop again and refuel. That would be the first chance for CHUSI to grab our data, and we'd have a good half day's travel for the analyses to run before then. Tons of time to figure out what exactly we had found.

I popped the inside maintenance hatch on my probe's little launch bay and ran diagnostics on each of the instruments. Recovering this thing would be next to impossible, even to fix badly calibrated or malfunctioning instruments. This baby could analyze particle samples with its spectrometer; gather all known wavelengths of electromagnetic radiation, including radio waves and gamma; record radioactive decays; and, the reason it was so expensive, detect neutrinos. Not individual neutrinos, obviously, but it would return any statistical anomalies in neutrino density. It would send us the data in real time so I could get straight to work on it. The only thing it couldn't measure for us was gravitational waves. Our research vessel had some cutting-edge gravitational wave sensors, mostly because Oort Research Centre was developing them. No way to get them on a tiny probe, though. We'd have to do without.

I slammed the maintenance hatch, and it auto-sealed. Fancy ship didn't require any levers. Once, an old seal on our research vessel wouldn't stop leaking and we'd had to weld it shut. So there were some upsides to this curvy lady, besides aesthetics, obviously.

I tramped up to the bridge and set the probe's course for the research centre. It was way too expensive to be a single-use piece of equipment. The return trip would take—according to the ship's calculations—seven years from launch to arrival at the centre, but it would get back there.

"Can you double-check my probe for me, Yarrow?" I said. If I messed this up, there would be no data for us, and we wouldn't get another chance.

Yarrow tapped around on the controls. "The configurations are correct."

I punched in the launch sequence and turned to look out the side window to watch the little probe pop out of the hull and float off toward Pardus's last known location. I could practically taste the sweet, sweet data it was already sending back to the ship's server. Not that there would be enough to analyze just yet.

Yarrow watched over my shoulder. "How long would you like to stay? Are there any readings we should obtain with the ship's instruments?"

"Let's take some from a few different locations. Wait for the probe to be out of range, though. I don't want our wake to taint its data."

"If I have thirty minutes, I'd like to get a double nap in," said Yarrow.

"Please, take your time. I can get the readings myself, so let's say this is my shift," I said.

Double sleep was Yarrow's way of saying that he would be completely asleep, both parts of his brain, as far as I understood it. He could last for weeks resting one part at a time, but having both parts asleep at once seemed to be like getting a full eight to ten hours of unbroken sleep for me.

"I appreciate it, Carolina, but thirty minutes will be fine," said Yarrow.

Right. We weren't together anymore. Just colleagues, professionals. No need to do each other unsolicited favours. One of his roles on this voyage was data collection, and he intended to fulfill it. Nothing more.

Once the probe had fed back enough data to be getting on with, I hunched over my screen, propped on the narrow wooden desk. Lancaster had been right about the server. It was lightning fast. But that just meant my useless results had come back in a few short minutes.

I chewed my lip. There was more analysis to do. There must be. What was I missing? I'd already redone all the regressions and statistical analyses that I'd used for the original dataset and...got exactly the same results. Normal section of empty space. No anomalies, nothing unusual at all. Not what I'd been hoping for. At least it wouldn't be hard to give up this data when the council caught up with us.

Wait, the neutrino data. I hadn't had that in my old datasets, so an initial basic analysis would get me started. I put in the parameters of my visualization and set it to run. Shouldn't take long on this beefy server. Yarrow passed me on his way up to the bridge to collect the data I'd requested now that the probe was well out of range.

"Has anything interesting become apparent?" he said.

I shook my head. "Not yet. Still getting the neutrinos sorted out."

"The ship isn't capable of collecting neutrino density data."

"I know. I'm hoping the stuff from the probe will be illuminating on its own."

"Do you still require the other measurements?"

"Yes, please." If only to make it look to the council as if we cared about the data we were collecting. If he thought we'd found something but didn't know what, it would drive Miller to distraction.

I went to the galley and reconstituted some food while waiting for the neutrino analysis to finish up. Yarrow must be flying around the little corner of space we were currently obsessed with, but I didn't feel a thing. He was a hell of a pilot.

A success message flashed across the screen while I was finishing up my food. Was it for my neutrinos or from the data Yarrow was collecting? I tossed out the packaging from my meal and went back to the desk.

The neutrinos...had a pattern. There was something there. Probably. The standard code that had come with the probe wasn't enough to tease it out, though; I'd have to write something proprietary. *Crap.* Hadn't I done enough of that in grad school? There was no one on board to pawn it off on, so it would have to be me.

I set the analysis running on the new data from the ship's instruments, even though it was practically guaranteed not to turn anything up, and got to work finagling some code for my neutrinos.

Just as I was finishing up my weird half-assed code, Lancaster called.

"Miller is on his way to you," he said.

Good morning, Caro. How are you? Nope. He must be freaking out.

"We're at the Pardus site."

Miller wasn't going to come all the way out here; he was going to stop us on our way back.

"I know, and so does Miller."

Shit! I'd only have until he got here to run my analysis. "How long do we have?"

"About an hour. His ship is fast." He rubbed a hand over his face. "And Carolina? Don't make any backups. If they find top secret data on our server..."

"Of course, I'd never put the research centre in that position. I think I've caused enough trouble for the time being." Guilt choked me.

"Nothing I can't handle, Carolina. I'm the one who told you to pursue this. They weren't happy when you didn't come straight here, but they'll hoover your data happily enough."

"As long as they don't blame you for everything I'm doing," I said.

Lancaster looked over his shoulder at something out of frame. "I gotta go, Carolina. I'll talk to you when you get back."

"Sounds good," I said, waved, and ended the call.

"You really intend to delete all of the data we just collected?" said Yarrow. He'd been sitting just out of frame, listening in.

"It's lucky we have such a monster of a server on board. We have an hour to do the analysis, and it might be all we need."

"Need for what?"

"To determine whether or not this data is even useful."

"And then what happens?"

If it was useless, the council could take it all, and it wouldn't matter. If it was useful, the council would still take it all, and I might cry. The thought of such a huge discovery being crammed in a locked cabinet (metaphorically) and buried (also metaphorically)...

"I'm going to finish analyzing the neutrino data. I don't think there's anything useful in the stuff we collected from the ship."

"Let me take a look," said Yarrow. "If we only have an hour left with this dataset, we need to extract all possible information from it as quickly as possible."

"Fair enough," I said. It wouldn't hurt to have another set of eyes on the data I'd already dismissed, especially an expert like Yarrow's.

Twenty minutes of alternating boredom and hair pulling later, I paced across the moulded polymer floor from the desk I'd been hunched over to the galley and back.

"It's a torus," said Yarrow.

I surfaced from my analytical haze and turned to him where he was hunched over his own screen at the galley table. "What's a torus?" I said and frowned.

"There's a pattern to the minute vacuum particles in this area, and it's a torus."

I crossed to look at his screen over his shoulder. "Shit," I said, "it's a torus. What the hell does that mean?"

Yarrow shook his head. "I don't have an inkling."

I scanned the density rendering he had made from the points sampled by the ship around the area. The extrapolation fell within acceptable error; there was never such thing as 100 percent certainty, but this was reliable at the very least.

"Make sure you delete that before we transfer the data to Miller," I said. I went back to my own screen to finish up my as-yet fruitless neutrino analysis.

"He can do the same analysis I did," said Yarrow. "Why bother deleting it?"

"One, let's not make it too easy for him. Two, then he'll know that we know about this." Why did that thought make me uneasy? The council wanted this kept quiet, probably at someone else's behest, and as willing as I was to cross the council, not all powers in the universe were to be taken so lightly.

Yarrow and I moved up to the bridge to watch for the CHUSI ship.

My neutrino program was still running, and Yarrow and I both propped our screens on the dashboard. We didn't have to wait long.

"Lepton and Dawn," said Miller, the annoyance clear in his voice, "we understand that you have collected data from this site. The previous project connected with these coordinates is now closed. Please turn over any data you've obtained and purge your servers. You will be required to leave the area." The *And don't come back* was obvious.

There had to be a way to stall them. A couple more minutes, and my program would spit out the new neutrino results...Damn the giant dataset I'd collected using the probe. I had forgotten to take into account that my analysis time was limited and had gone for the highest accuracy. After all, any anomalies could be tiny, any trends very slight—and I had been determined to get it all.

"Please begin transferring your data," said Miller. "I'm obligated to inform you that any copies remaining in your possession subsequent to the transfer will be considered leaked or stolen and prosecuted accordingly."

"Which data exactly falls under this rule? Surely the trip logs and other unrelated—"

"Ms. Dawn, I have already endured far more of your so-called cleverness than I have had any desire to. Please transfer the data you collected at this site. Either using your ship instruments or the probe that we are fully aware you launched. That includes but is not limited to electromagnetic spectra, gravitational data, and particle analysis."

No way to tell how long my program would take to run. When exactly were they going to check for copies? If they waited until we

arrived back at the research centre, we'd have time to run all the pro-
grams in the world, but if they checked now and found copies...We
couldn't risk it.

I started the data transfer with the measurements from the ship's
instruments. Yarrow had dutifully deleted his analysis. With any luck,
they'd think we hadn't had time to look at this data, what with the
giant datasets from the probe. They probably didn't know exactly how
fast the server on *Lepton* was, and the data transfer would be limited
by their no-doubt slow ship's computer.

The progress bar on my neutrino program inched up. "Come on," I
said under my breath. Maybe it was a damn good thing I'd cranked the
probe's data acquisition settings, since transferring its useless datasets
could potentially take half an hour; a half hour I'd have to finish my
work.

The ship's data transferred, then the particle and EM data from the
probe. The radioactivity measurements were on their way over to the
other ship when my neutrino program finished running. I scanned
them quickly, trying to memorize any anomalies.

But the results wouldn't compute in my brain. It was like nothing
I'd ever seen. "What the...?" I muttered. At least it wasn't frustratingly
normal anymore.

What even was that? Were they bouncing?

"Yarrow! Look, quickly!"

He leaned over my shoulder, his fresh-air scent engulfing me. Good
thing I wasn't trying to think clearly at the moment. *Crap.* I tried to
breathe through my mouth subtly as we stared at my screen.

"Neutrinos do not...act this way."

The other data transfers were ticking down. I had to wipe all this
before transferring the neutrino data.

"It's kind of round..."

"Does it perhaps align with the particulate distribution?"

Our time was up. I cringed and wiped the analysis along with my shitty program that had spat it out, but better deleted than let Miller have any of it. The less he thought we'd found, the more likely he'd leave us alone.

Once the council ship was satisfied that they had all the data and had double-checked three times that we'd wiped our copies, Yarrow and I practically collapsed at the table in the galley. I mean, I collapsed, and he slid gracefully into his seat and rested one set of elbows on the table, his chin on his interlaced fingers.

"What would you like to do now?" said Yarrow. "Shall we return to the research centre?"

"Anything else would be suspicious, right?"

Yarrow nodded. "It would."

"They'll be watching us," I said.

"Most likely."

"Any idea what was up with those neutrinos?" I said.

"No more than I did initially," said Yarrow.

We no longer had our data, so we couldn't check around with Lancaster and the others, see whether any of them could make heads or tails of it. We couldn't run any more focussed analyses for the same reason. What did that leave?

"I wonder if anyone's ever seen anything like that pattern," I mused. "Okay, take us back to the research centre for now. I'm going to dig into the literature, see if I can find any precedent for our weird readings."

"And if you find anything?"

"Depends what I find," I said. I swallowed. If the council planned to cover this up, was it possible that they'd done it before? They certainly hadn't seemed as clueless as usual around our data. They had known what to ask for and had made no bones about forcing us to delete our copies. They'd used threats to prevent us from circumventing their orders in exactly the way I'd planned. As if they had experience with stubborn academics in precisely this situation. Time to hit the books.

Chapter 3

Miller's office was, thankfully, on the moon. He couldn't have handled Earth gravity right now. Getting attitude from both sides on this one had been spectacularly aggravating. CHUSI hounding him for the data, Dawn trying to keep it from him with her little games. He'd slept on the way home, but not nearly enough, and sleeping sitting up was never as restful. Still, he had to deal with these datasets before passing out.

He bopped through the quarantine procedure for their database and then shot a copy off to the concerned party. Their security was not his problem.

T he first author I messages didn't respond, and I figured it was a fluke, but after the third one didn't answer, I started to wonder. It's not as if it was a weekend. Most researchers would be in their offices right now, that or their labs. I had left my contact info for all of the folks I reached out to.

There weren't any papers that mentioned disappearing astronomical objects, at least, not directly. If anyone had looked into a similar incident, they had been sworn to silence, same as us. What I had found was a reference to a paper that outlined a toroidal particle distribution in a seemingly empty region of space. I tried to follow up on the reference, but...nothing. The link itself gave a "page not found" error, so I searched the title of the paper, and all I got were references to the thing, but not the actual paper. I searched the publication's database for the authors' names, Sycamore and Proust. They'd published a few papers with the journal prior to the one in question, but none since.

Had they published anywhere since?

I spent about an hour futilely searching through aggregate data for Sycamore and Proust and following up on their various publications, but after the toroidal paper, neither had published again. Their contact information was, accordingly, about a decade old, so it wasn't surprising that they weren't reachable. The institution they'd worked for when they'd published their findings made no mention of either researcher, and their area of research wasn't listed on the department website: interstellar particulates, same as Oort. Same as me.

Not surprising, I guess, since we were looking for the same information. I called Lancaster.

"There's a paper I can't find from some researchers prominent about fifteen years ago, Sycamore and Proust? Do you know them?" Maybe I'd get lucky and he'd met them at a conference or something.

Lancaster blanched. "Proust passed away around then. Shocked the whole community. I think Dr. Sycamore left academia after that. I used to follow them closely. They were doing fascinating work. Why do you ask?"

I could tell Lancaster what we'd found, tell him about the paper, explain to him what we were trying to do. I opened my mouth to tell him—

He glanced out of frame.

Someone else was there.

"It's okay. I'll fill you in when we get back." I wasn't lying; I *would* fill him in when we got back. We just weren't coming back right now.

"Sounds good, Carolina. See you soon!" The screen went dark.

I stood and stretched my arms over my head and then trudged up to the bridge. The low strip lighting highlighted the view out the wall to wall viewports, stars in every direction.

Yarrow turned. "Any luck?" he said and yawned. Likely, he'd been half asleep.

"I've reached out to a few people, but I only found one reference to our toroidal pattern in the literature," I said.

"What caused it, according to them?"

I shook my head and stared out at the faraway stars. "No one has responded. And the paper seems to have disappeared."

"It was retracted?"

"No, there's no retraction notice. It just...doesn't exist. I guess they didn't think to purge the references in other papers, that or it was too much effort. But that's the only sign that a paper on toroidal distribution of interstellar particulates ever existed."

"And the neutrinos?"

"Cut me some slack," I said. "Banging my head against that donut-shaped brick wall was enough for the moment. I'll get back to it in a bit."

We both watched empty space go by, lost in thought. Not that there was much to see. It looked as if we were sitting still; only the instruments quietly ticking away the kilometres indicated that we were moving at all.

Yarrow rolled his shoulders. "I know a librarian who may be able to help us."

"They might have a copy of the missing paper?"

"Perhaps, or something better."

I could only access a fraction of the research in the universe. Humans were very big on gatekeeping, a holdover from the academic system that was dominant when we'd taken to the stars. Not all species were like that, but I didn't have any contacts outside human-dominated space.

The possibility of accessing a pool of data that dwarfed anything I'd yet experienced had my heart beating faster. The council couldn't be controlling the research of all other species.

We turned the ship around and headed the exact opposite direction from the research centre for a day before Yarrow and I reconvened at the table and shared a meal.

I projected a chart of our course onto the bulkhead. We were about to cross into space I'd never visited before. Pardus Station had been remote, by Solar standards, but the Solar System was small and remote itself, from the point of view of most species.

I took a bite and watched the charts click over into space I'd never visited.

"What brought you to the Solar System?" I said absently.

Yarrow didn't answer. He was literally staring into space.

"You don't have to tell me. I was just making conversation," I said. "I've never been here before. I've only been outside the Solar System once, and that was on a student exchange program. I guess my research placement counts as outside the Solar System as well, but it was just an interstellar station, probably similar to Pardus." I trailed off. Yarrow didn't seem in the mood to chat.

I ate my food and watched our little ship creep across the wall.

Yarrow surprised me. "I believed it would be best for everyone if I left my home system. I didn't want to be there, and they didn't want me there. So I found somewhere else to do my research."

"Fair enough." Local trends and anomalies in the vacuum of space could be studied from anywhere. Yarrow's and my research had some crossover, since the effects of constructed objects on the surrounding vacuum was pretty much just a specific case of his more general area, but we hadn't actually worked together before this project. Lancaster's choice of companion for me was well thought out, even if it was mostly based on Yarrow's other capabilities.

His piloting skills. Not his *other* capabilities. All the uses he'd found for his four hands whipped through my head. I cleared my throat.

He'd just revealed something about himself that I'd never known.

I pushed down all the intrusive questions I wanted to ask Yarrow. They might seem innocuous enough—When was the last time you went home? Why didn't you want to stay? How do you like the Solar System?—but there was obviously tons of history behind Yarrow's comment that I had no right to pry into.

"Want to tell me more about your librarian friend?" I said.

"If you're expecting a librarian, she might not be at all what you're picturing," said Yarrow with a smile. "You'll see." He pinged the chart at our destination. It was coming up fast.

Yarrow got us docked while I cleaned up and popped the hatch.

He offered me his arm as we stepped off the manufactured gravity of the ship and onto the real gravity of the moon, only slightly weaker than the conventional Earth standard. The moon seemed small to have such strong gravity. It must have a high density.

We'd gone away for a weekend together, back when we were a couple, to Mars—I'd never been there, despite having grown up on Earth—and I'd had to cling to Yarrow half the time. Turns out, no matter how often I took a step in 38 percent gravity, my body still expected 100 percent Earth grav.

I smiled up at Yarrow and took his arm, our skin touching, probably for the first time since we'd broken up. I'd been surprised, the first few times we'd touched, how human-like Yarrow's skin was; it had a mottled look to it that suggested tough hide. I'd tried to bury my reaction back then, but he insisted on my telling him what was wrong until I haltingly explained my mistake. He'd just smiled wryly and told me he understood why I had been trying to keep it to myself. Not that he'd learned anything from the incident; he still tried to ferret out everything I was thinking. He had tried. When we'd been together. Which we were not.

I looked down as my smile soured, and we walked together silently up the gate's tunnel. By the time we got to the egress, I was feeling steady on my feet, and I dropped my hand from Yarrow's elbow. I wasn't quite stable enough to slide it into my pocket, but I no longer required external support.

Yarrow led the way across a smooth black chamber with a transparent ceiling, the stars scattered over the inky sky like lights on a dashboard. The moon's planet arced overhead, awash in swirling blue and green gasses. I snapped out of it, shut my gaping mouth, and already on the far side of the room, Yarrow raised his eyebrows. One set of arms was across his chest; the other hands were on his hips. He tapped his foot pointedly. I started across the chamber.

"You've seen this before, have you?" I said.

"Yes, many times," he said as I reached him. "I used this library to research my thesis."

"Then I don't feel bad for stopping to gawk," I said. "It's remarkable."

"Yes, I think that's why she chose this place to spend eternity."

"Your librarian friend is going to live for eternity?" I said wryly. An immortal librarian? He had to mean for the records to spend eternity in the library.

"The moon's orbit is opposite the planet's rotation, so it won't decay, but the star itself won't last forever."

"Hopefully, they can back the whole thing up and move it before then," I said.

Yarrow didn't answer, just led the way down a flight of stairs. At the bottom, there were no books. The circular room contained a giant pillar made of some rough grey material, and that seemed to be it. A slight rushing sound, like a white noise machine, staved off the silence. Probably the air circulation system. Yarrow crossed to the pillar and motioned to me to come and feel it as he pressed a hand to the stone. Except it wasn't stone. I was touching something warm and soft and...alive.

The second my hand made contact with the skin of the pillar, my eyelids drooped. My head jolted up twice before I finally gave in to the drowsiness that swept through me. And then I was in a library. An old library from Earth with shelves of actual books on two levels, ladders reaching up to the highest shelves, carved wooden bookshelves, and filled with the smell of old books.

An older woman bent over the circulation desk and looked over her spectacles as I approached. A human woman. The tension left my shoulders. A dream. It had to be. Since this was a dream, I'd treat it like one. The first book I picked would probably be exactly what I was looking for. I wandered into the nearest aisle and pulled a book with a green leather spine from the shelf.

The librarian cleared her throat. "You're not even going to introduce yourself first?"

I tucked the book under my arm and sauntered to the desk. "I'm Carolina Dawn. I'd like to take out this book."

"You don't even know what it is yet. You'll find that book is completely empty without my assistance."

I glanced at the cover of the book in my hand. The gold-leaf title was too peeled to read.

"This isn't a dream, you know, Carolina," said the librarian.

I frowned at the librarian. People in dreams seldom acknowledged their dream existence.

"I fell asleep," I said.

"Merely a trance state," said the librarian. "Yarrow didn't explain my library to you?" Except that she didn't say Yarrow; she pronounced his name the same way he did, something a human larynx would never be able to manage.

My mouth went dry. Not the best first impression, wandering into the stacks uninvited and grabbing a random book off the shelf.

"No need to be embarrassed," said the librarian. "Let me help you find what you're looking for in my archive." She smiled and didn't seem the least bit offended, but how could she not be?

I took a breath to quell my urge to hide in the stacks and avoid the librarian for the rest of my life, and I explained what I was looking for: the missing paper or any other relevant research on the same topic. She led the way up a circular stairway to the far end of the library. I followed her down a long dusty aisle, and she rolled a ladder along the tall shelf.

"You're certainly convinced this information is hard to find," she said.

"I'm convinced? Seems like it's pretty obscure." I wiped a layer of dust from the nearest shelf.

"You constructed this library from the library archetype that lives in your mind. That means you shelved all the information."

"So it is a dream. How can it contain information that I don't already know?"

"I provide the information. You just do all the indexing," said the librarian. She climbed back down the ladder with a spiral-bound book in hand.

"That looks like a thesis," I said.

"I provide the information. You provide the binding," said the librarian. She handed me the book.

Carolina's research request: Toroidal particle distributions in vacuum.

"Anything else?" said the librarian.

I flipped through the pages: primary research articles, at least one thesis, and some kind of owner's manual? Nothing I recognized, but somehow all in English.

The librarian smiled at my no-doubt stunned expression. "I take it you have a few more requests."

After I made my requests and hauled them back to the circulation desk, the librarian helped me check them out. She used an old-timey date stamp to stamp them and pushed them across the counter. Already, the library was fading around me.

I jolted fully awake, still standing, and peeled my sweaty palm from the librarian's...skin? Yarrow sat across from me, scrolling on his screen.

"Where are my books?" The floor at my feet was clear. Where else could they be hiding?

Yarrow waved his screen, and I snatched mine from my pocket. There they were. All the documents the librarian had found for me, streaming from *Lepton*'s server.

We headed back to *Lepton* and set a course for the research centre.

❖

We were still two days out when I found it. My feet thumped down from where they'd been resting on the desk, and I clutched my screen closer to my face, scanning the fine type carefully. I tossed my screen aside and clambered up to the bridge. My foot slipped on the steps, but I caught myself, and Yarrow turned as I reached the top.

"If we go back to the research centre..." I wasn't exactly sure what would happen, but...

Yarrow cocked his head and fixed me with a hard stare. "What did you find?"

"The death certificate for that researcher, the one Lancaster told me about. One of the authors of the missing paper."

"Humans die fairly regularly," said Yarrow.

"During legal action to get the paper republished?" I said.

"Only one of the authors? Not both?"

"The other one wasn't named in the legal documents. I guess Dr. Sycamore didn't fight back."

Yarrow shook his head. "This is far-fetched. Who was the defendant?"

"It was censored."

That got a reaction out of Yarrow. "The librarian's information was censored?" He peered out the front windows, brow furrowed, as though he might be able to see officials waiting to take us in when we arrived at the research centre.

"Say we don't return to Oort. Where do you propose we go?"

I shrugged. I hadn't thought that far yet. If we went back, *Lepton* would be seized, the records we had unearthed would be buried once more, and we might never find out what they were trying to hide. Our best bet would be to talk to someone who already knew. Luckily, the librarian had given me Dr. Sycamore's contact information, because our options on that score were limited, at best.

We had no choice. Oh yeah, just keep on repeating that and maybe you'll believe it. After five hours of research, I was very sure this was the only option.

I flicked through the research notes from the librarian; maybe that would get my mind off the guilt of bringing up all this ancient history for Dr. Sycamore. She lived on Earth now and hadn't published in a decade. She was the only one who could point us in the right direction, but she didn't want to see us. I had figured that much out. Which was why we hadn't called ahead.

The owner's manual was for some kind of machine that must be mass-produced; otherwise, there wouldn't be a manual, at least nothing this nice. This was clearly tech edited with professional layout and design. Yeah, whatever this was a manual for, it wasn't a prototype. But the instructions were more opaque than an undergraduate's lab notes. The schematic and diagrams showed parts of the contraption, but never the whole thing, and the instructions almost exclusively consisted of diagrams, arrows, shapes, and warning signs. Even the title was simply *Manual JH98373-34*. Maybe it was a machine that ate space stations and left no trace behind. Yeah, right.

I put my screen on the desk and went to get a snack. On my way to the galley, I glanced out a viewport and paused. That distinctive blue halo of our atmosphere, squishy creatures that we are, and artificial lights winking from the dark side. *Earth. Home.* No other planet was quite like it, and I wasn't just saying that because it was mine. The spaceport crested the planet, and Yarrow matched velocities with it. We'd dock there and take a shuttle to the surface. I grabbed my snack and took it to my cabin to munch while I threw a few things in my duffle and tossed my screen on top. The handheld screen couldn't store nearly all the information I'd gathered from the librarian, but my most recent document would be cached to read on the shuttle.

A bump and clunk preceded the hiss of the hatch sealing to the port. We could pop our side when we were ready. I hung on the railing and poked my head up into the bridge.

"I'm ready when you are," I said.

Yarrow watched Earth flow by beneath us. "It's a beautiful planet," he said.

I padded up the stairs to stand beside him. "Yes, it is."

"This is your last opportunity to change your mind. We spoke about not endangering anyone."

I sighed. "I know. Dr. Sycamore doesn't deserve this."

"And if she refuses to see us?"

"Then I guess we've hit a dead end."

"Okay," said Yarrow. "Let's go."

The shuttle was probably built for four humans, two-person benches on either side. A tear in the cushioning on one had been mended with duct tape. I took that side and slid to the intact end. Yarrow slid onto the opposite bench and took up most of it.

Yarrow launched the shuttle while I typed in Dr. Sycamore's address as our destination. A red padlock flashed on the screen. Denied. The little sphere shuddered to a halt, and a lined face surrounded by a halo of iron-grey hair popped onto the shuttle's screen. I leaned into the tiny camera's frame so that she could see me in return.

"You came all this way for nothing," she said. "You should have called. I got in touch with Dr. Lancaster, and he let me know in no uncertain terms that you don't have his permission to be here."

"That's true, doctor," I said. "We didn't want to involve him or the Oort Research Centre in this visit."

"It's too late," said Dr. Sycamore. She sighed. The lock turned green, and the shuttle started moving again.

"What's too late?" I said, worry gnawing at me.

"We can talk about it when you get here. Just be aware that they know about you, if they didn't before." The screen went blank, and I sat back on the bench.

Yarrow, across from me, watched the scenery go by outside the window. We were buried in a cloud layer at the moment, but when we popped out the other side, a carpet of yellow and red trees spread out below us. He nodded.

"Very beautiful planet," he said.

"It's fall in this hemisphere. The trees reuptake all the chlorophyll from the leaves, which also drains their usual green colouring, leaving them orange and red. The leaves can't survive in the cold winter, but the chlorophyll is too costly for the trees to make every year. So..." I gestured to the fiery colours beneath us.

"Seasons caused by an axial tilt," said Yarrow. "Not something I have personal experience with. Very interesting to see their effects firsthand."

"Your planet doesn't have a tilted axis?"

"Nothing to speak of. Cold poles, warm tropics, hot equator. Just your basic latitudinal bands. Here you wait a few months and it goes from cold to hot in the same place."

"At higher latitudes, yes."

We sat in silence. Neither of us had any more energy to pretend that we weren't worried about what would be waiting for us. They know about you, if they didn't before. What exactly did that mean? Had *they* been arriving at Dr. Sycamore's when she ended the call with us? We would find out in—I checked the timer on the shuttle—under twenty minutes.

I pulled out my screen and continued reading the research that the librarian had put together for me until we landed.

Dr. Sycamore met us on her deck overlooking a sparkling lake and surrounded by rustling red leaves. She pulled her cozy sweater more tightly around her shoulders and set a camera on the railing where it could see all of us. There was no screen.

"I signed an NDA, and they want to be sure I don't violate it," said Dr. Sycamore. She didn't give her first name or introduce herself at all. She motioned us to a couple of chairs across from her and sat in an Adirondack chair herself, half facing the gorgeous view. "Ask your questions so that I can tell you I don't know anything and then you can bugger off."

Why did she agree to meet with us if she was going to be so hostile? I cleared my throat. Might as well do as she'd asked. I pulled out my screen and opened my notes, just in case I wanted to take anything down.

"I noticed a reference to a paper by Sycamore and Proust about toroidal distributions of particles in vacuum, but the paper seems to have disappeared. I tracked down your name as the Sycamore in question. Would you be able to tell me about your research?"

"Nope," said Dr. Sycamore, glaring not at me but into the camera.

"Can you give me any references who might know about your research or where to find your data? Even an old copy of your paper?"

"I can't," she said.

"Okay," I said and glanced at the camera myself. Damn. This couldn't be a dead end. If we didn't get any more information from this trip, all we would have accomplished was to alert *them* that we were looking into things that they quite obviously wanted left buried.

"Have you heard of a Moritz distribution?" said Yarrow.

Dr. Sycamore's gaze snapped to him. "I have."

I haven't.

I'd almost forgotten that Yarrow had been with the librarian almost as long as I had. I'd never even thought to ask what he'd found out.

"In the context of the vacuum?" said Yarrow.

Dr. Sycamore licked her lips, glanced at the camera, and shook her head. "Mere speculation."

Yarrow nodded. "It certainly seems that way."

I fought the urge to ask a million questions. The camera was still staring blankly at us, after all.

"Is that everything?" said Dr. Sycamore. "I'll show you out."

I tucked my screen into my pocket. No need to take any notes after all. Dr. Sycamore rose and led the way back to the waiting shuttle. She stood aside for me to pass through the shuttle door and jostled me with her hip as I brushed past. Unnecessarily hostile, this whole exchange. I huffed and sat on the bench. She actually shook Yarrow's hand as he passed, and he ducked into the shuttle and sat across from me again.

The door banged shut and hissed to seal, and the shuttle took off, back that way we'd come. I pulled out my screen, mostly to avoid talking to Yarrow about that disaster of a meeting. Whoever *they* were, they knew exactly what we knew now. A document popped up in my notes. Probably just the blank one I'd started in case Dr. Sycamore had any information for us. The title wasn't blank, though: *Long-term effects and side effects of...* It trailed off, too long for the title field. I opened the document.

A list of names, a list of publications, a location, and...a warning.

Watch that mouth of yours, Dawn. If you don't shut up, they'll shut you up. It's not a threat, it's a fact. My partner learned that the hard way, but you don't have to.

"Good thing I had NFC on," I muttered.

Dr. Sycamore must have transferred this page to my screen when she'd bumped into me. It hadn't been enough time for a long data transfer, but Dr. Sycamore had known this text file would only take a couple of seconds to download. Not such a useless meeting after all. We had a lead.

The interior of the shuttle was being monitored, so I waited until we were back on *Lepton* to show the list to Yarrow.

"I believe you overlooked this section," said Yarrow. He gestured to the warning at the bottom and then paced the length of the ship.

I sat at the little desk in the corner and propped my screen on it.

Yarrow waved at it again. "Whoever they are, they most certainly know that Dr. Sycamore gave you this list. It's a test. They're trying to get you to do something obviously in violation of their policies so that they have an excuse to neutralize us."

"Neutralize? Now who's being paranoid?" I retorted, leaning back in my chair.

"You forget, I did my research, too," said Yarrow. "Do you know what I found? More missing articles, news articles."

"More ships have gone missing, and the articles about those incidents were deleted?"

"If we're lucky they were ships," said Yarrow. He popped a ration packet into the reconstitutor with excessive force.

I leaned forward, elbows braced on my knees. "Do you have evidence otherwise?" I said.

He shook his head.

Evidence or not, had there been stations? Moons? Planets? We still had no conception of the mechanism involved, and it was fully possible that whatever had made Pardus Station disappear was scalable to larger objects. Of course, some strange natural phenomenon wasn't completely out of the question. But then why would someone go to all this trouble to hide it?

"I still say we explore the coordinates from Dr. Sycamore. Who knows when the council will decide to ground our ship? Or when Lancaster will get fed up with us and order us back to the centre. This might be the only chance we have."

Yarrow threw up two of his hands. The reconstitutor beeped, and he snatched his packet and dropped onto a bench in the galley. "Dr. Sycamore has warned us of the consequences of pursuing this. The cost has gone beyond damage to our careers."

I laced my fingers in my lap. "You're right. I shouldn't ask you to risk everything for this just because I've latched on to it."

Yarrow grumbled in his chest. "I didn't intend to object on those grounds. Carolina, I left my people and my family behind. If we change course now, neglect to return to the research centre, you may be required to do the same. It's not easy."

He was trying to protect me. And I'd thought chivalry was dead.

His expression softened. "On the condition that you contact some of the people on the list. If you can narrow down who or what we're dealing with, then I'll be much more inclined to go along with this."

"Done," I said. There was no contact information on the list, but it should be easy enough to track academics down by their names, particularly if their area of research was related to what we were looking for.

Chapter 4

Yeah, it was not *easy enough*. I had expected some of the folks on Dr. Sycamore's list to be unreachable, but three out of the five still seemed unreasonably high. No auto-responders this time; all three academics' most recent publications led to out-of-service numbers at old affiliations.

I moved on to the fourth name, which rang a bell. Maybe I'd heard them speak or had read something of theirs. It was likely that we were in related fields after all.

Prof. Grell Morbit. I did a quick literature search, and fifteen papers came up. Most of them had the professor as the lead author, not the corresponding author, so there was no contact information, just an institution: Martian Institute for Vacuum Engineering. On their faculty list, it showed Prof. Morbit as *on sabbatical*, but I clicked through to the professor's website, which listed them as resident researcher on...

"Pardus Station," I said under my breath. No way. Had they been on the station when it disappeared? No publications appeared under the dates of their sabbatical, which had started over a year ago and had no end date. Maybe they'd been in the middle of their research? Or their experiments had been the cause of the disappearance. My gut knotted. Or someone didn't want their research to see the light of day. None of the information we possessed ruled out any of those options.

I scrolled down to the contact form on their website, added my information and selected the Type Your Message box. The cursor blinked at me. I'm looking into a conspiracy to cover up the disappearance of Pardus Station. Yeah, no.

I popped over to their publications and read a few abstracts to get an idea of their area of research and what I could plausibly ask them. Maybe the Pardus Station sabbatical was a coincidence. Maybe Dr. Sycamore had put their name on the list because of their research area: refining and miniaturizing neutrino detectors. I would say that was relevant, after the weird neutrino patterns we'd found. If only we still had that dataset, I would have sent it along to the professor as an excuse to get in touch, but that was one of the datasets the council had appropriated.

I'd have to make do with describing the thing. I drafted a message and read it over. Maybe name-dropping Pardus was a bad idea, considering that if the professor had worked there, they had probably known more than one person who'd disappeared along with the station. On the other hand, it would get their attention. I settled for including the rough coordinates where we'd gathered the data, in hopes that if they did know about the disappearance, they would realize what I was talking about, and if not, they might recognize the coordinates' proximity to Pardus Station and, at the very least, respond to ask me about it.

I signed the note, included my affiliation as a member of the Oort Research Centre, and clicked off my screen. I laid it on the desk and shook out my hands. Why was my heart pounding after writing a simple message to a colleague? I'd done it a million times. But this time, if someone wanted to construe my message as overstepping the top secret restriction on all things Pardus, it would not be a leap.

Looking up the coordinates Dr. Sycamore had given us would be a good distraction from refreshing my inbox.

"I'm aware that I agreed to plot a course to these coordinates, but I'm having second thoughts," said Yarrow.

The sites were utterly empty, at least, according to the chart that covered the wall across from the table in the galley. We were already heading that way, but it would take a few days.

"Where are we right now?" I said.

Yarrow pointed out a spot on the wall. "I've set the chart so Earth and the research centre are in-plane." He poked each one.

Earth, the research centre, and our ship were clustered at the bottom of the chart. The flagged coordinates were way up at the top.

"Do we even have enough supplies to make it there?" I said.

"We do not. We'll have to stop. There are some way stations."

"Our track record with way stations is less than stellar. Okay, how long will it take us to get there? How many stops will we need to make?"

Yarrow tapped on his screen and a glowing line showed up on the wall, broken into three sections. "Two stops."

"Two? That's like two weeks' travel!"

"Just about."

"Lancaster is never going to let us keep his baby that long."

"What choice does he have?"

"He could report *Lepton* stolen."

Yarrow didn't answer.

"Whatever we find at those coordinates better be worth it. What else is over there?"

"Some systems I'm unfamiliar with."

"I'll do some research," I said, as if I didn't have enough on my plate. The last person on the list Dr. Sycamore had provided had been impossible to find, and the smattering of publications she'd referenced were mostly missing, but I'd collected the few available abstracts—all in the same ballpark we'd been poking around in: interstellar vacuum composition and manipulation—and still had information the librarian had found for me to read.

"I'll set a course for the first way station," said Yarrow. "I'm also still going through my research from the library. So far, anything that has initially seemed useful has hit a dead end. Too many news articles are missing."

"Same thing on the academic research side. How far back do yours go?"

"Those I've found go back about a century."

A hundred years of random disappearances, all covered up by...some as-yet-unknown entity. "The papers only go back fifty. But that's not surprising since detector technology has advanced rapidly in the last fifty years."

They must have had a much easier time covering up the disappearances before researchers like us started poking around and realized that there was a pattern. Sure, the families of those that were gone would have noticed, but since when could miners and colonists get any traction with governments to look into disappearances? Besides, everything that happened in deep space still seemed risky and mysterious to folks on Earth. It wouldn't have been difficult to convince the families to drop it.

During the trip, both Yarrow and I focussed on trying to absorb as much information from the librarian's files as we possibly could, but I got a bad feeling as we pulled into the first of the two way stations. They—whoever they were—couldn't possibly know that we were going to stop at this way station, out of the thousands available to us. Couldn't possibly know we were going in this specific direction. Unless Dr. Sycamore had planted the list as a trap. But she had also warned us. Not very trap-like. Still, we took our time.

The way station loomed ahead, lights blinking rhythmically along its length. Yarrow docked seamlessly, and the seal hissed. I pressed the pad, and the latch clicked over to solidify the mechanical connection, and Yarrow appeared just as the hatch popped and swung open. Auto-hatches were expensive but so damned slow.

Shadows obscured most of the grubby corridor. This dock must have been used for ships coming directly from the surface of the planet below; that was one of the only ways grit could get onto a space station. Yarrow paused at the dock's fuel pump and punched in instructions to fill the tank while we were gone, and I settled my empty duffle bag more comfortably on my shoulders.

As he finished up, I led the way through to the main station, and the corridor opened into a two-storey promenade crowded with shops but mostly devoid of people.

A few grungy crew members lounged at the restaurant, its tables spilling onto the main thoroughfare through the centre of the station, and we slid past, ignoring their pointed looks. We passed the shuttle dock and a row of call booths to get to the general store. Some of the larger stations had specialized shops, but most out-of-the-way places like this one had one small store run by a—

"Come in, how can I help you?" said a gruff voice from behind the counter. I hadn't even noticed her in the chaos of shelves covered with everything from ration packs in slick stacks to machine parts piled haphazardly on a pallet. A sign behind the counter listed the entertainment material available for download—always the same three videos and dozen books at these places. The gruff woman waited while we got our bearings. Yarrow strolled between the shelves and collected some ration packs from the pile.

"Just restocking," I said.

"On your way to...?" She must have caught my guarded look. "Just curious. Always like to hear about where folks are headed. The farthest I've been is Flockrin, you know, the far moon opposite us."

I didn't know, but I nodded. Probably something everyone in this system was familiar with.

Yarrow stacked an armful of ration packs on the counter. "Will you select your own?"

"Sure," I said. I nodded to the cashier again and turned to the ration packs. I scanned the flavour labels down the column of boxes and wiggled a box of the best flavour they had—butter chicken—loose. I grabbed a couple individual packs in different flavours for variety and piled them on the box. We'd need to stop and fuel up again, so no need to get too many of the things at once. I'd probably want a change next week when we got to the second way station.

"And how will you be paying today?" said the cashier after ringing everything through.

I brandished the fob around my wrist, and she scanned it. Yarrow laid a hand on my arm. He looked stricken. Shit. The fob was tied to my expense account at the research centre. By this time, Lancaster would be required to report on our location if he became aware of it, and the location of this store would show up clearly on the expense statement. If whoever wanted Pardus's disappearance kept quiet hadn't known where we were before, they would now.

Yarrow and I got everything stowed in my bag and tried not to hurry back to *Lepton*. The last thing we needed was for someone to stop us and ask questions.

"More time will be required for the ship to refuel completely," said Yarrow.

"We'll be more inconspicuous on board than hanging around here," I said. "How long will we need?"

"How long will we have?"

We skirted the restaurant again. The patrons stared as they had before, that's all. Even if my fob had alerted Lancaster, surely he'd dawdle in passing the information on. That would give us maybe an hour, and then whoever they were would have to get a ship out here. And we were pretty much in the middle of nowhere.

"Let's just make sure we have the fuel to get us to the next way station."

"You don't expect them to be waiting for us there?" said Yarrow as we turned into the corridor that would lead us back to our ship.

The corridor was deserted, and our voices echoed down it in both directions and out of sight. I didn't answer until the ship's hatch was shut and latched behind us. Once the fuel connector was released, we could get out of here.

"Set a course for the research centre," I said.

Yarrow stared at me silently. He thought I was backing down.

"We'll change course once we've left this station behind. Our registered flight plan will, hopefully, throw them off for long enough that we can reach the second way station, refuel, and get going before they catch on."

"You don't think they'll catch on faster than that?"

"Space is big, and we're a small ship. Statistically speaking, we will be very difficult to find."

"It's worth attempting," said Yarrow and disappeared up the steps to the bridge.

I stowed the food packs in the galley and climbed slowly to the bridge myself. "Are you still sure you want to be dragged on this voyage with me?"

"I am," said Yarrow.

How could he be sure, though? Neither of us had any idea what we were getting ourselves into. He was going along with my suggestions, giving his input when I asked for it, but acting like my subordinate, my assistant on this venture. If I said it was time to return to the research centre and give up pursuit of Pardus, he'd agree just as easily. But if I asked him again whether he was sure, he'd give me that grumpy look as though I wasn't listening to him.

The speakers crackled. "*Lepton*, please stand by."

Yarrow looked at me, his antennae jerking back and forth. He punched a button on the dashboard. "Sorry, station, we've already completed preflight checks and are preparing to depart. Please direct any messages to us in flight," he said. His twenty fingers danced over the dashboard, releasing the fuel connector, completing the preflight preparations, and setting in the flight plan for the Oort Research Centre, presumably.

I buckled myself into the co-pilot's chair.

The ship detached from the way station and floated gently, the actuators lining the engines up with our set course, and then I was pressed back into my seat as the engines kicked in and we rocketed away from the station.

"*Lepton*, we will be relaying the message to you shortly. That was not very professional behaviour." The speaker crackled again and then cut out.

"They're right. That wasn't very professional," I said. A grin crept over my face, and Yarrow returned it.

"Fuel is at eighty percent, enough to get us to the next way station, even with this little detour," said Yarrow.

"You think the message is from...them?"

"We shall see when they forward on the recording," said Yarrow.

The chime came through about half an hour later, just as Yarrow was making the course correction to put us back on track to the way station and the coordinates Dr. Sycamore had sent us. I pulled up the video recording and glanced over the metadata. It wasn't from the council, Lancaster, or some shady private entity.

The person who'd wanted to talk to us was Prof. Grell Morbit, the researcher I'd been trying to get in touch with for days.

I shut myself in my cabin and watched the message, then dragged myself back up to the bridge and slumped into the co-pilot's chair.

"Did you watch the message?" said Yarrow, not looking at me.

"Yup," I said, not looking at him.

"Who sent it?"

"Professor Morbit."

"What did he say?"

I shrugged.

"I apologize for taking it upon myself to decline the call," said Yarrow.

I sighed and turned to him. "I'm not angry with you."

His antennae twitched.

"I'm mad at myself for being so paranoid. We can call Professor Morbit back when we get to the next way station."

"Until then, what did he say?"

I shrugged again. "Thanks for my interest in his work, I can visit his lab anytime. Pleasantries."

"You suspect he would have been more forthcoming in a live call rather than a recording?"

I nodded. "It's a minor setback. I'm disappointed more than any-thing." Both Yarrow and I had let our paranoia and fear rule our actions, and though the consequence was probably nothing more than an inconvenience this time, there was no telling what the future consequences might be. I needed to get my feelings under control and concentrate on our objective: following every avenue of research and determining the fate of Pardus Station. "If you want to have a double sleep, I'm fine to keep watch for a few hours."

Yarrow nodded, and my half of the dashboard lit up as he switched control over to me. He left me alone with my thoughts. I pulled out my screen and opened the next file on my list from the librarian.

I had all week to regret our rash actions and talk myself down from our overblown paranoia. We were in no way important enough for these shady characters to follow us halfway across the Galaxy.

Yarrow was taking another double sleep on the run-up to the second waystation, so I was alone on the bridge, my screen propped on the dash, as usual, when a warning light flickered on the dashboard. I tapped it, but the explanation text must have been missing, because nothing happened. Hopefully, it wasn't urgent. It was probably noth-ing. We could have it checked out at the way station.

Yarrow's head popped up from below as he mounted the stairs.

"I thought you were sleeping—"

"What's wrong?" he said.

"It's just a light. There's no..."

The entire bank of warning lights flicked on. Yarrow and I sat frozen for a half second. We both dove for the lifeboat, and I reached it a second ahead of him. He squeezed in after me, slammed the hatch closed, and I punched the launch button, rocketing us off *Lepton*'s hull.

We were only a few metres away when the ship winked out. Not the lights on the ship. *Lepton* winked out of existence in its entirety. One second it was there, and the next it was not.

I cursed quietly to myself.

"The lifeboat is stocked. We'll make it to the way station," said Yarrow. He let out a breath and covered his eyes with his hand.

"It's not that," I said. "Do you realize we just witnessed the same phenomenon that likely transpired at Pardus Station?"

"Forgive me for being more focussed on our survival."

"If they had that little warning time…what would you estimate the interval was between the warning lights and the disappearance?"

"Less than a minute," said Yarrow.

Less than a minute to evacuate an entire space station. Whoever was controlling this phenomenon, assuming for the moment it was being consciously controlled, had been well aware that the station would not be evacuated prior to…whatever it was that had happened. Acid crawled up my throat. We had barely evacuated the bridge with so little warning. If Yarrow hadn't sensed my confusion and come up to check on me when he did, he wouldn't have had time to evacuate, either. I would have had to leave him behind. Otherwise, he and I both would have suffered the same fate as *Lepton*.

Whatever fate that was.

We didn't have to debate going to the way station; it was our only option in the tiny lifeboat. Our knees practically touched across the narrow aisle, and yes, it was stocked, but not beyond emergency rations stored under our seats.

And so, the moment we latched on, we hunkered down in the dim back corner of the way station bar. I'd paid for the drinks with my fob—we had no choice anymore—and it was just a matter of time before Lancaster, at least, knew that we'd arrived here.

I sighed. "He's going to kill me," I said.

"Who is?"

"Lancaster. He offered me his baby so that I could try to keep the Pardus project at the research centre. We failed at that before we even made it to Pardus Station's coordinates and then gallivanted off with his ship without even asking." I took a long pull of my drink.

Yarrow didn't argue with me.

"And now his ship is just gone." Had there been time for an automated distress signal to be sent out? Did Lancaster know the ship had disappeared, or would he just assume we'd docked at the way station? He could send us a message, but without a proper ship, the way station would have no way of reaching us. Unless we wanted to sleep in the cramped pod, we'd have to get accommodations, and Lancaster would be notified of that as well, as long as my fob was set to charge everything as research expenses. Getting switched over would be complex without my screen. Which had disappeared along with *Lepton*.

What avenues were still left to explore? Beg a rescue from Lancaster and prostrate ourselves—myself, honestly—at his feet for losing his ship. If I could switch my fob over to my personal account, we could buy our own passage back, but that would be about it. Buying another ship was far beyond my means, and there was no way I was going to beg it off my parents. Or we could stay here in the bar. I took another gulp of my drink.

I had yet to get in touch with Prof. Grell Morbit for a live call, and I still hadn't combed through all of the librarian's data—

Data that had been stored on the ship's server. Which had abruptly disappeared.

I cursed to myself. "We're right back where we started."

"We know more than we did," said Yarrow. "The coordinates of interest, we have Dr. Morbit as a contact, we know about the toroidal distribution and the strange neutrino patterns."

"And we have someone hunting us who can make an entire ship disappear without a trace in under a minute," I added.

"But we don't have a ship, so that's less of a threat now."

Was he trying to be funny? "You're listing that as an asset?"

"We currently have nothing except our clothing, a sparsely stocked lifeboat, my screen, and your fob that reports to Lancaster, who reports to the council, who reports to Miller, who in turn reports to whoever is trying to keep us from following this trail. Or so it would seem. Being in possession of a ship that could be...disappeared...without consequence was unquestionably a liability."

Fair point. A star liner disappearing would get way more attention than some little cruiser. Maybe we *would* be safer now going...wherever we were going. Dr. Sycamore's coordinates were out. Star liners would only run where folks wanted to go, and some empty corner of space wasn't exactly a tourist spot. First, now that we were at a station, I could call Dr. Morbit back.

I told Yarrow I'd be right back, crammed myself into a call booth, and waited for the call to Prof. Morbit to connect. My elbow pressed against the faded wall of the booth on one side, and I double-checked again that the door was properly latched on the other. No guarantee that the operator wasn't recording the call, but our options were exceedingly limited.

Frizzy white hair popped into the bottom of the frame in front of a shelf stacked with piles of unfiled papers.

"Hello?" said the professor and adjusted the camera so his entire face was visible. His green skin was so pale as to almost be grey. He must have been over a hundred to be that washed out.

"Hello, Professor Morbit. It's Carolina Dawn. I reached out to you about your neutrino detector. I'm sorry I missed your call last week."

"Hi, Carolina, yes, I remember. You got my message! You should come visit me. I'm at Exodus Labs now," he said. Right to the point.

"I'm a bit far afield at the moment," I said, smiling.

He tapped his screen a couple times, mouth agape in concentration. "Oh, yes, I see that now. What are you doing out there?" He glanced back at the camera and knit his brow. "Never mind. Next time you're in the area, come on by. I'm sure I can find time to show you around my lab and answer all your questions."

Only very slightly more forthcoming on a live call, then. I groped about for some way to get information from him without being too obvious. "I'm really curious what you thought of the readings I described to you. Have your instruments ever shown readings like that?"

"I'm not sure, Carolina, I'll have to check my records and get back to you."

Why had he called last week if there was nothing he felt he could say? Mentioning Dr. Sycamore's name would be a sure-fire way to get noticed, if this call wasn't already being monitored. Who was I kidding? Whoever had made our ship disappear out from under us would be monitoring this conversation, no matter how careful I was.

"Dr. Sycamore seemed to think you were the one to talk to about neutrino distributions. Whereabouts is Exodus Labs? I'll drop by next time I'm in the area."

"Back the way you came a ways. You are absolutely welcome anytime. I'll pop the location information in the chat window for you."

"Thanks so much, professor. My current area of research is fairly obscure. Not many publications seem to have explored it." And the ones that were out there have disappeared.

"I'm not at all surprised, Carolina. Best of luck out there," said Prof. Morbit, and his smile seemed genuine. "I hope to see you soon!"

"Thanks. Good luck with your research," I said.

Prof. Morbit waved, and the screen disconnected. I popped over to the chat window and found the location the professor had mentioned. I looked up Exodus Labs, a research lab with a focus on particle physics, and there was Prof. Morbit's profile. He specialized in neutrino entanglement, which I'd honestly never heard of. I printed out the coordinates and tucked them into my pocket. If I'd still had my screen, I could have transferred it over instead of using paper like a dinosaur. But I hadn't thought to cram my screen in my pocket while fleeing for my life, so the paper would have to do. On the other hand, paper was nearly untraceable, unlike digital files. Maybe the general store at this way station had a pencil. *Yikes.* Next I'd be buying a notebook. Maybe an abacus.

By that evening, I'd painstakingly switched my fob over to my personal account, and I needed a bit of a sit-down and a drink to recover. The clerk could have just checked my biometrics and called it a day, but he'd apparently taken it as his responsibility to verify my identity unquestionably and asked me for the passcode I'd set up a decade earlier when I'd opened my account. When I'd told him I had no idea, he pulled up a long list of security questions, and the exam began. Maybe he'd expected me to give up and leave, but he'd clearly never dealt with a post-doc before. I had done much more difficult exams in my time.

Still, it had taken most of the afternoon, and a victorious drink to toast my meagre savings was in order.

I grabbed a starshine mixed with some carbonated blue sugar water concoction and tucked myself into a back corner of the half-empty bar. It was just coming on evening, and the locals wouldn't be in for another hour or two. If I'd had my screen, I would have shot Yarrow a message to join me so I could let him in on what I'd learned, see whether he wanted to visit Prof. Morbit with me. I'd never even asked whether Yarrow had managed to save his library files. *Shit.* Had I always been so uninterested in his life? Must be some strong 'shine to get me thinking like this already.

Lucky for me, Yarrow found me before I hit the bottom of my drink. He ducked into the booth so as not to bump his antennae on the low ceiling, sat across from me, and set his drink on the table.

"What did you get up to today?" I said, definitely not out of guilt from my realization that I never asked him about himself.

He raised his brow-ridges. "How many drinks have you had?"

"This is the first one, and it's not even finished yet, thanks."

Yarrow sipped his and set it carefully on the laminate tabletop. He traced the faded star pattern with his finger. "Tell me why you're so determined to follow this trail."

"I'm not. I'm just curious."

"You're risking your life, my life if I accompany you, to find out what happened to Pardus Station. That isn't simple curiosity."

Risking my life. What would have happened to us if we hadn't escaped *Lepton*? My gut knotted. Would it have been like getting sucked through a black hole? Stretched apart and obliterated into nothingness? Or more like the elusive teleportation that the entire physics community had been trying to pin down for a century: just winking out of existence somehow? Would we have had time to wonder what was happening—or maybe even find out—before ceasing to be? Yarrow was right. We had almost died. If we weren't stodgy academics who insisted on keeping a watch almost constantly, we probably would have. But I still didn't want to give up. Yarrow was right to ask why.

The thought of going home to my little white office in the research centre and durdling with datasets soured my stomach even more. What right did I have to sit there safe while people were disappearing out here in the middle of nowhere? And not only that—no one would ever know about it. Pardus, like most interstellar stations, had been populated with mostly miners, poor folks looking for a better life for their kids, and the support staff that ran the place. The odd ship passing by would have used it as a makeshift way station, but for the most part, they would have been on their own, and no one would have asked after them when they disappeared.

No one but me.

I tipped the last of my drink into my mouth, thumped the glass onto the table, and gulped.

"I don't know how you grew up, since you never tell me, but I was a sheltered kid. I didn't know about interstellar migrants or asteroid miners, way station attendants or long-haul pilots. And my friends were the same. As far as we were concerned, food just appeared in our house, and a new screen was something that showed up one day. If I thought about it at all, I assumed machines did all that kind of work. But it's not machines, it's people. So let's treat them like people." Damn, that had been a strong drink. "You think everyone would look the other way if the Oort Research Centre disappeared? Not a chance. We're fancy academics. But what do we do?" I rubbed my palms over my face. I wasn't saying this right.

"I take your meaning," said Yarrow. "It is morally unconscionable for one life to be held more important than another, and even more so for a life to be regarded as disposable." He finished off his own drink. "The purpose of determining Pardus's fate is to prevent the same befalling another station."

I nodded.

"Preferably prior to the same befalling us," said Yarrow, but he was smiling.

"I'll drink to that," I said and waved down the server.

Chapter 5

We were a handful of drinks deep when we staggered back to our tiny cabin on the way station. We'd done the calculations: star liner fare to Exodus, the fare home to the research centre, plus a new screen for me, and we could only afford one room. To be fair, I'd already been two drinks deep when we'd made that decision, and every time Yarrow gestured with his hands, I'd had to deliberately direct my thoughts away from how they felt wandering over various parts of my body. But to be even more fair, I'm perfectly capable of doing basic math while slightly inebriated. So there. I'm pretty sure I said that to Yarrow as I leaned on his arm while he checked us in.

He led the way into our room and collapsed onto one of the twin beds, supporting himself with two of his hands behind him. But the other two were still free. I straddled his thighs, and he rumbled in his chest.

"You are intoxicated, Carolina."

"Yep." I leaned in, close enough to feel his breath on my face, but he held me back from bringing our lips together. I whined and squirmed.

"Carolina, you and I will not be intimate tonight."

I squirmed harder in his lap. A certain part of him definitely wanted to be intimate with me. "We won't?"

"No. I'm no expert on human relationships, but my understanding is that physical intimacy is conventionally accompanied by some sort of commitment, a commitment we no longer share."

"Not all humans need that." Why couldn't he just go with it instead of being all logical and considering the future?

"Have you forgotten that we had many conversations on this subject when your mind was clear? You seemed very certain then that you desired some measure of commitment from your sexual partners."

What a boring conversation. I just wanted those four hands all over me. Was that really so much to ask? "I've changed my mind. No commitment necessary." I leaned in again, but Yarrow didn't let up.

"I'm afraid I can't accept such a modification until your system is free of intoxicants." He smoothed a hand down my arm. "As much as I might like to."

I squeaked as he lifted me far too easily and set me down on the other bed. He was really turning me down! Heat crept up my neck and over my face. I'd just tried to drunkenly jump Yarrow, and he'd ever so gently saved me from myself.

I scrambled off the bed and locked myself in the bathroom. When I came out, we silently switched places, and by the time he came back in the room, I pretended that I was already asleep. He was right, of course. Indulging this would only make it harder in the morning when we stopped pretending and went back to being awkward—in that case, very awkward—colleagues.

By morning, my stomach roiled, but meds quickly took care of the hangover part, leaving only the guilt part. I'd put Yarrow in an incredibly uncomfortable situation last night. I could practically still feel his hardness on my thigh through our clothes. *Yikes.* Time to get out of here.

I muttered something about meeting him at the shuttle and went in search of a new screen. I hemmed and hawed over the model as long as possible to avoid having to sit in a silent waiting lounge with Yarrow, and finally landed on last year's HGNT PicoDot 3. By then, I had to rush to the gate.

Yarrow was already there, of course. I tapped my fob to pay for my shuttle ticket and stepped aside for Yarrow to pay for his. Chances were they would still be able to track us this way, but at least Lancaster wouldn't be roped in with us anymore. I took a deep breath. We were risking our careers, but we didn't need to risk him as well, especially without his permission.

I stepped through the gate, and Yarrow followed me down the walkway to the shuttle. I tapped the glowing button on the doors, and they whooshed open, releasing a rush of cool, processed air. Should I wipe the waystation grime off my shoes before stepping over the threshold onto the subtly patterned white floor? There was obviously nothing to wipe them on, so instead, I found a pair of empty seats, and slid in next to the window.

Yarrow settled himself beside me. It was odd not to have any luggage. I'd picked up a little backpack, my new screen, the notebook and pencil I'd considered in the video booth, and a change of clothes from the way station general store. We'd also crammed the emergency rations from the lifeboat into my bag before selling the useless boat for scrap. Since Yarrow had had his screen in his pocket when we fled *Lepton*, resupplying had made considerably less of a dent in his account than it had in mine.

I couldn't hold it in anymore. "You're sure you want to do this?"

Predictably, he gave me an annoyed look. "I stated earlier that I am part of this endeavour."

"I know," I said. "Sorry."

He shook his head. "There's no need to apologize, Carolina. You did nothing wrong." He chuckled softly. "I doubt I'll ever get accustomed to your quirk of double-checking."

"It isn't just me. Lots of humans double-check." But I smiled as well. "What were you able to save on your screen?"

"I found a few notes in the screen's cache last night, along with two documents from the librarian, both of which I had already read, unfortunately."

"Your notes are a good find," I said. "I may be able to extract more information from your documents from my alternative perspective, if you wouldn't mind sharing."

Yarrow nodded. "I didn't write them to be intelligible to others, but you're welcome to consult me on the unclear points." He transferred the rescued files to my screen with a tap, and I dove into them.

The two documents were obituaries for miners, who had apparently passed away in a mining accident on an interstellar station a few years back, across the Orion Arm from Pardus. I cross-referenced with Yarrow's notes; there had been a headline about their mining operation in the librarian's records, but the actual news article was missing, like my academic papers. If these folks had disappeared like the people on Pardus, that would explain the missing article. The obituaries were vague, but they did mention some surviving family. Had they been fed the mining accident story? Had they been told the truth and sworn to secrecy like Dr. Sycamore? Interrogating the families of tragically deceased miners ranked at the bottom of my list of avenues to explore.

I scrolled to the top of Yarrow's notes file and skimmed. A lot of it was unintelligible, especially the translated version I was reading. The automatic translator worked best on documents with full sentences, and point-form notes with lots of technical jargon left tons of words translated phonetically.

"What's a gh'ratal?" I said, turning my screen to Yarrow.

He knit his brow and looked where I was pointing. He snorted at the translator's spelling attempt. "*Quark.*"

I nodded and kept on. Soon, I knew the words for *toroid*, *electron*, *neutrino*, and the equivalents of electron, muon, and tau neutrino generations.

"I thought you said you'd mostly looked up news articles at the library," I said when I ran across *photon* and added it to my mental dictionary. Which maybe should become an actual dictionary at this point.

"Mostly," said Yarrow. "You'll find a list of suspected disappearance events at the end of my notes, based on the missing news reports. I took more notes on the little I discovered about the data we'd already analyzed. You searched the experimental and practical measurement side, and I went for a more cosmology-based approach. Neither of which had much to offer."

I had recreated my research notes from the library as best I could from memory and shared the file with Yarrow. It seemed he was finding them as enlightening as I was finding his, which was to say, a total dead end except for all the holes filled with question marks. Still, hope bubbled in my chest. We were researchers. Holes filled with question marks were building blocks with which to construct hypotheses, experiments, and eventually, theories. I opened up a new document and shared it with Yarrow, then titled the thing: "Question Marks."

Once we got from the way station to the nearby transit hub, we booked passage a few systems over, where we'd be able to reach the lab itself.

It would be easy to get a ride out to Exodus Labs. The labs' website had all the information we needed, addressed to students since their program was one of the most popular in the region.

The journey would only be overnight by star liner, so we didn't bother to pay for a private room—private rooms—or anything. We'd make do with a table in the atrium or wander the viewing deck to make the time go more quickly.

After boarding, we gathered with all the other passengers on the viewing deck to watch the launch and the swirling orange moon retreat into the distance. I rested my forearms on the rail and leaned into them as passengers trickled away to gamble or eat. Yarrow stood beside me, one set of hands spread on the rail, the other crossed over his chest.

"Are we making a mistake?" I said.

"Is that the reason you continue to ask me if I'm sure I want to participate in our venture?" said Yarrow. "You aren't sure yourself?"

I hadn't thought of it that way, but maybe Yarrow was right. He was sure. Whenever he made a decision, he was always so sure. I tried to be like that. Sometimes too much so. I'd completed my master's under a supervisor I could barely stand by the end because I'd put in so much effort to convince him to take me on. After all, what would my parents have said if I'd given up and found a new supervisor? But there was no doubt I would have been happier working with someone else.

The planet we'd left behind was now no wider than my little finger, just big enough to let us know it wasn't really a star. Soon it would disappear completely, and the star it was orbiting would become just another speckle, one of millions spattered across the sky.

"We need to do something," I said. "Dr. Sycamore signed an NDA. She gave up. But she still passed us information when we needed it."

"Dr. Proust didn't. And he's dead."

"Exactly."

Yarrow sighed heavily. "You are questioning whether you'd die for this research if it comes to that. That is very important to determine. I've made my decision." He smiled out the window. "But I don't tend to shy away from tussles, even when outmatched. And you need to make your own. Either way, you've already accomplished so much in the pursuit of Pardus Station. No one would blame you for putting the project to rest."

If by *accomplished so much* he meant implicating him, annoying a retired researcher, getting Lancaster surveilled, and losing his ship forever, then yes, I'd accomplished plenty.

We were already on our way to see Prof. Morbit, so there was no point in turning around now.

"Okay," I said. "After we talk to Professor Morbit, I'll make my decision." Going to see him would be safe enough. Exodus Labs was open to the public and filled with students. It wasn't some shady operation where they could make us disappear.

The star liner dropped us off at a port with small shuttles to the labs running every ten minutes, and the platform was packed with undergrads staring at standard-issue screens. They barely looked up when the shuttle pulled in, and Yarrow and I were practically swept aboard as they all seamlessly packed onto the thing. How did they find seats without looking up from their screens? I found an empty one near the door, and Yarrow motioned for me to take it. I didn't resist; he could hold on with all four hands if he wanted to.

Exodus Labs came into view, and I leaned forward to get a better look through the front of the shuttle. The tube-shaped megastation rotated slowly, distant stars just visible through its centre as we approached one end. Five Oort Research Centres could have fit comfortably inside the thing, and appendages housing independent labs, either temporarily visiting or privately run, bristled off the main tube in all directions. The shuttle flew straight in one end of the tube and latched on inside.

The doors popped and then slid open, and the students once again exited while barely glancing up from their screens. Just a commute for them. The shuttle we had vacated was quickly filled again. Stations had a strange way of feeling like constant rush hour, since there was no day and no night. Shifts and classes were scheduled round the clock.

Not a single student stopped to admire the lobby, and we had to move to the side so as not to impede foot traffic. Glowing translucent curves reached up at least five stories. Huge protrusions, like burls on an old tree, swelled out of the walls every few metres, seemingly at random, and their walls thinned to near transparency.

I went straight for the directory terminals lined up on the opposite wall. We wouldn't get anywhere simply asking around for Prof. Morbit; the likelihood of bumping into someone who knew him specifically out of the hundreds of researchers working here was slim to none. I did a quick search for his name, and a Call button popped up. No floor, room, or directions were indicated. On a station this big, some areas would be restricted from public access, and we'd need proof of visitor status to get through security; Prof. Morbit's office must be in one.

I didn't call the professor ahead of time for the same reason that I'd surprised Dr. Sycamore: I didn't want anyone else to know that we were coming. I'd underestimated the scope of this lab and, likely, of Prof. Morbit's work. I'd never heard of neutrino entanglement, so I'd assumed it was a tiny offshoot field in a backwater station. Apparently not.

We'd come this far.

I hit the Call button.

The call rang five times before I gave up and closed it. Maybe the professor was out or away or even just asleep. There hadn't been an option to leave a message. Maybe I could message him from my screen. How had it not crossed my mind that he might not be available? I'd simply assumed that he'd have let me know if he was going to be away when he invited me.

Across from the main information desk, we found a bench and sat. Yarrow hadn't said anything. I pulled up the professor's contact form and shot off a message letting him know that we were at the station and would appreciate a meeting.

"So now we wait," I said.

My screen pinged. Prof. Morbit had replied already? I pulled it up.

Thanks for contacting me. Unfortunately, I will be out of the office until...

"Out of office" auto-reply. He wouldn't be back for a week. I turned my screen to Yarrow, and he read over the message. Leaving now seemed a lot like giving up, and finding a place to stay for the week wouldn't be hard. With all the lab visitors and students cycling through the station, there would be places available. The trick would be ensuring I had enough credits left afterward to book passage home. Research didn't exactly pay well.

"I propose a tour of the lab while we wait," said Yarrow. He jerked his chin toward the desk opposite us. A large Tour Group Assembly Point sign flickered beside it, cycling through various languages.

"You expect to gain new insight from a public tour?" I said. Everything would probably be too low level to get much out of it.

Yarrow shrugged and crossed to the desk. We potentially had a week to kill, and what harm could it do to learn more about this place? Maybe the tour guide would be able to tell me something about neutrino entanglement and the tour wouldn't end up being a complete loss. We could sort out our next moves after we knew more about this place. Professor Morbit led a whole research group. For all I knew, someone from the group might be willing to talk to us and save us the wait.

Yarrow turned and waved me over, and I crossed to the desk next to him. The clerk wore an Exodus Labs uniform, complete with a little hat over her short hair.

"The next tour starts in fifteen minutes. Just come to the assembly point. Your tour guide will be a grad student here at the lab."

"One who's not a fan of TA'ing?" I said.

The desk clerk smiled. "Exactly. Neither am I. Between you and me, hosting the public pays better as well."

"Doesn't everything?" I said.

"Sounds like you're in academia."

"Yes, both of us are researchers," I said, gesturing to Yarrow. "We're here to consult with a professor at the lab, but turns out he's away for a while."

"Which professor?" said the clerk. "Maybe I can point you to their students or someone in a related field."

"Professor Grell Morbit? Neutrino entanglement."

The desk clerk tapped her lip with a bright-orange nail. "I think I had him for Intro to Quantum Entanglement back when I was doing my master's. He was away so much that the TA practically taught the course. I think I've seen him around, if you want to look him up. Jasper Gorsch. He might still work at Exodus."

"Thanks so much," I said and gave her a genuine smile. We had fifteen minutes to kill before the tour, so I pulled out my screen and shot off a message to Dr. Jasper Gorsch.

The tour guide was already talking to a family when we walked up fifteen minutes later. The kid was busy asking a million questions, wildly waving her hands as the tour guide nodded, beamed, and answered almost as emphatically, even though she was about two feet taller.

"...when they're finished, the spokes often hitch a ride on an outgoing shuttle and take a star liner back to their permanent research lab," she was saying as we came in earshot.

"They just stick off the side?" said the kid, who couldn't have been more than ten.

"Yes, they're designed to attach securely to standard hatches." The guide looked up from the kid when we stopped next to them. "You must be the other folks for the tour! I'm Rica. I've already got to know a bit about Jaylin and her parents here, but I like to know a bit about the interests of my tour group. Where are you from?"

I looked at Yarrow. He'd got us into this, so he could be our ambassador.

"We're researchers at the Oort Research Centre in the Solar System," he said.

Rica's face lit up. "What's your field? It must be something interstellar-related to be affiliated with the Oort Centre."

"I explore local trends and anomalies in the interstellar vacuum," said Yarrow. "Mostly just analyzing huge datasets and doing statistical analysis."

"Doesn't every practical field boil down to statistical analysis?" said Rica with a giggle.

Yarrow smiled back, the two of them pretty much talking right over my head. Literally.

Rica dropped her gaze to me. "What about you? What's your area of concentration?"

"My PhD was on actuator fluctuations in nebulous gasses and gas transfer to the vacuum post-contact. My post-doc research is also focussed on effects of constructed objects on their surrounding vacuum."

The little kid was staring at me and Yarrow open mouthed. Most of the people who worked here probably had research areas that sounded just as impressive.

Heat crept up my neck. "That's just a fancy way of saying *What happens to space when ships move through it?*" I turned to Rica. "What about you?"

"My thesis is"—she waved her hand in front of her face—"about something to do with neutrinos. Let's not talk about it." She grimaced, and I chuckled. She started the tour, assuring us and the little kid that she would get into as many technical details as she was able, then winked at the parents and assured them that she would tell them all about the interdepartmental drama at the lab.

The tour, while edifying, was also not terribly useful to our current project. Exodus Labs specialized in research on lepton interactions, with a focus on neutrinos and the weak bosons. It had a number of affiliated institutions across the Galaxy, including the Europa Institute, where I had done my master's work. I hadn't heard of Exodus when I'd been there back in...last decade? *Yikes.* No wonder.

As we left the neutrino detection wing and headed for the neutrino production wing, the corridor opened into a huge concourse, giant viewports up one side, and a vaulted gallery in the middle where the floor was six decks down and about four more up.

Jaylin ran to the railing, her parents trailing her, and Rica fell into step with me.

"What brings you and Yarrow to our humble station?" she said.

If Rica hadn't been chattering away and asking questions of every member of our little tour for a half hour already, I might not have answered her. But she seemed to be one of those people who was genuinely interested in strangers.

"We're meeting a colleague, and we had some time to kill beforehand. Yarrow thought a tour might be interesting."

"And has it been interesting? I really hope it has been. I want to keep my five-star tour guide rating."

"Yes, I'm glad he dragged me into it," I said. "I don't get to see this side of academia very often." I gestured at the little kid, walking ahead of us between her parents, waving wildly at the stars out the huge multi-storey viewport. "It's nice to be around someone who hasn't had the wonder drained out of them by post-secondary education."

Rica laughed. "That's part of the reason I like to run these tours," she said. "Watching undergrads gradually have all their enthusiasm worn away over the course of the semester gets me down."

"Some of us enjoyed our post-secondary education," rumbled Yarrow from behind us.

"So when did you have your sense of wonder drained out of you?" I said.

"I still possess my sense of wonder," said Yarrow.

I was about to scoff, but I held myself back. How long had it been since I'd really looked at Yarrow? Not just seeing what I expected to see but taking him in as a person? I nodded instead.

Rica hurried to the front of the group. "We're entering the strange world of neutrino production! When we step through these doors..."

The rest of the tour didn't include any private labs, and it turned out that was where Dr. Jasper Gorsch was currently working. When we got back to the front desk, I checked my screen and found a one-line response from Jasper:

Room 4354 —J

I took that as agreement to meet with us, and after thanking Rica and bidding farewell to our tour companions, Yarrow and I made for the elevators.

We waited for our turn with a few other folks. A set of doors slid open, and though there was space for four people inside, only one student entered. When no one else made a move to do so, neither did Yarrow and I. Maybe it was a convention not to share here?

Finally, our elevator arrived. Inside, there were no rows of numbered buttons, just a keypad with a label peeling off that said *Room Code*. I dutifully typed in the code Jasper had sent along, and the elevator doors slid shut.

The elevator slid sideways, and I stumbled a step and reflexively grasped the rail. I had been ready for the thing to move upward, but this explained the personal elevator convention; they moved around the tube-shaped station as well as up and down.

"Did you know this thing was going to toss me at the wall?" I said.

Yarrow casually held the rail with all four hands. "I had a hunch. I wouldn't have let you get tossed too badly," he said.

"Thanks so much," I said. "Really makes me feel better that you'd only let me get slightly tossed."

Yarrow chuckled. The elevator slowed, and I braced myself for another lateral move, but the elevator dinged, and the doors slid open on a long white hallway, exactly like all the ones we'd seen on the tour, except that a row of hatches studded the right-hand side of this hall with room numbers listed beside each. When we reached 4354, the hatch stood open.

Should I knock on the frame or something?

The open room inside was scattered with desks, some occupied by silent folks, heads bent over their screens, headphones on. A few office doorways ranged on the walls. Somehow, I'd thought high-tech Exodus Labs would have equally fancy grad student offices. Apparently not. On the other hand, this was one of those bristles that I had noticed coming in: an independent lab attached to the side of Exodus, not part of the main lab itself.

A student with artfully tousled hair and light brown skin stuck his head out of one of the offices, waved at us, and then disappeared. I looked at Yarrow. Were we supposed to follow? The student slouched out of the office before I could make up my mind and met us at the door, sticking out his hand to shake.

"I'm Jasper, I got your message. Carolina, right?"

"Yes, I heard you work with Professor Morbit," I said.

"Not anymore. I did at one point, then I changed my research focus." Jasper glanced around the lab, and I caught a glare from one of the students. "Let's head to the caf. We can talk there. Our lab is a mandated quiet area." He cracked a smile when he said that. Maybe the mandate came from the glaring student more so than the supervisor.

I fell into step with Jasper, Yarrow a few steps behind.

"So what's your concentration now?" I said.

"Quantum teleportation."

I didn't formulate an answer from my jumble of questions until we'd filed through the short caf line and found a table in the corner. The caf was moderately busy but, as with the shuttle, probably would have been no matter what time of day we'd shown up, since everyone at the station was on a slightly different schedule. I sat next to Yarrow, and Jasper sat across from us.

"Any luck solving quantum teleportation?" I said, trying to keep my voice light.

Yarrow huffed quietly. I was not being as subtle as I'd hoped. Or maybe my anxiety was only obvious to Yarrow, since he knew why I was asking. Was it possible that someone had solved quantum tele-portation and Pardus hadn't disappeared, it had been teleported?

Jasper laughed, thankfully missing or ignoring the tension in my voice. "It's still the same old problem. The cosmic rules about trans-porting matter faster than the speed of light are unbreakable, and if you make an exact replica at another point in space, what do you do with the old copy?"

"Why bother studying it, then?" I said.

"Ah, I just like to say *quantum teleportation*. Sounds impressive, and it's a conversation starter. I actually work on transmitting large data packets via neutrino entanglement, hence my work with Pro-fessor Morbit. He's more focussed on establishing entanglement over long distances as opposed to passing information. But if you have questions about quantum entanglement, I can probably help you out."

Telling Jasper that we were trying to uncover a conspiracy to hide disappearances of large objects in interstellar space wouldn't give us much credibility. Sitting at the dinged-up caf table, eating synthesized mashed potatoes, I barely believed it myself.

Yarrow jumped in. "We discovered a strange neutrino distribution pattern in interstellar space, something we'd never encountered be-fore, and we've been looking for someone more experienced to exam-ine it for us."

"Sure, I'm happy to help out. Transfer your analysis to my screen, and I'll give it a gander."

I looked at Yarrow. Not only did we no longer have the data—it had been deleted by the council what seemed like months ago—but we didn't even have our notes from *Lepton*'s server, which had disap-peared along with *Lepton*.

"Unfortunately, the data was lost," said Yarrow.

"Shit, I'm sorry. It sucks losing work. So, are you planning to describe your lost data to me and have me magically tell you what it means?" said Jasper, raising an eyebrow.

"When you put it that way…" I said. Coming here had been a silly idea. How had we thought someone could interpret data we didn't even have anymore?

"Is there any process you know of that could leave traces as a pattern of neutrinos?"

Jasper put down his fork and propped his elbows on the table. "Neutrinos, by and large, are far too random to appear naturally in a pattern, so I would think some sort of process was involved, yes. As to what sort…it could be anything. Not natural, but anything else. There are tons of processes these days that use neutrinos to transmute matter, power ships and other machinery that requires a large power draw." Jasper shrugged. "Sorry I can't narrow it down." He took a bite.

"No, we appreciate your input," I said. "If we can get our hands on another similar dataset, can we send it your way, along with our analysis?"

"Absolutely. I read a literature review recently on some kind of detector that could extract information from traces of neutrino patterns. They don't hang around for long, most of the time, so it's not a popular topic."

"What don't hang around for long?" I said. Was he talking about neutrinos? We'd picked up the pattern days after Pardus's disappearance.

"The pattern diffuses into the background within minutes, usually, so you'd have to be using whatever detector pretty much directly after the event, and if you knew the event happened, then why bother to determine its properties using the neutrino pattern, you know?" He speared a cube of tofu with his fork and popped it into his mouth.

My fork hung in the air, and I lowered it and tried to clear my features. Did that mean whatever neutrino pattern we'd picked up had somehow been preserved for all that time, or had we done our scan within moments of some event occurring at the exact site where Pardus had disappeared? Either one seemed impossible.

We'd come to Exodus Labs for answers, but Jasper's kind information dump just raised more questions. He was adamant that neutrino patterns don't hang around. They are unstable and easily diluted with background radiation, and they just don't have the capacity to leave long-term imprints. He finally made an offhand remark about checking our equipment calibration and changed the subject once we'd badgered him enough. I didn't blame him. Arguing with people who didn't have the background for their claims was one of the worst parts of being a physicist.

Still, that left us on our way to hunt down accommodations with no more clue about our neutrino patterns than we'd had before. Was it possible that it had been a calibration error? Could the pattern we'd observed have been essentially imaginary? We hadn't taken any control readings in other parts of interstellar space, and the probe that had collected the data was long gone now and not available for calibration.

The lobby was slightly emptier now, and Yarrow sat beside me. Like me, he had his screen tucked away and was staring into space, both literally and figuratively. Dr. Morbit would be away for almost a week, so we'd have to get a cabin. Cabins. If we could each afford our own. Then again, why waste the money? We were adults who could bunk in the same room without any lingering awkwardness, right?

Beating my head against the brick wall of Pardus's disappearance was more appealing than imagining spending a week sharing a room with Yarrow and what might happen between us.

Dr. Morbit would be back in a few days, hopefully with more information in person than he'd been willing to part with over our call. And there was also Yarrow's Moritz distribution idea that Dr. Sycamore had seemed so nervous about. I'd been so focussed on the list of contacts Dr. Sycamore had given me at the end of our meeting that I'd never even thought to ask Yarrow about the distribution. It hadn't shown up in his notes, strangely.

"What's a Moritz distribution?" I said.

Yarrow blinked and turned to me.

"Sorry, I didn't mean to interrupt."

"No need to apologize," said Yarrow. "It's something akin to the toroidal distribution we observed, at electron substructure scale. It's based on a theory that electrons aren't point particles but composed of a toroidal distribution of smaller charged particles, the Mortiz distribution."

"And the toroidal particle distribution we observed resembles the Moritz distribution, except with atoms in vacuum instead of sub-atomic charges?"

"Exactly."

"Sounds like coincidence to me."

"Might be."

There were altogether too many maybes and perhapses, loose threads, and outright dead ends in the lines of inquiry we were trying to follow. Without more information, more data, another avenue to explore, would we ever be able to work it out?

My gut twisted. Was it time to give up? I wandered the port's viewing deck, where a star liner outside was gearing up to launch. I picked at a scratch on the railing. The other gawkers swarmed the windows farther down, watching the star liner test its engines, but I stared into the blackness of space punctuated by a few flickering specks of distant stars, the splash of a nebula. Somewhere out there, Lancaster waited to chew me out, maybe fire me for almost getting killed and getting my associate killed. Losing his ship, his baby. When he'd lent me *Lepton*, I'd thought he was encouraging me to break the council's rules, but what if I'd been wrong? What if he'd expected us to come back when he sent that warning that the council was on their way to appropriate our data?

A light tread passed behind me and stopped. Someone leaned on the rail in my peripheral vision. It wasn't Yarrow. The person was shorter than me by a foot, willowy, with semi-transparent lavender skin and huge black eyes. They didn't speak. Though the rail extended unoccupied on either side of me, this person stood barely an arm's length away. The star liner's engines rumbled the deck as it finally launched, and I turned back to the vastness of space and my forthcoming doom.

At the very least, I could state with confidence that Yarrow had nothing to do with my complete and total disregard for the council's dictates. I didn't have to take him down with me. Where to go and what to do when I was released from my position at the research centre would be a problem to confront when it arose.

"Nice day for a voyage," said the person next to me.

I suppressed my sigh. "I didn't check the weather. Astral wind peaking?"

"Oh yeah," she said. "Nice and strong today." They gestured out the window as though they could see the astral wind. Maybe they could.

I nodded.

"Ever been on a star liner before?" she said.

"Yes, a few times. You?"

"Oh, yes! I travel constantly."

"How does that ship compare?" I said. Maybe completing the conversation would be the fastest way to end it.

"That one's a long route, so a pretty big ship, as star liners go. It doesn't have much in the way of luxury, but it's practical. The Solar System tends to favour economy, overall. They don't favour anything too flashy."

"You've been to the Solar System before?"

"I'm there all the time."

"Me too. I grew up there."

She chuckled. "I figured you for a human."

I nodded again and took a breath to make my excuses so I could escape.

"I have no idea how I found myself so enmeshed with Solar culture. The Galaxy is so huge and..."

"The Solar System is so small," I finished with a smirk.

Another ship's engines rumbled the floor, and something rattled in one of the on-board shops behind me.

"I came halfway across the Galaxy to work at Exodus, but my work takes me all over human-centric space."

Exodus labs was the largest settlement in this sector by about five to ten times. Most of the folks on this star liner worked here. Bumping into another Exodus researcher was less than surprising.

"I don't travel much for my work. Mostly just analyze data gathered by the rest of my group," I said.

"Do you work at Exodus as well? What group are you in?"

"No, I'm here to visit. Just looking for some expertise on neutrino entanglement."

"You don't look as though you've found it. Which is odd because Exodus Labs is the pre-eminent neutrino research facility in the Orion Arm."

"The person I came to consult is away, actually. He won't be back for a week." Which was strange. He hadn't mentioned that he'd be gone when I'd talked to him a couple days ago.

"So you'll be here a while, then? My research is more particulate focussed, but if you need anything, I'm more than happy to help out. Or if you want a tour of Exodus. I'm Trix. Look me up in the directory."

"We actually took the tour already, but that's very kind. I do have some vacuum particulate distribution questions I'd love to get some eyes on." How had Trix known that? What were the chances of a random stranger being able to help with our torus problem?

"I knew it!" Trix grinned.

Shit! Did she know about Pardus?

"My cards never lead me astray. They said come talk to you, and here I am, ready to answer your questions." She pulled a deck from inside her robe pocket and brandished it at me. "Everyone makes fun of me. You humans, always so concerned with proof."

Her *deck of cards* had led her to me? Did the people who were after me really think I'd fall for this?

"I'll do a reading for you, if you want. I can tell that you don't believe in oracle cards, but sometimes, one reading is all it takes. Here!" She gestured to a nearby empty high table with two stools, dusted a few crumbs onto the floor, and spread her cards in one long sweep. She folded her hands and stared at me.

"Um, what do I do?" Was I really doing this?

"Pick a few."

"How many?" *A few* was a very nebulous quantity.

"How many feels right?"

Was she trying to annoy me? I could just say *none*. Why not just tell me the optimal number? "Um...three?"

"Wonderful! Pick three."

"Should I look at them?"

"If that feels right to you, then go ahead."

I gingerly tapped three cards, evenly spaced along the deck, and crossed my arms.

Trix snatched the three cards and placed them face down on the table, sweeping the rest of the deck back into a perfect stack to one side. She flipped the first card. The art showed a bright-pink nebula, dumbbell shaped, three stars hidden behind the dust, somehow flickering. A chill snaked up my spine. No, the flickering must be my imagination.

"A nebula. Things are in flux right now. Murky. There's nothing definite when you get a nebula. This one in particular represents a descent into the fog and eventually coming out the other side."

Obviously, that could mean anything. I'd humour Trix while she looked at the other cards. Two more wouldn't take that long, and I had nowhere to be. She flipped the next card.

It was a planet, blue-green and gaseous. *Let me guess, another wishy-washy prediction?*

"Planets have firm gravity and steady orbits. This one knows where it's going and pulls others along like moons."

Again, what could that mean? Whatever.

Trix flipped the last card. My nails dug into my palm.

"Pardus," I murmured.

A lone space station over a scattering of stars, a smaller ship just coming in to dock with it. Trix wasn't saying anything.

She was staring straight at me.

Chapter 6

"Pardus," she said. "Where do you know that name from?"

Shit. Had "they" caught up with us? Did she know what we were doing here, after they'd told us to back off? How had she ensured the card that looked *exactly* like Pardus Station turned up? She must have done some trickery with the card shuffling or something.

She was still gazing thoughtfully at me. "What are the chances that I'd bump into someone who knows that name here at Exodus?" Trix mused. The words could have come out of my mouth, because I was definitely thinking the same. "I guess my cards did lead me to you." She squared her shoulders. "I am a collective consciousness species. I have beings all over the Galaxy, one of whom was on Pardus Station. Since you know the name, I assume you're familiar with what happened to the station. The being who was aboard...we haven't been able to feel her in weeks."

If this was a set-up, it was extremely elaborate.

Trix had opened up to me, so it was only fair that I do the same. "Pardus Station disappeared three weeks ago. I'm..." Might as well go all the way. "I'm here to ask around about some of the data we collected from the site."

"What do you mean by disappeared? It's lost? Did they go off course? No, I'd still be able to feel my being." She shook her head, the hope that had briefly shone in her eyes dimming. "By *disappeared*, you mean it was vapourized?"

"None of the evidence supports that. But no, they didn't just change course." Trix was a particulate scientist. She'd know what to do with our findings. "I determined that the station was gone by looking for wake traces at their last known location. Wake traces that simply ended abruptly. My colleague and I went to that location and took further measurements, and we found a particulate cloud, albeit a subtle one, in a toroidal distribution."

"Trix was nodding. "As though a magnetic field had orbited the station."

"What?" There was an obvious explanation for that random torus we'd found?

"It's usually on a much bigger scale, when a satellite with a magnetic field orbits a planet, it leaves behind a kind of trail, a torus, where its orbit is."

Orbited? Pardus Station had been orbited by another body and then disappeared?

"Oh, you weren't about to say that! Go on, I'm sorry for interrupting. Where did the torus come from?" Trix squared up her cards and shuffled them.

"We had no clue. I think you just solved our particulate problem."

I exchanged info with Trix and assured her that I would be in touch with any other Pardus news.

When I finally got back, exhausted, to our shared room—our budget was even tighter now that we needed accommodation here as well—I found Yarrow deep in double sleep, one arm thrown over his eyes, the others crunched into his body by the narrow bunk. His antennae relaxed across the pillow, though as I watched, one of them jerked. Was that like REM for Yarrow, or did he know I was here?

I slipped into the bathroom (that doubled as a shower stall) to get ready for bed, then climbed to the top bunk, my back practically brushing the bulkhead as I ascended the ladder. I loosened the tightly tucked top sheet and slid under the thin blanket. The pillow barely dented when I rested my head on it, but it's not like I had a selection, so I closed my eyes.

"Goodnight, Carolina," said Yarrow.

I gasped and sighed it out. "I thought you were asleep." I pried my eyes back open. The ceiling loomed in front of my face in the dark.

"I was."

"Double sleep, I mean."

"Yes."

"But you knew I was here?"

"Yes, of course."

"Humans don't. Not when we're asleep."

"Hmm."

I didn't think he was going to answer, so I closed my eyes again, all too aware that Yarrow was lying in bed only a few feet below me.

"You're very vulnerable when you're sleeping," said Yarrow.

"Hence, the individual rooms with locked doors while we do it." Was this really the time to have a conversation about the unique properties of humans?

"You aren't locked away from me." What the hell was he getting at?

"I trust you."

"We're no longer romantically involved."

Heat bloomed in my core, but I shoved it down. "I am aware of that," I snapped. "I trust several people I'm not romantically involved with." Not that I could name any, but there had to be someone. Everyone had someone.

And now I was lying in bed practically within arm's reach of Yarrow, thinking about when we'd been romantically involved. At this moment, I couldn't remember why we'd broken up at all. Something to do with him sensing my emotions too much, but how could a partner be too sensitive? What kind of maladjusted adult was I?

"I value your trust," said Yarrow. He sighed. "I don't always recall that you aren't aware of how you are emoting."

He knew that I was thinking about how we used to be together? Or did he know that I was questioning why we'd broken up? He couldn't read my thoughts. Just emotions. "What level of granularity can you sense, with respect to emotions?"

"I am currently aware of your nostalgia, which I can only assume was triggered by my mention of our romantic entanglement."

So yes, he did know that I was thinking about how good our relationship had been. Or he could easily infer that from my nostalgia. And that's why we broke up. Humans treasure their private thoughts, and having my privacy invaded like this constantly left me exhausted, especially with no reciprocation. There was one way to fix that.

"What are you thinking about," I said. "No, wait, what are you trying to *emote* to me right now?"

Yarrow chuckled. "Finding words to represent emotions seems futile." His sheets rustled, and the bunk shook. "I will attempt it."

I rolled onto my side, toward the opening of the bunk so that the bulkhead was a little farther from my face.

"I believe that my emotions are tangled together at the moment. I am glad you are here with me, as I always am when you're around. I am disappointed that our voyage seems futile, in the end. I am slightly angry that we will likely be heading back to the research centre empty-handed. I am honoured that you trust me enough to enter your vulnerable sleeping state in the same room with me and consider a locked door to be unnecessary between us.

"And, Carolina, I'm also nostalgic when I recall our relation-ship. I very much enjoyed it, and I...I still like you very much."

My heart leaped, almost into my mouth, and I took a deep breath, trying to get my pounding pulse under control.

"But I am very much aware of the challenges inherent in an interspecies romance."

Maybe challenges that couldn't be overcome. There were reasons we'd broken up. Good reasons. "Unless you're willing to constantly narrate your feelings to me using language..." I laughed. They were good reasons.

"Hmm," said Yarrow again.

If he said anything more, I wasn't awake for it.

The next morning, I rolled out of my bunk and found a note from Yarrow on my screen: *Meet me at the Creature Café.* We'd passed it on our tour of Exodus, and I'd made some comment about how cute the little dragons were. (They weren't really drag-ons, but tiny lizards with wings counted, as far as I was con-cerned.) And I guess he'd remembered.

The clicking of mugs, the hiss of steam, and the soft babble of voices made my shoulders drop before I even turned the corner. A warm mug in my hands and cavorting dragons would let me forget about Pardus, losing *Lepton*, and this weird situation with Yarrow for a while.

As soon as I stepped into the café, Yarrow beckoned me over. I waved back and went to the counter to get my tea. I grabbed it and beelined for Yarrow's quiet corner. He put down his screen and picked up his mug.

"How was your day yesterday after we parted?" said Yarrow.

"I actually met someone who..." How did I explain that a part of Trix had been on Pardus? Probably just like that. "Part of her being was on Pardus, and she's also trying to figure out what happened."

Yarrow knit his brow. "You stumbled upon this person?"

"Yes, but she had these cards." I held up a hand. "It's not as suspicious as it sounds. Plus, she gave me a lead!"

Yarrow rumbled.

"She's an interstellar particulate expert, and she knows what might have made our torus." I quickly explained what Trix had told me. "So, not quite as stuck as we thought. And we can get in touch with her if we want more info." I blew on my steaming tea. "How's your tiny corner of space looking? Any luck getting Lancaster to approve your voyage request?" Unlike me, Yarrow had been brave enough to get in touch with Lancaster since our *Lepton* debacle. I'd subsequently sent him a message, but he'd never responded, and I hadn't tried again.

"Not as yet. Besides, the vessel's schedule is booked for months in advance."

"You've been waiting a couple years by now, what's a few more months?"

"That's after approval and registration." Yarrow sipped from his mug and stared into it. The steam curled up and dissipated.

"He's retaliating for Lepton, isn't he?" I said.

Yarrow shook his head. "I have no evidence of that. But I suspect having lost a ship upon which I was a crew-member, he is more reluctant to grant me authority over another."

My jaw spasmed. "I'll talk to him." No matter how horrible it would be. Yarrow didn't deserve this.

"I would prefer if you refrained. I plan to apply to crew the forthcoming voyage and petition the lead to allow one of my projects as a side activity."

Smart. Go around Lancaster without actually going around him.

"Besides, Lepton's disappearance was not your fault, Carolina. The perpetrator could have killed you. There's no need to put something right when it was never your wrong."

I clenched my teeth. He could say that all he wanted, but that didn't make it true. It have certainly never mattered for me growing up. Yikes. Subject change time.

If Yarrow was going to disappear for a couple months, Lancaster wasn't speaking to me, and I couldn't even wedge my foot in the door for my own research—not that I was totally sure what my research was about anymore—maybe it was time to put some serious thought into leaving the research centre and looking for another position. Maybe here, with Dr. Grell Morbit, whispered a little voice in the back of my head. Which made no sense, because my specialization had nothing to do with neutrino detectors. But I'd be lying if I said I wasn't interested.

I made an appointment with Lancaster, since that seemed to be the only way for me to catch him.

Yarrow left to meet Jasper Gorsch for lunch, and I found a quiet corner of the café. A little brown-streaked dragon fluttered by the window in their enclosure. I tapped Call, picked at my nail, and tried to swallow the lump in my throat. The screen flickered on, Lancaster's drawn face filling most of it. His office was barely larger than mine, but the little guest nook at the end of his desk marked him as someone who had folks come to him instead of the other way around. The chair there was empty, but that's where I'd sat countless times while he patiently helped me through snags in my projects.

"All the information for my sabbatical request was attached to the meeting entry, so I just need your formal approval."

Lancaster sighed. "I reviewed your request, but I didn't see the connection with your area of research." The drinking bird on the ledge above Lancaster's desk dipped its head. It rested on the edge of the cup of water; the liquid inside its body slid down, and it tilted upright.

"I'm exploring marginally related fields at the moment, and I have a contact at Exodus who's offered to show me around," I said. Finally, our eyes met, and Lancaster's tightened.

He puffed out a breath. "I understand." He pulled up the official request in the corner of the screen and tapped to approve it. "If you find greener pastures at Exodus, I'll be sorry to see you go," he said.

I nodded. "Thanks, me too."

I managed to keep the lump in my throat contained until my screen went dark. I let out a shaky breath and shook myself. This was good. This was progress instead of stagnation. Lancaster was on the same page as me about my future at Oort and didn't hint that he wanted me to stay. *Good.* I swiped my sleeve under my eye and blinked the rest of my tears back.

By the time Yarrow arrived back at the cafe, I was deep down the Pardus rabbit hole again. I'd had a long chat with Trix, and the resulting correspondence and research, therefore, had pretty much consumed the intervening hours—for both of us.

I started chattering to Yarrow about five seconds after he got his drink and sat down.

"So, do you want to collaborate with us?" I pulled up the agenda Trix and I had drafted for the next few days, but Yarrow was silent. I turned to him and finally looked.

He'd pulled up a seat beside mine, and he had his arms crossed over his chest, the others resting on the chair's arms. His head was cocked to one side, no doubt trying to figure me out.

"What?"

"I learned something of interest from Jasper."

"Oh yeah?" But all our data was gone. "Did he have another dataset from somewhere?"

Yarrow blushed and fixed his gaze on the table. "I recreated our data for him." He hurried on. "The neutrino pattern was characteristic of entanglement. Neutrinos don't hold their patterns, not on their own. They were generated by entangled particles. I haven't looked into it deeply enough to really understand, but somehow, a whole sea of neutrinos were generated by very specifically arranged entangled particles."

"Specifically arranged? Like in the shape of a huge station?"

Yarrow shrugged. "The arrangement itself was unclear. My memory of the dataset was vague at best."

"You spent all that time reconstructing it and then meeting with Jasper, so can I assume you're on board for our conference with Trix?" I added another attendee to the conference room booking. "Jasper is welcome to join us as well," I added. "If he's now been sucked into this Pardus thing, too."

"I'll let him know," said Yarrow.

I sent off Trix's information to Yarrow's screen and then opened up the "Question Marks" document I'd created and shared with Yarrow. I added *entangled neutrino generators* to the list.

Trix and I had decided that if we were having an unsanctioned meeting about Pardus, we were going to do it right. I still had my list of leads, and I would gather all the information I possibly could before our meeting.

Spending a few days with Yarrow at the Exodus was actually really nice. We headed for the concourse for a change of scenery the day before our conference, and there was only one big chair free in front of the giant viewports. Maybe it would have been big enough, if cozy, for two humans, but Yarrow and I were not going to both fit.

"I can find another seating arrangement—"

"That's not necessary," said Yarrow and patted his lap. "If you're amenable."

We'd spent days, back when we were together, curled up quietly with our research projects back at Oort. He opened his arms to me. Yup. Seemed like he remembered.

I cuddled into his lap. I wasn't *intoxicated* this time, so I was able to make this decision.

I tried to ignore how wonderful it felt to be snug and warm here again and started at the top of my list. For all that Yarrow and I had been trying to get to the coordinates that Dr. Sycamore had sent along, I'd never really looked into where they were beyond the chart: what was around that location, or what else could possibly be happening in the vicinity that might give us a hint as to what Dr. Sycamore was trying to tell us. It said a lot about how paranoid we'd been that my first instinct had been to go to the seemingly empty coordinates rather than research what was nearby. I just assumed that I'd come up empty, that anything Dr. Sycamore wanted to point us toward would be blacked out, top secret, and completely inaccessible. I was wrong.

The coordinates housed a Dyson ring, or one section of one. It had never actually been completed; whoever had been running the project had probably come up short on money and left the section to orbit the star. Since it had been sitting there for decades, tidally locked with no protection from the star's radiation, no doubt it was ablated almost beyond recognition at this point, just a tiny piece of space junk. Tiny in the hugest of terms, of course. The thing was the size of Luna, or thereabouts, albeit a thin sheet instead of a round clump.

I added all of this information to our shared notes and moved on to the next question on my list. The mechanical owner's manual from the librarian. Unfortunately, I had lost the model number on the manual, and searching for random manuals didn't yield any promising results. The rest of my leads fizzled in similar fashion, and I put down my screen and stared out into the field of stars.

I would have to follow up on that Dyson ring and see who had been building it. Maybe that was what Dr. Sycamore had wanted us to find. Trix had been collecting potentially useful data about gas tori, the ionized gasses found in the wake of orbiting bodies with magnetic fields, and why in the world or out of it we would have found one in the middle of interstellar space. Granted, it was tiny, as gas tori went, but it was still a very unusual formation to stumble on without a corresponding orbiting body.

Every time it seemed like we were making progress, we'd find ourselves up another cul-de-sac, stumbling on more information that just didn't make any sense. And yet, here we all were, ready to meet up and discuss all of this strange and disparate data that someone didn't want us to have our hands on in the first place. Poor Miller. Trying to hide things from the most curious and dogged demographic in the Galaxy: scientists.

Once Yarrow also gave up on his leads, we meandered back to our cabin. After some awkward hemming and hawing, I ended up curled next to Yarrow, and I fell asleep with my head on his chest, his steady heartbeat and two secure arms lulling me into dreams. Sure, I woke up in the night and moved to the other bunk so that I could stretch out, and sure, we hadn't so much as kissed, but physical contact is a human need that I had been without for far too long. I'd never asked Yarrow whether he needed physical contact as well, but he was always just as likely to put his arm around me as I was to snuggle up with him.

By the next morning, we weren't even trying to keep a professional distance. We weren't together, or if we were, we hadn't talked about it, but time apart had made both of us realize, I think, how much intimacy had grown between us. We held hands as we walked along Exodus Labs' wide concourse, stars on one side, a rail that overlooked the gallery on the other. Yarrow laid his other arm comfortably around my back, and I squeezed his hand. We chatted about something unimportant and laughed at each other's silly jokes. We didn't talk about Pardus.

We found a spot to eat some lunch and sat near the huge windows, watching the stars hang there in the sky.

Someone behind Yarrow caught my eye.

"Carolina?" said Yarrow, his antennae twitching, no doubt picking up on my trepidation.

"One sec," I said. Someone was staring at us from two tables over. I snapped my gaze back to the table. They could be staring for any number of reasons. Yarrow was, as far as I knew, the only one to even leave his planet. Besides, plenty of humans would see a human and an alien together and stare the way that guy was.

"Are you planning to tell me what's got you so agitated?" said Yarrow.

I forced a smile. "Just someone staring." I shrugged. "I guess I'm still paranoid, jumping at nothing."

Yarrow rumbled in his chest. I picked at my food.

"It seems to be seriously troubling you," said Yarrow. "Perhaps paranoia is the wrong word."

"I don't think it is," I said. "Folks stare all the time for all kinds of reasons."

"We haven't been trying to hide our interest in Pardus's disappearance these past few days. We've been speaking of it openly with Jasper and Trix on channels that, while not public, could easily be monitored by someone who wished to do so. There is no reason whatsoever that they would not be aware that we're present at this port and take steps to monitor us." Yarrow gripped my hand on the table. "I think it's time that we accept that what might be considered paranoia in another case is likely to be fact for us."

"We still don't even know that someone is trying to cover up Pardus's disappearance."

Yarrow gave me a pitying look. "We unequivocally do, and it's time we give up denying it. Remember that we are not members of the press. We are researchers. We wish to understand the mechanism by which an entire space station, or ship for that matter, could disappear without a trace. That is all."

"Is it?" I picked at the thumbnail of my free hand. "Would we really keep it to ourselves if we found out that someone had intentionally killed hundreds of people, no matter what the mechanism?"

Yarrow looked past me at the dark sky behind my head.

"Would you?" I said.

"I don't share many values with my home system, my culture of origin." Yarrow still looked over my shoulder, as though he could stare through the darkness all the way back to the system he grew up in. "I made a few attempts to change things there, but there was little support for my viewpoint. I told you once that it was best for everyone that I left, and I still believe that is so. But in doing so, I gave up on those I was trying to defend. If they lost their lives in the interim..."

I couldn't let that silence hang between us. "But you said yourself you couldn't have saved them. You tried."

"But I still left." He finally met my eyes. "There are complexities, Carolina. It is rarely as simple as evil people making others disappear out of malice."

"And you think there are complexities that might make it okay for someone to have removed Pardus from the Galaxy without warning?"

Yarrow sighed. "Would you think less of me if I said yes?"

A little bit, yeah. "I don't know," I said. "Let's figure out what's going on first, then we can assess the ethical questions it raises." I pulled my hand back from his to take a sip of my drink and clasped my hands in my lap.

Yarrow left his hand loosely on the table, just within reach.

◈

The next day was conference day. When we got to the Creature Café, Trix was already there and waved a lavender two-fingered hand frantically in greeting. Waving was the universal greeting between alien species that weren't familiar with one another's customs: It was visible and could be felt through infinitesimal air currents—anything involving contact or bodily fluids was generally reserved for later meetings.

"Caro!" said Trix. She dashed across the café to us and stopped just within my personal bubble, bouncing on the balls of her feet. "Humans hug, right?"

I grinned. "Yes, a hug would be great." I opened my arms, even though hugging was a little much for me. But Trix and I had talked so much, and her excitement was contagious.

Once we broke apart, Trix turned to Yarrow, and I quickly introduced them. Yarrow put out a hand—for a handshake?—and Trix ran a long finger down the inside of his forearm. Possessive jealousy rattled around in my chest, but the gesture didn't seem to be as intimate to either of them as it was for humans, and Trix immediately turned on her heel and bounded away, her chatter indicating that she wanted us to follow.

"The meeting room is amazing. I already checked it out. We'll have it for two days since you said that's how long you have. I confirmed already..." Trix didn't let up all the way to the back of the café and down a narrow corridor. Hopefully, her chatter was mostly due to excitement and would die down a little.

Jasper wouldn't join us until later in the day; he was on a slightly different day-night cycle than we were. Trix led us into a bubble she'd "found" containing a forest ecosystem, complete with animal, insect, and fish life. Many of the species were from Earth, considering its proximity, but some I hadn't seen before. As we walked, a dragon, larger than the ones I'd watched through the windows, swooped to a perch near the door and cocked its scaly head at us. No human could resist having dragon-like creatures around if the opportunity arose.

We followed Trix up a wooden staircase to a platform overlooking the wider bubble that had a smart board at one end and a big table in the middle. A boardroom in the rainforest.

"I've already added some notes to the board," said Trix, gesturing at the smart board. "But we don't have to get into everything now. Maybe it makes sense to wait for Jasper? Are we all on the same time clock at the moment? I think we're all on Earth days, right? Do you want to eat together?"

Trix simmered down on the way to the restaurant—nothing fancy; we'd chosen this place since we were all academics and on a budget—and her stream of questions finally abated.

Once we were seated and had some semblance of privacy, Trix finally spoke calmly. "I didn't want to tell you over chat, but there's been another disappearance."

I gulped down my bite of pasta and stared at her.

"A research vessel and all her crew. Almost a week ago. Vanished, just like Pardus. I heard some folks talking about it. Some of them worked here."

We tried to keep talk about Pardus to a minimum in the restaurant and then hurried back to our conference room to get down to business.

By the time Jasper arrived, we already had a conspiracy board going. The smart board was covered in notes and lines connecting them like a spiderweb.

"Woah," said Jasper when he saw it. "What'd I miss?"

The research vessel, *Kepler 6*, had been on an expedition somewhere in the Sagittarius Arm of the Galaxy. The voyage plan itself had been a bit hush-hush, and no one seemed to agree on their purpose or their exact coordinates.

"Do we know they really disappeared?" said Jasper, sinking into a chair and leaning his elbows on the table. "They're not just stranded somewhere without comms?"

"Their transponder hasn't been located, and that would work without comms," I said.

"But that's like a thousand light years away from where Pardus disappeared," said Jasper.

"The time elapsed between the disappearances of Pardus and *Kepler 6* would have allowed for travel between their last known locations," said Yarrow. "Assuming such travel is necessary to effect a disappearance." He tapped the board. "Our own ship also disappeared subsequent to Pardus."

Jasper rubbed his eyes. "If we want to gather data from that location, it would take us a year to get there by star liner. Not practical."

"Is there anyone we can ask? Someone closer by?" I said. I'd ask Dr. Morbit when he got back. He seemed to be the only one willing to talk about Pardus at all.

Yarrow turned to the rail overlooking the rainforest, Trix frowned at the board, and Jasper rubbed his eyes again. Apparently, he *was* the only one.

"Barring that, we could go back to the Pardus site, gather another dataset to replace the one we lost," I said.

"And have the council confiscate it again?" said Jasper. "Waste of time."

Yarrow turned and leaned on the rail. "In addition to the risk from the council, may I remind you that we are currently without a ship?"

"So we have no way of gathering data from the *Kepler 6* site, the Pardus site, or the site of *Lepton*'s disappearance. That's okay. We can work with the data we have," said Trix.

"And what data do we have?" said Jasper.

We glanced blankly at one another. We had no concrete data. I'd asked Trix about the toroidal particle pattern, and Yarrow had recreated what he could to ask Jasper about the neutrino pattern, but we didn't actually have either of those datasets.

"There isn't actually any data..." I began.

"That is technically incorrect," said Yarrow.

I frowned at him. "You have copies of the data?"

"I do not." He raised his eyebrows at me.

True, we didn't have the datasets, but they did still exist. Miller had them.

I didn't want to bring up my contact at the council. Or rather, my parents' contact. But we'd already been mulling over strategies to get our hands on that dataset for hours now, and no one else had come up with anything even remotely viable.

Jasper leaned back in his chair and shrugged. "I still think it could work." He crossed his ankle over his knee.

"Breaking in like in some pre-space-age spy movie will not work," I said. If I'd thought Jasper would be the reasonable one, it was only because he hadn't loosened up yet. "They don't have some warehouse full of file folders or some server full of file folders, for that matter. If Miller took over this project, it's Miller who has the datasets. His office might be where projects go to die, but technically, he's a researcher just like us, not part of the council."

"You know a lot about the council, Carolina," said Jasper.

"I've applied for a lot of grants," I said, but my tone was far too defensive.

Jasper just shrugged.

"Miller's office is on Luna," said Yarrow. "It's quite accessible."

"Getting to the office won't be the problem," I said. "But he'll take one look at us and laugh us off the moon."

"Let's just explain the situation to him," said Trix. "I'm sure he'll understand what's at stake."

"I'm willing to bet he already knows what's at stake," I said.

"Even if he did want it looked into, why would he give the project to us?" said Jasper.

"Miller does not have the authority to assign projects," said Yarrow. "He follows the council's commands just as scrupulously as we must."

What we needed was someone with enough clout at the council itself to assign the project back to one of us and give us clearance and access to all of the datasets. Maybe even permission to gather more data. Maybe even funding and resources. But the council were the ones who were trying to keep this under wraps in the first place. Even if they were acting at the behest of some other organization—maybe especially then—they had reasons for keeping this project locked away, and we had no idea what those reasons were.

"I feel like we're going in circles on this council thing," I said. "Maybe we should take a break."

Our best bet was still to get those datasets back. And to do that...I was going to have to go crawling to my parents. But it was too important now. It wasn't about me or my career anymore. Tracking down this tech and getting it regulated or banned outright was the priority.

I didn't ask the others whether they wanted me to call in a favour with my parents. They would obviously tell me to do it—they wouldn't understand the dynamic that made me hesitate. Besides, if I told them that I was going to, I'd have to tell them if my parents refused to help, and then I'd never be able to look them in the eyes again.

The call rang and rang. I checked the time: 8:49 p.m. That should be in their window between dinner and bedtime, unless they were out for dinner or visiting friends. My finger hovered over the End Call button. No way was I leaving them a message. Then the call clicked over.

"Carolina?" said my mother. The camera stayed dark.

"Hi, Mum," I said and waved.

"Hi, darling. I only have a moment. Did you need something?"

I cleared my throat. "Remember that project I was assigned?"

"The one you summarily lost?" said my dad's voice. So they'd heard about that.

"Yes, that one. I tried to keep it, and I'd still really like to get it back. I'd really appreciate your help...anything you're able to do at CHUSI." I picked at my nail while the blank screen looked back at me silently.

"I don't see why we should burden Noel with this," said my dad. "You lost it the first time. Who's to say you won't lose it again? Connections are not to be abused, Carolina."

I visibly deflated. Shit, my camera was on. I straightened up. "I understand," I said. "Thanks for considering it."

"We have to go now, dear," said my mom.

"Okay, bye!" I tried to look cheerful. Why had I left my camera on? The twisted rictus on my face was in no way cheerful.

The call ended, and I closed my eyes and held my breath for a count of four, then sighed it out. Okay. That had been worth a shot, but I'd never expected it to be a sure thing.

Noel. I popped over to the council staff list and searched: *Noel*. Noel McRea. The portrait was of an old white guy. That was probably him. If they wouldn't help me, then my best bet was to bypass them and hope that Noel recognized my name.

I typed up a request, careful not to imply that my parents endorsed it, but I also avoided mentioning that I had contacted them at all. I read it over three times, tweaking it here and there. Chances were I wouldn't get a response before our little conference ended tomorrow, but we could keep collaborating virtually, especially if we managed to legally acquire the datasets we needed and formal permission to work on the project.

I read over the message one more time and hit Send.

We gathered in our rainforest conference room for the last time; our booking was almost up. We weren't really working, just chatting, really, when Miller's face popped up on the screen beside our smart board.

"Am I interrupting something?" he said. The room was set up for virtual conferences, so no doubt he could see us all sitting around the table. He didn't wait for an answer. "I thought I'd pop in and tell you in person, since you don't seem to be getting it, Ms. Dawn. The Pardus Station data, and any other related data, is and will remain unavailable to you and anyone working with you. It is classified, top secret, not for public consumption, and it won't be released. Yes, even if you contact your parents' pet council member and try to pull strings. Do you want to try to convince me and get it out of your system?"

My stomach knotted. They were all looking at me.

My last ditch effort would be to convince Miller that keeping this to ourselves—since he no doubt was fully aware of what was going on at this point—was ethically reprehensible. There was no sense in keeping the extent of our knowledge secret anymore. If Miller himself didn't know about Pardus being purposefully disappeared, then it was time someone told him.

"You're telling me that you would rather watch stations like Pardus get intentionally disappeared, along with all of their inhabitants, than let us have the data that might stop that from happening?"

"Oh, Dawn," said Miller, and his smile was twisted. "You think you can stop it? You think for one second that they wouldn't make you disappear, along with everyone working with you?"

"If they're so quick to do that, why are we still here? I'm sure you know we've all been working on this problem," I said.

"I've been able to shield all of you so far. It is technically my project, but if you keep going over my head...I won't be able to protect you," said Miller.

Miller had been protecting us? *Miller*?

"Why would you protect us?" said Jasper.

Miller shrugged. "You're all so adorable, paddling around in the shallow end, thinking you're diving in the ocean. I have a soft spot for cute, innocent, idealistic kids, I guess."

Trix stood up, leaning toward the screen on the table. "So you pop in here with your threats, and you expect us just to back down? After these people almost *killed* Carolina and Yarrow?"

Miller chuckled. "I don't do threats. You are in over your heads, and you don't seem to have any idea that's the case. I'm letting you know that even I have limitations. I have no control over whether this project gets taken away from me, and if it does, the new lead will take you down without a second thought."

"So you let us keep working on this because you don't think we have a chance of figuring it out," I said.

"Just so, Ms. Dawn, with one modification. I know for a fact that you don't stand a chance of figuring it out, and even if you did, what difference would that make? Plenty of people are in the loop, know exactly how this technology works, and are powerless to stop it from being used." He held up a hand to forestall Trix's and my stammering. "You are, of course, free to heed my warning or not. I am perfectly aware that you have no motivation to do so. I would appreciate if you'd dial back your attempts to get the project transferred away from me. Take that as you will." Miller hung up, and the screen went back to a slow carousel of ads for this port's many highlights and services.

"You contacted a council member?" The disappointment in Yarrow's voice nearly choked my reply.

"I didn't see how it could make things worse for us." But apparently, I'd been wrong about that.

"It could have worked," said Jasper.

"So, do we believe him?" said Trix. "He said we should stop, that we could be disappeared ourselves. I know that, Carolina and Yarrow, you've been in that position before, but it's so creepy. One second you're there, and next second..."

What? What actually happened to people who were disappeared?

The law of conservation of energy stated that if that much matter was really turned to nothingness, enough energy would be released that they wouldn't be able to hide it. In the case of Pardus, it would have taken out half of human-dominated space. So if the matter wasn't turned to energy, it had to have gone somewhere, maybe been transformed somehow. Our measurements of Pardus's remains had been very clear on that point. There wasn't any debris, certainly not enough matter to have been a disintegrated space station.

I looked at Jasper. "I think we need to seriously consider the possibility of teleportation."

"We'll have to do it over chat," said Jasper, hitching his messenger bag up on his shoulder. He waved his screen at me: Our room booking was over.

Chapter 7

"What's the status of the Pardus report?"

Miller jerked his attention back to the CHUSI meeting that had been running all morning.

"We've had reports that Dawn remains involved despite explicit instructions to desist."

"I can confirm that. She contacted me personally."

It would be a bad idea to cut in now. "That's partly my fault. I've been using her as a contractor, since she was already familiar with Pardus." Dammit. His mouth, apparently, didn't get the memo.

"So you've said. The concerned party doesn't want to pursue this project any further, and I think it would be wise not to provoke them unnecessarily. Close the project."

With the project closed, any human researcher's involvement would be beyond suspicious, and there
was no longer anything Miller could do about it.

Yarrow was out of our shared room for the evening, so this was
the only privacy I was going to get. I called Miller.

He picked up, but he huffed as he did it. "Ms. Dawn, you are not
going to change my mind. I've already told you that I can't alter—"

"I know what you told us. Was that all true? You've been protecting us?"

"When certain interested parties asked about your very suspicious and badly concealed interest in Pardus Station and its
associated disappearance, I told them that you were under very
limited contract with me to study a few things. If I hadn't...we
wouldn't be having this little talk right now. And before you ask,
no, I'm not authorized to grant contractors clearance or access
to datasets. Since all you've been doing so far is engaging in wild
speculation, I invented some excuse about...It doesn't matter what
it was exactly."

"I guess I should thank you," I ground out.

"Yeah, probably." He raised his eyebrows. "Was that it? As hard
as it may be for you to believe, I actually do have work to do."

"You never answered Trix. You don't have any ethical problems
with this technology and how it's being used?"

"That's true, I never answered." His face softened as he said,
"As my contractor, you've done good work." Then, his glower was
back. "Goodbye, Carolina. I hope it's never necessary for us to
speak again. You're on HGNT's radar now, and not in a good way."

"Okay," I said. "Bye." My screen went dark, and I was left staring at my own reflection.

HGNT? The screen company? Next stop, doing as much research on HGNT as possible.

After an hour of research, I almost believed that Miller had been trying to help. Not only did HGNT own Pardus Station, but Exodus Labs was one of their subsidiaries. If I was going to find answers, Miller had tipped me off exactly where to look.

Crap, was that the time? Pardus and HGNT could wait. I was meeting Yarrow at the studio in two minutes. He'd booked a slot for us, out of the blue, and I couldn't miss it.

I hustled down to the studio and had time to print my viola before Yarrow got there, so I was playing when Yarrow entered our booth. His instrument was custom, but the specs he'd spent so long iterating were saved on his screen, so it was as close to the ga-ruth from his home world as he could get out here. He manoeuvred his long instrument case through the doorway, sat silently across from me, and popped it open. He fitted his ga'ruth together and rested it on his lap. Fingers settled over the sixteen evenly spaced holes, he closed his eyes and joined in with me.

It could have been a strange combination, the low, mellow tones of the ga'ruth and the slightly strident way my viola playing always seemed to turn out, but I'd been hooked since the first time we'd played together. They blended, my viola adding a brightness to take the edge off the taciturn quality of the ga'ruth. Or maybe it was just the way that Yarrow played it; I'd never heard it played by anyone else.

I paused, and Yarrow took over the tune, fading into a mournful song I'd heard him play before. I popped in a few pizzicato notes, swayed to the new rhythm, and layered a quick, cheerful melody overtop. We were meeting with Dr. Morbit tomorrow, and I was going to ask him whether I could stay at Exodus. This might be the last time we played together. We were both aware of it, but there was no need to wallow. Yarrow's antennae twitched, and he stuck to his original melody, ponderous and measured.

When the song ended, Yarrow put down his ga'ruth. "I'll miss playing with you like this. It's evident that you don't want to talk about it, but I'm attempting to communicate my emotions verbally," he said.

I chuckled. "I appreciate it. Do you want to play another?" I plucked a lively jig. More of a fiddle tune, but I could make it work.

Yarrow bobbed his head and fitted the ga'ruth's mouthpiece between his lips.

We played three more songs, alternating leader and follower. The last one I chose was slower, more plaintive, and it was Yarrow's turn to jazz it up with a syncopated beat and some unusual note combinations. After a particularly dissonant section, he seemed to lose the thread of my melody, and it sounded a little like he'd dropped his ga'ruth down the stairs. My laughter shook my viola almost too much to play, and Yarrow's unhinged trumpeting cut off as he spat out his mouthpiece and dissolved into guffaws. I ended with a flourish, and set the tail of my viola on my leg.

"So," I said.

"So?" said Yarrow and raised his eyebrows.

"Do you think you'll find someone else to play with when I'm gone?" My smile was strained.

"You expect your placement at Exodus to be permanent?"

"No." I looked down and focussed on putting my viola safely back in its case. "But there's not much left for me at Oort, not since I lost *Lepton*."

Yarrow grumbled in his chest, and his hard case clicked as he opened the latches. "*You* lost nothing. The ship was taken out from under us. There's no need to take on that responsibility."

I shrugged. "Besides, if I can be more subtle, stay under the radar, maybe the Pardus investigation won't be quite as...lethal."

Yarrow cocked his head and nodded. "That seems plausible." He clicked the latches shut on his case and straightened up. "Perhaps best not to rely on it."

"I'll still be careful," I said. "And I won't implicate you this time."

"I appreciate that, but it isn't necessary. Don't hesitate to reach out if there's anything I can help with."

Warmth filled my chest. "Of course," I said. "Thanks."

Yarrow jerked a nod. "I also want to know what happened to Pardus. And the other ships." His smile bared his teeth. "And I'm not afraid of being implicated."

I laughed. "You're braver than I am, then. I don't want to get blinked out of existence."

Yarrow laughed, but his smile faded. "Nor do I. When I return from my voyage, if you're still here, I'll visit you. We can discuss your findings then."

I nodded, a lump in my throat. "Sure," I said.

"I hope Exodus is a fresh start for you," said Yarrow. His eyes went hard. "Oort will be poorer for your absence."

I stood and paced to the viewport. "It's not like I was doing much there." I crossed my arms and huddled in on myself. "Besides making trouble for Lancaster."

Yarrow followed me to the viewport and looked over my head at the scattering of stars. "Wherever you learned that you have no value, you must unlearn it." The Sun was indistinguishable from the rest of the stars unless you already knew where it was. Yarrow rested a hand on my shoulder, I leaned into his body, and he wrapped his lower arm around my waist.

"Where will your voyage take you?" I asked. I wasn't touching his comment.

"The middle of nowhere," said Yarrow. "That's a definite drawback of studying interstellar space. Very few opportunities to visit desirable destinations."

I chuckled. "Will you even be able to receive messages out there?"

"Possibly not," said Yarrow and sighed. "But I'll check every time we resupply."

It would only be two months or so, but even the research vessel couldn't last more than a month between resupplying. "Thanks," I said again. This hunt for Pardus Station was surprisingly hazardous, and bouncing ideas off of someone would be welcome. Particularly without having to implicate yet another innocent researcher. I would miss him so much, but who could blame him for wanting to get far away from me?

Yarrow didn't come with me to see Dr. Morbit. His star liner was leaving in the morning, so tonight would be our last night together, if I was accepted here.

Prof. Morbit waved webbed fingers as I stepped off the public elevator, and I waved back and slouched toward him, past three metal benches and the closed grate of a café window. The exhaustion from the past few days was catching up with me all at once, but I tried to channel my excitement for this new opportunity as I smiled at Dr. Morbit. This entryway seemed newer than the surrounding corridors with their industrial metal floors and exposed infrastructure.

"Thanks for meeting with me yourself, Professor Morbit," I said. "I hope I didn't keep you waiting long?"

Up close, he was a couple inches shorter than me, the panels of his robes brushing the floor.

"Please, Grell will be sufficient," he said. "Not long. I'm sorry I wasn't here to meet you last week." He beckoned me after him into an elevator and punched in the room code. Woah, fast walker. "I had a last-minute expedition I had to take care of. I'll show you around the lab. My group will be happy to help you out with any questions after that." Dr. Morbit must have noticed me gripping the rails in the elevator. "The gravity directional shifts here on Exodus certainly can be jarring if you're not used to them."

Grell's group was divided into a practical team and a theoretical team, though the practical team was just him at the moment.

"I'm looking for the right co-conspirators," he said and chuckled. "My office is right here." He waved to a hallway flanked by two security guards and passed then with a nod. Both doors were shut and he entered the one on the left with his biometrics.

Dr. Morbit's office was even more disorganized in person. Stacks of papers teetered on the shelves behind his desk, but they also dotted the floor and covered another bookshelf across from him. I pulled the chair out, crushing some uneven sheets.

"How are you enjoying the institute?" said Dr. Morbit.

"I'm learning a lot," I said, which was true. Everyone I'd met at Exodus from the tour guide to Jasper and Trix had been lovely and helpful. Dr. Morbit's team would surely be no different.

"I've looked into your publication history, and it seems as though you'd make a good addition to our theoretical team, what with your thesis and your independent research."

Independent? He was referring to the Pardus stuff. "Thank you."

"Would you be at all interested?"

I glanced at the viewport. "I'm thinking about it."

"You come highly recommended by Dr. Lancaster, and I know for a fact that you have initiative in droves, from our primary contact."

"About that," I said. We hadn't had that conversation in person yet, wherein he might feel comfortable addressing Pardus Station directly. "Would you mind telling me more about your time on Pardus Station?"

Dr. Morbit sighed. "I knew you'd come back to this eventually. Add persistence to your list of qualities. I'll tell you right now though, Carolina, you won't get far barking up this particular tree." He smoothed his hands on his desktop. "I worked at Pardus Station for a while, on their neutrino detector. I got it online, calibrated and refined it for them a little. That's all. I recorded my experience as a case study. It's under submission at the moment, actually. I'll send you a copy when it gets published. I know the station was lost. Tragic, really. I saw no signs of the kind of neglect that would have led to their incident while I was there. I understand you're looking for a more satisfying explanation for the loss of the station, but I'm afraid I don't have any information for you."

"Incident?" Dr. Morbit made it sound as if there were an established cause for the station's disappearance. Neglect wouldn't have made the damned thing poof into the ether as it apparently had.

"The explosion?" said Dr. Morbit gently. "Did you lose someone close to you?"

Explosion. I scrabbled for something to say. "Are you sure you're talking about Pardus Station?" Apparently, I'd landed on the most useless question in existence.

"Of course," said Dr. Morbit. "The core overheated and vaporized the whole station. What else could incinerate a station so completely?"

I had seen the data, and both Yarrow and I had studied every reading we could get our hands on. There had been no evidence of vaporization, no evidence of any kind of explosion, no debris field... Either Dr. Morbit was lying, or he was vastly misinformed. Maybe the same way that those miners' families would have been misinformed about their deaths. Either way, I wasn't going to get any information from Dr. Morbit that I didn't already have. If he knew anything, he wasn't about to tell me. And if he did know something, he would definitely pass along my interest to HGNT. Best that I pretended to have lost interest.

"Of course," I echoed. "I was just following up on our conversation. I know the whole thing is closed." I tried to smile.

"Let me know when you decide whether you'd like to join my group. Neutrinos are a burgeoning field, and my understanding is that you could benefit from more focus to your research."

"That's certainly true," I said and smiled for real this time. "Thanks—" Someone knocked on the doorframe and stuck their head in.

"Professor Morbit?" said a student.

"Is that the time?" said the professor. "Nice chatting with you, Carolina."

I stood, pushing the chair into the crushed papers on Dr. Morbit's shelf again, and slipped past the student into the corridor. I paced past security, around the corner, and into a low hallway, where I leaned against the bulkhead. A round floor-to-ceiling viewport capped the end of the corridor, and I stared at my silhouette reflected in the glass. Maybe I could stay here. Lancaster had given me a good recommendation, maybe hadn't even mentioned how I'd lost his baby with no plausible explanation. The folks here were nice, friendly. I could fit in. I could make friends, maybe, this time.

Something moved outside the viewport. No, it had to be a reflection. I glanced behind me, then stuck my head into the corridor. Nothing. I gulped back the bile rising in my throat. It was my imagination. Nothing could survive out there. I shuddered.

Nothing could live out here, at least not without some kind of apparatus.

An eerie feeling crept up my neck. I'd had that thought before. On Lepton. I'd been alone on the bridge, keeping watch, and I'd caught something out of the corner of my eye. I'd dismissed it as paranoia then, too. I shivered. It was paranoia. Nothing could live out there in space, and nothing—nothing—could live unassisted in vacuum. Everyone knew that.

My screen chimed. Trix wanted to meet up for lunch.

We met at the Creature Café again. I was quickly becoming a regular here. If I stayed, I would be a regular for real. Maybe I'd even adopt a fuzzy little companion. The blue weasel thing looked very cuddly.

Trix waved as she hurried in and dropped into the chair opposite me.

"I've been looking up Dr. Morbit," she said.

"Hello to you, too."

"Oh, yes. Hello! Good afternoon. I hope you're well. Dr. Morbit is always off on those unexpected little missions to who knows where."

I shrugged. "He's a practical researcher. Of course he's in the field a lot." But he'd also seemed to think Pardus had exploded. "He's assisting with installing and optimizing more neutrino detectors." That's what he'd done on Pardus, so probably what his trips were for.

"That doesn't sound like a job for a preeminent neutrino entanglement expert. Nowadays, there are technicians more qualified to tune the detectors. I'm sure you have an idea of what sort of work Grell's group is up to from talking to them. I'm just saying, you should be careful, Carolina."

If those trips weren't technical assistance with neutrino detectors, and Dr. Morbit had waved away my questions about Pardus as simply a routine visit that he might have made to any station to get their neutrino detector up and running, then Dr. Morbit had lied to me. *Okay, slow down.* Neutrino detectors were still specialized equipment. Even *Lepton* hadn't had one, and it was brand new, top of the line, and custom built for an interstellar scientist. Pardus Station had been an interstellar long-haul colony and mining base. What on Earth or off it would they have needed a neutrino detector for? Either Dr. Morbit had lied to me—and why would he?—or Pardus hadn't exactly been a regular long-haul station. Either way, I'd be more likely to find out by staying on Exodus.

"I'll be careful." Dr. Morbit was a pre-eminent researcher, not some snake oil salesman. Researchers had ethics. Either he didn't know about Pardus or he was working on the same problem I was and he'd give me the details when I was ready. "How's your research going?"

Trix sighed, but she accepted my subject change and dropped Dr. Morbit for the rest of lunch.

Once I'd waved goodbye to Trix, I just had to call Lancaster. I didn't actually *have* to; we'd already talked about me staying on here at Exodus, for a while but I'd worked with him for years, and he'd been something of a friend. I wanted to say goodbye.

"Hey, Carolina, I'm glad you called," said Lancaster. He had dark circles under his eyes. Maybe that was just the crappy camera or the crappy office lighting.

"We talked about me staying on here, and I've decided I will," I said. Why had I thought this call was a good idea? Something was bothering

Lancaster, but it wasn't my business. Unless it was about CHUSI or HGNT... "What's been going on at the centre?"

Lancaster sighed and rubbed his eyes. "The usual council breathing down our necks while simultaneously refusing necessary funding. I've been telling them for years that our research vessel needs an overhaul, but they wave me away for another year and tell me to fix it. With what money, I have no idea."

Nothing bad had happened. It was fine. "On my last voyage, Frixel showed me how to weld a leaky hatch shut. It's a chance for nerds like me to learn practical skills."

"If I have any questions about that probe, I'll be in touch," said Lancaster, attempting another smile. "Otherwise, best of luck at Exodus."

Probe? Oh, the probe with the Pardus data, still seven light years away from Oort Research Centre. Were they going to hound Lancaster until it arrived back there?

"Thanks," I said. "Good luck with the council."

Was it my imagination, or had Lancaster been about to say something when his gaze flicked to the side and he bit it back? Dr. Sycamore had done the same thing when we'd interviewed her. When someone had been watching her every move through a camera.

"Thanks," said Lancaster, gave a half-hearted wave, and shut the call.

I called up Dr. Morbit right away, and he was jubilant. I was going to be joining a team working on simulating pinches in space through neutrino signatures.

"Your background in ship wakes should be invaluable. I believe the pinches will show up as anomalies in the ship's wake. We just have to prove it."

We'd have to build a simulation of a pinch to do that. "I've never heard of a space pinch before..."

"Don't worry about that at all. The team has the parameters to plug into the simulation. They need you for the wake part."

That...actually made a lot of sense. A bubble of excitement swelled in my chest. I was going to be doing work again. Not just something random that came across Lancaster's desk that he shunted off to me, and not a doomed project like Pardus, but something related to my specialization with funding and a prominent researcher to champion it. While also looking for the key to Pardus's disappearance, of course.

I thanked Dr. Morbit and ended the call.

Time to go and find Yarrow and tell him I wouldn't be going home.

When we sat down to dinner that night—our last night—it was clear that he already knew.

"So, what should we have?" I said. "Our last night eating out before I get my permanent quarters on Exodus."

"Carolina, I'm aware that you're not telling me something," said Yarrow. "I can only surmise that you have a plan you have declined to share with me. I...wish that you would share it. You don't have to do anything foolish on your own."

"You're assuming it's foolish. I wonder how the salmon is? We're pretty far from the ocean," I said, but I didn't laugh at my own joke.

"I consider cutting all of us out, your only supports in this endeavour, to be foolish on its face. So no, I'm not assuming anything."

I slapped my menu flat on the table. "I understand you want to be a part of this, and if you could join me, I would ask you to, but you want to go on your voyage. You have this whole plan to get on Lancaster's good side. You don't want to stay here with me. Jasper already left Dr. Morbit's group once, and Trix has no interest in neutrinos. This is a good research opportunity for me."

Yarrow shook his head. "I don't believe that's the whole truth."

"Fine, I want to do it alone. Is that what you wanted to hear?"

"Yes, it seems to be more honest, at least." He spread two hands on the table. "Carolina, there is no need for you to avoid us. None of us are judging you for any mistakes you believe you've made."

I sighed heavily. This wasn't the way I wanted our last night together to go. "I'm sorry," I said, picking at a corner of my menu. "From the beginning, I haven't wanted to put anyone else in danger. I've gathered you and then Jasper, then Trix, and I'm not sure they understand the danger that they're putting themselves in. They see this problem to be solved as though, because we're on the right side, nothing bad can happen to us. Maybe I'm projecting. I'm afraid I still don't understand what I'm getting myself into. But I tried to back away, I tried to leave it be, and it took almost nothing for me to dive back in head first and pull other folks in with me. This question is going to keep pulling at me. So I've decided to let it."

"Okay," said Yarrow.

"Okay?"

"Yes. I think the mos'ricol is supposed to be pretty good here, since it's naturally meant to keep for long periods of time. You should try it."

The first time Yarrow suggests food from the Perseus Arm—much closer to his home system than Sol—is possibly the last time that we're going to see each other. "This is one of those times for you to explain what you're trying to emote."

Yarrow didn't look up from his menu. "I'm hurt that you're not including me in this, but I understand. Sometimes, one must take action alone, for oneself, and not be beholden to anyone else. Trust me, I understand. I would appreciate it if you kept in touch, not about your work, whatever it ends up being, just...as friends."

Friends.

Yarrow laid his hand on the table between us, and I took it. Very much something friends did.

I ended up ordering the mos'ricol, and Yarrow was right: It was delicious.

"Here, try a bite," I said, brandishing my laden fork at him.

He shook his head. "I'd rather not."

"I like this, but I have no baseline. Is this 'good' like the honey-mustard salmon is 'good,' surprisingly good for space food, or is this 'good' like as good as mos'ricol gets?"

Yarrow glared at me but took my fork. He could have just said It's good for space food, but I promise it isn't as good as it gets, but he didn't. He closed his eyes as he chewed and handed my fork back to me. His antennae twitched as he swallowed. He opened his eyes and stared into his plate, seemingly intent on getting the perfect bite of his salad put together. He stabbed at the tomato three times before he gave up on it and put the imperfect lettuce, cucumber, olive, and feta bite into his mouth.

I shouldn't have pushed him to try the mos'ricol. He'd never seemed homesick before; he'd always talked about his home system with resignation, never with affection. But then again, he'd always refused to let me make any food from his past, always deferred to whatever I was eating.

Once we left the restaurant, Yarrow's shoulders dropped, and he wandered with me up to the observation deck. We picked out a bench on the port side, and Yarrow laid an arm along the back of it behind me.

Would it really be so bad to tell Yarrow my plan? He could help me develop it, maybe save me some problems down the road. But he could also poke so many holes in it that I'd realize it was a terrible idea, and then I'd have nothing. My plan may be terrible, but it's better than nothing.

"What will you do next?" I said instead.

Yarrow shrugged. "Keep working toward a fellowship at the research centre. That's what I came to the Solar System to do."

A couple walked past behind us, holding hands, their reflection wavering across the stars in the window.

"I suppose there's no point in asking what you will do next?" said Yarrow.

"The usual, these days," I said. "Something incredibly foolish and needlessly reckless."

"That's usual for you now?"

"I stole my supervisor's custom luxury space cruiser to chase down a lead that the council had forbidden me to follow and ended up almost getting winked out of existence, but instead of giving up and going home, I kept following the trail until it went cold, at which point I recruited other folks to help me revive it and got a clandestine warning from someone who I thought was my enemy, and even he thinks I'm being so foolish that he's currently saving my skin."

"Yes, I suppose that does sound incredibly foolish."

We both laughed, and I scooted closer into Yarrow's side. He slid his lower arm around my waist and let the other fall from the back of the bench and around my shoulders.

I leaned into his body. "Any chance you'd be willing to do something foolish and reckless with me tonight?"

Our last night together for a long time, maybe forever. If the reasons we broke up were ever that big a deal, they meant nothing in this moment. I just had to turn my head a little and our lips met. Yarrow's arms tightened around my shoulders and waist, and I turned so I was practically in his lap. Our bodies pressed together, and I let the tension ebb from mine, let Yarrow cradle me and make me forget, for a little while, Miller's warning and my half-baked plan.

"That's it, Carolina, let me carry it, just for now," Yarrow rumbled into my neck. His antennae bobbed gently, and I stroked over his smooth scalp to the base of one. He gasped as I ran my finger lightly up the side. "Don't—" I paused, and his whole body shuddered. "If you want to do that, we should go back to our cabin."

I licked my lips. "So I guess I shouldn't see what happens if I..." I poked out my tongue, and Yarrow growled and jerked his head away.

"Not in public, no," he rumbled.

I wriggled on his lap. "Then let's not be in public anymore."

Yarrow swept me onto my feet. I grabbed his arm, and we booked it back to our cabin.

The door to our tiny cabin hadn't even completely slid shut as Yarrow lifted my shirt over my head.

"Tell me how to touch your antennae."

"One at a time, gently," said Yarrow.

I skated a finger up one of his antennae, and he shuddered.

"Was that bad?"

"Not at all."

I worked the clasps on his suit and slid my hands over his toned stomach, up to his shoulders, and he shrugged out of it. The suit rode his hips, catching on his hard length. I kissed him, sliding my hands under the jumpsuit and letting it fall to the floor. He stepped out of it as I grasped his throbbing hardness. I licked my lips and made to go to my knees, but he held me up and cocked his head at me. In all the time we were together, he'd never allowed me to suck him off, despite eating me out regularly. I'd never gathered my courage enough to ask him why outside of the bedroom, and to do it now would break the mood.

Instead, I undid my pants and slid them off. Yarrow tumbled to his back on the bottom bunk and opened his four arms to me. I slid in above him and immediately bumped the back of my head. Yarrow's antennae twitched, and he cupped my head gently to cushion any future bonks, which made me laugh quietly.

"Always looking out for me."

He nodded and lightly traced my breasts, then down my ribs. He would never rush me, would simply accept whatever I was willing to give him. I traced one antenna with a fingertip, and he shuddered but kept careful control and didn't so much as jerk his hips.

"I want you," I said and lifted my hips so he could line us up.

We joined together silently, and he picked up my rhythm, meeting me on every thrust until we peaked, and I collapsed on his chest.

We wouldn't be together much longer. This had just been a fling, something to remember each other by. I slid off him and shut myself in the bathroom. Could he still feel my emotions through the door? I kept everything swirling inside me tamped down, and if he could sense it, he didn't say anything when I emerged and climbed silently to my top bunk.

Chapter 8

D r. Morbit showed me around my new lab and introduced everyone, then left me to fend for myself. Margot had huge eyes and was always second-guessing herself. De-hua kept his tall frame hunched over his desk and only cut in if he thought they were barking up totally the wrong tree. Lami's smile was brilliant against her dark-brown skin, and she was constantly synergizing and simplifying the team's ideas. Frodli didn't seem to have eyes, but also didn't seem to have any trouble seeing, and her dark-purple hair floated on something other than air currents. I was dying to ask whether she controlled it or something else did, but that would have been unforgivably rude.

Frodli led me to an office at the back of the lab—a cramped meeting room. The whiteboard at the back had about a dozen little bubbles with *PLO* included, in various states of being slowly worn away. Frodli tossed a file folder full of actual papers on the table and gestured for me to sit. She sat opposite me and folded her hands.

"What is it?" I said. I'd already signed the expected NDA, employment contract, network usage policy, harassment policy, and code of conduct.

"Take a look," said Frodli.

I slid the folder over and opened it. My own ID photo stared back at me from the top of the stack of papers. I leafed through: my locations and movements for the past eight months, a list of my contacts, a list of the datasets I'd collected and the ones I'd had access to, the people that I'd contacted...and transcripts of my conversation with Dr. Sycamore, and my calls with Dr. Morbit and Lancaster. Printouts of my messages back and forth to Trix. Everything. So it hadn't been paranoia after all.

"You've already been through all this," I said.

"That's right."

"And why are you showing it to me?"

"Don't break your NDA," said Frodli.

So all this information was supposed to be intimidating. But if I could go through it and see what they had, then maybe I could figure out what they had missed, find some channel they didn't have access to. I closed the folder and pushed back from the table.

"I'm not planning to," I said. I tucked the folder under my arm.

"You think you're taking that?" Frodli shook her head. "We are happy to have an enthusiastic and competent partner on our team, but if you jeopardize our project, if you turn on us, we'll turn on you."

I nodded slowly. That actually made a lot of sense. Rethinking my entire plan was out of the question at the moment, but at least I had my own cabin here so I could stew in private later. "Sounds reasonable," I said. "I'm ready to get up to speed on the project." I handed Frodli the folder, and she used it to gesture to the door.

Had I thought it was going to be simple to waltz in here, snatch what I needed, and expose everything? If an opportunity to become a whistleblower arose, I would grab it, but until then, I'd have to lie low.

This new job paid better—and I mean five times as much—as my old research stipend. I had my own little suite on a sprawling station in the heart of Ursa Major that actually had restaurants and a theater. I'll admit I was getting complacent. My colleagues were brilliant, not to mention we were working on an intellectually challenging project. If

HGNT had hired me to get me out of the way, to stop me from asking so many questions. Over the past month, I definitely had.

Lami dragged us all out for drinks after work one night to a little pub a few decks over from our lab, even De-hua, who grumbled that he'd have to go back to work later but was summarily ignored. To my surprise, once we got to the pub, Lami, De-hua, and Margot immediately took over the tiny dance floor, leaving Frodli and I sipping our drinks at the table alone.

"You don't have to keep me company if you want to join in," said Frodli and gestured to De-hua's erratic version of the sprinkler. Margot dodged his flailing elbow, gave him a smack, and danced out of his way.

"That's okay," I said. "I don't really..." I gestured to where Lami and Margot seemed to be starting some kind of choreographed thing as the next song came on. "You don't have to keep me company, either," I said quickly.

She shrugged. "I don't dance near others. Can't stand anyone touching my hair."

I sipped my drink and grinned. Lami and Margot were indeed doing a prearranged dance—a few other folks had seamlessly joined them from around the bar. De-hua carried on doing his own thing on an open corner of the floor.

"Thanks for not trying to dig up dirt on our lab," said Frodli, staring straight ahead.

"No problem," I said. Not that I'd abandoned the idea of using this job as my in to HGNT.

"I know you're not just here for the project," said Frodli. "We've..."

Margot, Lami, and the other dancers struck a pose as the song ended, and De-hua cheered along with half the bar.

"People have used us before, so I know the feeling," Frodli finished. "You're replacing a Geometry spy, you know."

Shit. I wrapped my hands around my pint glass. My plan had in no way taken into account that this research was being done by people, that HGNT was made up of individuals. If I did find dirt on the company, if I did expose their involvement in the disappearance of hundreds of people, what did I really expect to happen? They would blame a few reckless researchers or a few ambitious underlings, get rid of them, and carry on. Maybe keep what they were doing further under wraps. But did I really think exposing the truth would slow the company down?

"I'm sorry," I said.

"Are you spying on us, Carolina?" said Frodli and cocked her head at me.

No one beyond Frodli was in a position to overhear what I said next over the blaring music, and if I didn't come up with a really good answer right now, Frodli and everyone would think I was from Geometry, trying to take their work and betray them.

"You're right. I'm not just here for the project. But I'm not a spy."

"Then why are you here?"

"Have you heard of Pardus Station?"

"I haven't," said Frodli.

Why would she have? HGNT certainly wouldn't want it all spread around. Maybe Frodli hadn't read through my file very carefully. But then again, why would HGNT put my work on Pardus in that file? They put together the info for Frodli and her group. Was it my place to throw Frodli's faith in HGNT into question? If I was going to tell her about it, now would be the time, with the pumping music covering our conversation.

I opened my mouth just in time for the three dancers to flop back into their seats, practically shouting over the music. I turned quickly and pasted a smile on my face. No point in ruining everyone's evening.

The run-in with Frodli reminded me why I was here. Our "pinch" research was coming along, and we were finally getting some good results, mostly for the neutrinos. The way that Dr. Morbit had set up the pinch simulation made it seem as if neutrinos would be most affected in its vicinity.

We'd finally put everything together and set the simulation to run overnight, so as we trickled in the next morning, we all congregated around Frodli, who had pulled it up on her monitor. And there it was. The pattern that Dr. Morbit was looking for. A neutrino pattern. A very familiar, persistent neutrino pattern.

I stepped back and caught my breath. Where Pardus used to be, we had found that exact neutrino pattern, the one that indicated a pinch in space. Dr. Morbit would be overjoyed when we showed him, especially since it proved that there was a pinch at the Pardus site. He hadn't seemed interested in discussing Pardus before, but this would change his mind for sure. I'd get it to him as soon as he came back from his latest voyage.

Yarrow and I had given the Pardus data over to CHUSI, and Miller had mentioned HGNT as an interested party. There was a chance that those datasets were accessible from somewhere at Exodus.

Everyone was looking at me.

"You should come with us, Carolina," said Lami.

"Come?"

"Yeah, she wasn't listening at all," said Margot.

"Dinner," said De-hua. "They're dragging me out, so you have to come, too."

The look Frodli gave me said I had better come, but if I hurt her lab mates, I'd regret it. "We're celebrating our progress on the simulation, in no small part due to your contributions."

"Uh, yeah. Sure."

At the end of the day, De-hua grumbled but joined us without anyone having to try very hard to convince him. We sat around a big table with a rotating tray in the centre and ordered dishes off circulating carts, dim sum style, except the dishes were far more varied than simply dim sum. It was very useful to be able to point at whatever I wanted try, instead of embarrassing myself trying to pronounce an alien food.

"I couldn't find anything on Pardus," said Frodli, out of nowhere, and I almost choked on the blueish chicken I was enjoying.

"What's Pardus?" said Lami, when I had finished coughing.

"Something Carolina mentioned the other day. I thought I'd check it out, see what she meant, but there wasn't much. It's a mining station? Care to fill us in?"

"I..." I cleared my throat and wiped my mouth on my napkin. "I'm not sure HGNT would want me talking about it."

"It's not included in your NDA, is it?" said Frodli.

Was it? I honestly hadn't checked that closely.

"Doesn't matter," said De-hua between mouthfuls of something actively wriggling. "We can talk to each other about that stuff freely."

I sighed. So, pleading NDA restrictions wouldn't work. Why didn't I want to tell these folks? They seemed to love working here. They had such stable, fulfilling lives. Did I really want to be the one to upend that? To pull back the curtain and show them what those lives were costing?

"So?" said Lami.

"The long version or the short version?"

Lami just gave me a look. I was stalling, and she knew it.

"Fine. HGNT sent the station out on a mission, at which point, it disappeared without a trace. When I tried to gather readings from the site, not only did CHUSI confiscate my data, but my ship got disappeared out from under me as well."

De-hua chuckled, but his laughter faded fast. "You're serious."

"A disappearing space station?" said Lami. "Sounds impossible. You must have misread your data."

I ran my hands over my face. "I thought so, too. I figured the probe was miscalibrated or something. But there's more. Are you sure you want to know about all this?"

"I do," said De-hua. He was still eating, not looking at me.

Margot nodded.

Frodli shrugged. "You have intrigued me."

"Fine, I can't be the only one who doesn't know about it," said Lami.

"There's no debris field, only a torus, as though an orbiting body was there, and a weird neutrino pattern. A persistent one."

"And you're an interstellar particulate expert," said Frodli.

"Which is why the data passed across my desk in the first place. I was pursuing it when"—I swallowed hard—"when our ship itself disappeared. We barely made it out."

De-hua stared at me, a couple noodles hanging from his mouth.

"I saw the thing disappear with my own eyes. Not fly away, not explode. Disappear. We tried to look into it more closely, but...larger forces were working against us."

"The council?" said Lami.

"Partially, though..." I shook my head. "It's bigger than the council."

"You think it's HGNT," said Frodli. "You're here to expose them."

I shrugged. "You thought I was here to dig up dirt using your research as an excuse, and I guess I am." I pushed the rest of my blue chicken around my plate.

"What *are* you going to do?" said Margot, her big eyes even rounder.

"Considering our simulation just spat out a neutrino pattern identical to the scans we took from Pardus's last known location, I'm going to hunt down those datasets and use them to prove that Dr. Morbit's pinch in space is what we found there." *And hopefully, that Pardus Station is still out there.*

"I'll drink to that," said De-hua, his cheeks already a little pink. He lifted his glass, and Lami followed suit with her mocktail. Frodli grumbled something and lifted her glass, too. Margot glanced furtively at me, but she joined them as well.

They were going to help me try to get those datasets back? Why? Was this whole thing a set-up so HGNT could catch me out? No, if they wanted me gone, I'd be gone, especially without Miller's protection. De-hua and Lami no doubt were interested in the implications of finding a practical example of our theoretical results. Frodli wanted to keep an eye on them. And Margot...was just following the group? Either way, where would we even start looking for HGNT's copies of that data?

I lifted my water glass and clinked it with all of theirs.

Apparently, we were a team now.

Our team was serious about the mission. De-hua had previously worked with a group that had used the Exodus repository of datasets that were freely available for staff to use in their research. I spent a few days searching the repository for neutrino patterns while also trying to avoid the name Pardus and its specific coordinates. If copies of our data were in there, I probably wasn't going to know without taking a look at a visualization.

I narrowed it down to three sets, and we were each going to grab one to cut down on transfer time to our screens. Or I should say *their* screens since I wasn't going to be grabbing any data myself. Frodli thought, probably correctly, that any activity related to Pardus was more likely to be flagged in my screen than the others', so Margot and I were just going for moral support.

I tried to pay attention to De-hua's and Lami's chatter as we sauntered into the library, since it was better than worrying about what HGNT had planned for me if they discovered I was still trying to expose their possible murders.

The tall viewports showed a panorama of stars; the white floor and walls gleamed. A handful of narrow preformed desks and stools housed ports for connecting a screen up to the repository, but no bookshelves, no circulation desk, and no librarian in sight. Which was good. No one was there to record our activities.

De-hua, Lami, and Frodli beelined for the desks, and Margot and I wandered to the viewports. Maybe we should be keeping watch. What would we even do if someone confronted us? We could claim that this was part of our research, surely Dr. Morbit would back us up on that?

Margot was watching her own feet.

"So, how long have you worked at Exodus?" I said.

"About a year. Let's see. I joined in April, and it's October, so a year and a half."

"What did you do before that?"

"I worked with Dr. Morbit at the Martian Institute."

"Cool, so you've really seen his research evolve, then?"

She nodded at the ground. Fine. I wasn't going to force a conversation that clearly neither of us was really interested in.

"Done!" said Lami.

Thank Heavens.

The others finished up, and we headed back toward the lab.

"Mine didn't have a location in the metadata," said Lami. "When you set up the probe, did you input the coordinates?"

Had I? I honestly had no idea. Even if we had, HGNT could just as easily have stripped them out again. The only way to be sure whether any of these datasets were ours would be to do the analysis. We'd do it when we got back to the lab, then if we found what I hoped for, we'd go to Dr. Morbit, and he could take it up with HGNT.

Except someone was blocking the door to our lab. A very serious broad someone wearing sunglasses in a *space station* and asking for me.

"Ms. Dawn? Please come with me."

De-hua and Lami stared, Margot backed against the wall, and Frodli glared at me. Was she suspicious of me? Still? If anything, this proved my story was true.

I didn't move. "What is this about?"

"I'm not the one to ask," said the guard.

"I'm sorry, Carolina," whispered Margot, so quietly that I might have imagined it.

Either way, there was no escaping this sunglasses person.

I followed them to the elevator, where they not only punched in a code but scanned their fingerprint and badge as well.

I wiped my sweaty palms on my pants and picked at my thumb. Was this it? Were they going to use whatever means necessary to put Pardus to rest once and for all?

The elevator slowed and stopped. I followed the security guard directly into an office. A giant viewport framed a businesswoman with a stark bob and perfect eyeliner. Every single thing in here was deliberate. Did she even use this office to work in? Her desk was clear but for a Newton's cradle and a lamp; one wall was a fish tank, and the knick-knacks on the built-in shelves opposite were perfectly spaced to provide visual noise while not looking cluttered.

The door closed behind me.

Even the floor was pristine.

This was not a place to try to play games. I'd be outmatched and outmanoeuvred.

"Just tell me what you want me to do," I said.

See? Not a good start. I should have said something like *Why am I here?* It would have sounded way less guilty. *Anything* else would have sounded way less guilty.

"What's your name?"

Really? That's what she was asking? "Don't you know that already?"

She shrugged and just kept staring at me.

So I stared back. "Dr. Carolina Dawn."

"Do you want to sit?" She jerked her chin at the chair next to me.

Sit? Why? She was about to pass judgment on me. I'd face it standing.

"Suit yourself." What was with the staring? She hadn't even asked me anything! Was I supposed to be running this meeting?

She reached across her desk and started the Newton's cradle. *Tick, tick, tick, tick, tick*...I clenched my fists to keep from knocking the thing onto the floor.

"How's your family? Talked to them recently?" What kind of cartoon villain crap was this? She was threatening my family?

Except that HGNT could probably actually hurt them. She was totally calm, still just watching me. What did she want me to say? No, I don't talk to them much. I'm sure they can take care of themselves?

Tick, tick, tick, tick...

"Not interested in small talk, I take it?"

I shook my head. Why was she doing this? *Just get to the point!*

"You've done some great work for Dr. Morbit," she said. "Good enough that he's insisted we keep you around. Unfortunately for you, he's not at Exodus at the moment. You must know your NDA with HGNT, along with trade secret law, means you can't share any information outside the company. I'm sure you didn't know that applies to employees not directly involved with the project. Otherwise, I'm sure you wouldn't have filled in your teammates about it."

"How do you know I told them?"

"I wouldn't have if that little mousey pet of Dr. Morbit's hadn't told me about your illicit project." Margot?

So now that I was working for HGNT, talking about Pardus was literally illegal? Rage boiled in my gut. "You expect me to keep the disappearance of hundreds of people a secret?"

The woman's face didn't change. She just kept staring at me. Why did she just stare at me? Her wooden desk—was it mahogany? In space?—gleamed. The damn Newton's cradle on the end just ticked away and would for the foreseeable future unless someone reached out and stopped it. But that seemed like a good way to lose a hand.

She had a freaking fish tank. In space. The school of tiny fish swam back and forth; one big one, with eyes that bulged as if someone was squeezing it, trailed behind them at half their speed, its mouth opening and closing, gulping water. Maybe it was like one of those little yappy dogs that thought it was a Great Dane, but the inverse.

"I have no particular expectations," the woman finally said. Her blouse rippled like silk, and its pearl buttons shone as she leaned forward. "You are bound by the contracts you signed with HGNT. It's actually very simple. Legal action is routine for such a large corporation, and contract law is very cut and dried on the subject."

"You're threatening me to shut me up."

She actually smiled, her perfect red lips just turning up slightly. There was nothing funny about what I'd said. I guess I should have expected threats from a huge evil corporation like HGNT.

"You know, I could reveal what I've learned, even though it's not much. You don't want it to get out to the public."

She cocked her head, her black bob tilting a bit, her smile still in place. Why didn't this woman ever just have a conversation? *Tick, tick, tick, tick...* She watched me with those unfathomable brown eyes until my stomach started to turn over. I'd said something wrong, something incredibly foolish, that much was obvious, but everything I'd said was completely true.

"What do you think would happen if you leaked confidential HGNT information to the public?" She sounded genuinely curious.

But now that she'd asked, what *did* I think would happen? That people would believe unquestioningly that a space station had just disappeared and HGNT was responsible? What was more likely: An evil corporation had secret tech that made ships and stations disappear, or an unfortunate accident had befallen a far-away mining station, as Dr. Morbit had said? When it came right down to it, it would be HGNT's word against mine. That's what was so funny.

I shook out my hands, finally feeling the burn of the little crescents my nails had been driving into my palms, and took a deep breath. She had me cornered.

"What will the company do if I keep going? What's the penalty for divulging company secrets?" I should probably have looked that up before signing my HGNT contract.

"What's the penalty for breaking any law? You and the others on your team—"

The others? "Don't bring them into this. I'm the one who started the whole thing."

"They signed their own contracts, and they are responsible for their own behaviour. That goes for all HGNT employees."

What? I'd told the others about Pardus; they'd felt obligated to help me, and now they had all broken their contracts, too? "They were just helping me out. They didn't know…" *that we were breaking our contracts.* At least I kept that last part inside.

"Nevertheless, the law is clear. You and your team's communications fit the definition of improper disclosure of a trade secret on your part, and misappropriation on theirs."

Tick, tick, tick, tick…

The woman tapped her chin, her long plum-coloured nail just brushing her lip. "I think Frodli would take the brunt of it."

My stomach lurched, and my whole body followed. I braced myself on the back of the chair. Frodli, who hadn't wanted to get mixed up in this in the first place, who had already been burned by Geometry, who wanted so much to protect her team. No question she would take the fall if given the chance. So I couldn't give her one.

"I'm the one who"—*stop admitting to breaking your contract!*—"asked her to look into the subject. She did nothing wrong." If I had refused to fill them in on Pardus, would this still be happening? Would I still have been called in here? I was the one who had screwed this up, so I was the one who would have to fix it.

"What do you want me to do?" They were the same words I'd opened with, but this time, I think I really meant them. She must have thought so, too.

"It remains true that ignorance of the law is no excuse for breaking it, but I think we'll hold off on any consequences for breaking your contract for the moment, provided you don't do it again. Same goes for your little squad."

That tracked. Get in line, or else. We'd already screwed up, and they knew it. Going forward, they would have that to hold over our heads, no matter how careful we were. If there was any going forward. They could charge us with that trade secret thing. I'd look into the penalty for divulging trade secrets at some point, but chances were that the company that had already tried to make me disappear once wasn't going to stick to legal routes. And if Dr. Morbit hadn't insisted on keeping me around, I might already know their methods.

"There's no need to answer," she said and stopped the Newton's cradle with one last tick. She gestured to the door.

I didn't move. I had to be sure my mistakes wouldn't hurt the others. "I'll sign anything you want me to sign. But I take all the blame for our activities. The trade secrets I told them are on me. If they get leaked, none of them get blamed." It would have been nice to have had a lawyer here to make sure I was saying the right things. This stuff all felt very legally binding.

"Very well," she said and nodded to the door. "I'll ensure your team is informed of the consequences of continuing their extracurricular activities."

"Okay, thanks!"

I was standing in the middle of her reception area before it hit me. Had I just...thanked her for making me sign whatever she wanted?

The important part was that Frodli and the rest of the team were exculpated.

The receptionist gave me a fake smile and pointed me toward the door, where a security guard stood watching me.

It wasn't until I was shut in a windowless room alone that it really sank in: I may have made an error in judgment.

Chapter 9

M y face stared back at me from a one-way mirror, my already pale skin washed out in the bright lights that made the stark surroundings practically burn my retinas.

The door latch clicked; the door swung open, and a bedraggled, gangly figure in a suit slipped through. They plopped their briefcase on the table, pushed at their bangs, and slipped a few sheets of paper and a pen out. They slid the stack toward me, and the pen rolled over on top.

"It's all standard," said the harried bureaucrat.

The buzz in my ears almost made me miss their rambling.

"They let me know you'd need a couple of special documents. Could have given me more warning, but they wanted them done up immediately, so there they are. I'll get someone to escort you back to your place once you've signed everything."

"Escort me?"

"Just until IT gets your new Exodus screen set up." They waved at the papers. "Page three, I think? You take your time with that paperwork, and I'm here to answer any questions. I'll need your screen now so that IT can get started on the transfer. All your personal data will remain confidential, of course. They won't touch that. It's in the contract. Which you might want to read. Don't you think?"

I slid the papers closer and fiddled with the pen. Standard. No slandering HGNT, no talking about anything I learned here, no sharing trade secrets—which I already wasn't allowed to do—no working for a rival corporation for eight months. No definition of a rival corporation was provided.

My screen. They were taking my screen and replacing it with one of their tracked ones. I'd said I'd sign anything. I slid my poor screen across to the lawyer, and they grabbed it up and passed it out to someone through a crack in the door. The urge to burst out and run after it made my leg jiggle. I picked at my nail.

My vision blurred, and my stomach sank. The new screen would be overflowing with tracking software so they would know where I was, what I was doing, and see every message I sent or received. And this paperwork was giving them permission.

But what was all that compared to my team getting disappeared? The sinking feeling in my gut twisted into nausea. How else could I keep them safe, keep them out of this? I probably should have thought of that before I joined HGNT. I wouldn't even be able to message Trix or Yarrow without HGNT knowing about it.

I flipped through the deal I'd wrangled from them.

Carolina Dawn assumes full liability for trade secrets exchanged by her team during her employment (see Appendix A).

It went on for a little while, saying the same thing a few different ways. Appendix A proved that Margot had been watching us very closely. Everything I'd shared with the team about Pardus was catalogued here. If anyone so much as stumbled on this contract in my files, I'd be breaking my NDA.

But this was it, the only thing that would keep HGNT from dropping the hammer on Frodli and the others.

My pen hovered over the signature line. The flustered lawyer paced on the other side of the desk, glancing over to the growing stack of papers on my left. The last sheet sat in front of me. I couldn't leave until this was signed, but neither could they.

I'd started the job here at Exodus to get to the bottom of Pardus's disappearance, and I'd discovered that the station might not have been destroyed at all, it might be in one of Dr. Morbit's "pinches" in space. Once I signed this, I wouldn't be able to talk to anyone about it, even Dr. Morbit wouldn't be able to argue for my protection then. Could I still help the people trapped in one of these pinches? Would gathering more information from Dr. Morbit about the pinches be allowed? That wasn't technically talking about Pardus. Maybe I could still help them. And if anyone would know how to say something while technically not mentioning it, a lawyer would. And I just happened to have a lawyer trapped in here with me.

"That whole trade secret law thing," I said.

The lawyer whirled, flattened their palms on the other side of the table, and hung their head. "Can't we just get this done with?" they muttered.

I tapped the blank signature line with the back of the pen. "You said if I had any questions..."

"Fine." They heaved a sigh. "Just know that this conversation is being recorded."

"Not a problem for me. They're about to record everything on my screen twenty-four seven."

"Trade secrets. The one-oh-one level. You know something that makes the corporation money. You tell someone else, they sue you for the money they would have made."

"Okay, say I know something that counts as a trade secret, then I accidentally give it away—"

"Improper disclosure. There are no accidents."

"Right, so if that information becomes public knowledge—"

"Or falls into the hands of a competitor."

"Then I would have to pay for the money they would have made, as you said."

"That's the gist."

"What about if the information implicates the corporation somehow?"

"You mean like in the case of a whistleblower?"

I shrugged. "Probably? You're the expert."

"I don't think I can help you, not without more details. Not to mention that you're not my client, HGNT is. I'm here as a courtesy."

"You work for HGNT. And it doesn't bother you to work for a corporation that routinely kills people?" I wasn't above guilting them into helping me.

"Let's not get slanderous, now." They raised their eyebrows.

What a spineless— "A corporation that is *suspected* of routinely killing people."

"I was hired to do a job, and I do it. Being responsible for gag orders isn't anyone's dream career. Some of us don't have the luxury of choosing where our next meal or cabin assignment is going to come from." They tapped the signature line.

As much as the option of running home to my parents was distasteful, it was there. Plenty of people didn't have that option, and I actually knew one: Yarrow, banished from his home system. Not to mention all the folks on Pardus. Being monitored didn't mean I would have to give up. Even without anyone's help, I could still figure something out. It was still out there, and I would figure out how to get it back by myself if I had to.

I signed the last page.

The lawyer slid the stack of papers over and focussed on squaring them up. "If the information that was improperly disclosed came to light another way—an unrelated way—then the trade secret would no longer be enforceable." They glanced at me, slid the papers into their briefcase, and walked out.

❖

Going out with my little team where Frodli could confront me about Pardus was just about last on my list of things to do with the day I'd had. Right after *Tell Yarrow that I missed him and wanted to stay with him forever*, and right before *Ask my parents for money to buy a ship*. That's why I avoided them all for two days before I broached the subject.

We were out for drinks again, the others tearing up the dance floor while Frodli and I watched from the sidelines. Maybe one day they would get me out there dancing with them. I could at least hold my own next to De-hua, who was doing some kind of disco poking manoeuvre even though the music was thoroughly modern and not twentieth century in any way.

"You've been quiet about Pardus since that secret meeting you had," said Frodli. "De-hua and Lami fought for an hour about whether you were coming back at all."

I froze, and my heartbeat sped up. "Well, I did."

"Yes." Frodli sipped her drink and laughed as Lami tried to learn whatever the heck dance De-hua was doing.

Hadn't the scary woman told her not to mention Pardus? "Your team is safe now." She might be willing to risk it, but I wasn't.

She turned slowly to face me, her blank eye sockets creepy in the dim bar lighting. "What?"

"It was a mistake bringing you all in on it. Just forget about it."

"Forget about...the possibilities you raised? How our research might be used?" Hundreds of people trapped in a space pinch."

"I'm taking care of it."

"And you expect us to just forget it," said Frodli. It didn't sound like a question, it sounded like an accusation of her own.

"There's every chance that pursuing it could be dangerous."

Frodli shook her head, watching Margot and Lami try to teach De-hua one of their dances. She wouldn't put them in danger. "You expect me to convince them to quit?"

"Yes, I do." I tried to apologize with just my eyes. "I don't want any more help." Besides, anything else we did would get straight back to HGNT via Margot.

Frodli shook her head again. "Margot won't be involved anymore." Had she read my mind?

Even if that was the case, I still couldn't risk these folks. "That's great...I'll let you know if there's anything you can do." Maybe. Probably not. "I'm taking care of it."

Frodli frowned, but she dropped it.

And now I *was* taking care of it, sitting across the Creature Café table from Pauli. She popped her gum and gave my HGNT-issued screen a look as though it were a toddler with cookie crumbs around its mouth. I fidgeted, hovering on the edge of my chair.

"So, can I circumvent the software?" I said.

She flipped her long black braid over her shoulder and rolled her eyes.

In order to avoid HGNT's eavesdropping, I'd used a call booth to put out an anonymous call for someone with the expertise we needed to meet me here in the pet café. Through the glass, I watched a kitten try to take down a chair leg, completely ignoring the catnip mouse abandoned on the floor.

"The screen is registered to Exodus Labs, two years old, hasn't been updated to the newest OS," said Pauli.

"Okay, and the network? Is that how they're getting their information?"

Pauli stared into space above my head and bit her lip. "Yeah," she finally said.

Across from the cat room, a host of enclosures and runs held a number of smaller creatures, mostly rodents, some rabbits. A fuzzy blueish weasel slept on a perch, its legs dangling. It looked so chill.

Pauli popped her gum again and gave me a pitying look. "You're gunna have to tell me what's up."

"What do you mean?"

"I work for HGNT, and they are not going to like you turning off their taps."

"I—"

"Yeah, no. Tell me what's going on or find someone else. But just so you know, pretty much anyone else would have walked out by now."

"Why?"

"I'll piss off HGNT. I don't care. Most people"—she raised her eyebrows at me—"are not like me."

Considering that merely being here with Pauli was probably violating the deal I'd just signed, telling her about everything was out of the question. And she looked young. Like, a teenager, with her distressed clothes and one earbud she couldn't bring herself to take out to listen to our conversation properly. No way should she be mixed up in this mess.

"I'm sorry, Pauli," I said. "I can't give you any more information. If that's a requirement for you, then thanks for your time."

Pauli glowered, shoved back her chair, and stomped out.

When I opened my door the next morning, she was standing there. I froze in the doorway. I'd contacted her anonymously, so how had she figured out where I lived? And why had she gone to all the effort?

She gave me a self-satisfied smile, and her eyes flashed, daring me to turn her away.

I let her in.

"I threw together something for you. Set it running, and then turn off your network access—"

What was she talking about? "What?"

"What you really need is a burner screen, but it's too late to get one now."

That was a good idea. "Why is it too late?"

"They're keeping tabs on you already. Enough silly questions. Here's my gift to you." She grabbed my screen right out of my hand, unlocked it, and installed something.

"How did you know my unlock code?" Had she hacked my screen?

"You punched it in yesterday." She'd been watching over my shoulder and memorized it? And now she was asking me to trust her with a program she'd just cobbled together and dumped on my screen...

"Just one problem. The monitoring software definitely just watched you install that."

"I fuckin' hope so. It looks like an addictive as shit merge game. They have to believe you're playing it the whole time your network is off, since that's all they'll see."

Holy shit. This might work. Why the hell was this stranger helping me? Asking would be ungrateful, but I had to be sure. "And you're helping me because? You said you work for them."

"I do. Family business. Who could resist pulling one over on their old man. Do you have any paper?" She looked around my place like she might spot some hiding behind the couch.

"Paper?" How was I supposed to keep up with all this topic jumping making my head spin?

"You know, ground-up trees squished into a sheet? Write on it with a pencil?"

I know what paper is! "Yeah, I do."

"Untraceable." She flopped onto my loveseat while I dug out the notebook I'd bought after *Lepton* vanished, when I'd been at my most paranoid.

She scribbled out a number. "That's one of my burners. If you need to get me from a call booth, that'll do it."

"Thanks." She was doing this to give her father, who ran HGNT, the finger. She certainly looked the youthful rebel. I'd have to test the program, and it would only work as long as I kept my network off, so no sending messages, but I could at least move around Exodus without being tracked.

I tried it out on a few casual strolls in the next couple of days. No security came banging on my door, demanding to know why I'd turned my network access off, which was as much assurance as I was going to get. Turning the app on regularly would help sell my game addiction in case I needed to use it for an extended period at some point.

❖

Dr. Morbit finally returned from his stint in the field and came down to check on our team's progress a few days after my meeting with Pauli.

As our team lead, Frodli got the materials together to present, and we all gathered in our conference room.

"Welcome back, Dr. Morbit," said Frodli as she motioned him to a seat. "I hope your voyage went well?"

"Thanks so much, Frodli. Yes, very well indeed. I hear you've been doing great things yourselves now that Carolina is on the team."

"Yes, her practical knowledge has been a great help." Frodli didn't meet my eyes.

"Good, good. Let's see what you have for me, then."

Frodli launched into her presentation, the visualizations Lami had come up with for the wake pattern around a pinch eliciting a crow from Dr. Morbit.

"Wonderful job, everyone. Now, if you don't mind, I'd like to speak to Carolina for a moment."

Everyone stared at me. I cleared my throat, but what was there to say? He'd heard about me dragging his team into my Pardus antics, and he was going to get rid of me. The rest of the team filed out, and Frodli shut the door on us. Another supervisor I'd let down. Another place I'd have to leave pretty soon from sheer embarrassment—and that was the best-case scenario. If he stopped protecting me from HGNT...

"You've done very good work here, Carolina."

Here it was. Good work, *but*...

"I don't want to lose you from my team, and I've told HGNT as much."

What?

"You seem determined not to let Pardus Station go. I must say, I don't see why Kronenberg is surprised after you've stuck to it this long. Rest assured, you are not the only one with an interest in Pardus."

Dr. Morbit had already known about the pinch keeping Pardus trapped. He must already be trying to free them.

"I would ask that you not bring my team into it, though, Carolina. They don't have the...drive that we have. I fear it would be too much for them."

I was already nodding as he spoke. "Of course." I would leave them out of it if it meant I could help with the research that would set the folks on Pardus free.

"I appreciate it. Don't forget, there's a practical side to my research!" He tapped the side of his nose and grinned.

A weight lifted out of my gut. I wasn't as alone in this as I'd thought. "Maybe one day, you can show me your experimental set-up or your data?"

Dr. Morbit's grin melted away. "I don't think Kronenberg would approve that, unfortunately. But I suppose if someone found out about my practical research...stumbled upon it, perhaps, he wouldn't be able to argue secrecy any longer."

Was he telling me to sneak into his lab?

He glanced at my screen sitting on the conference table. It was passing everything we said back to HGNT, and presumably to Kronenberg. Using Pauli's trick with Dr. Morbit sitting right there was a bad idea. I'd have to figure out how to *stumble upon* his lab all on my own.

Later that day, I hunched in a call booth, punching in Pauli's number from the piece of actual paper I clutched in my sweaty hand.

She picked up on the third ring, without video.

"Hello?" said a deep voice. Or maybe it wasn't her.

"Um...hi. I got this number..." Maybe someone had found her burner. Should I avoid saying her name just in case? What if she'd got busted?

"Carolina?" Pauli's voice, all of a sudden. "Sorry about the voice changer. Can't be too careful."

In a past life, I would have laughed, would have considered Pauli to be weirdly paranoid, but in the life I'd found myself sucked into, answering an unknown number with a voice changer actually seemed like a smart precaution.

"Yes, it's me. From a call booth, like you said. I need something." Pauli never seemed interested in pointless chatter.

"Oh yeah? Shocking. It turns out I do, too. I need to get off this station."

"You think I can help you with that somehow? Are you...being held against your will?"

"I'm freaking grounded, not shackled to the wall. Don't be so freaking dramatic," said the kid who answered my call with a werewolf-sounding voice changer. "And yes, you can. You have money. I want you to prep a spoke for me. Rations, a reconstitutor, life support."

"I'm being watched constantly. What makes you think I can do that without drawing attention?"

"What do you need help with?" she fired back.

"Exodus plans. I need to find Dr. Morbit's—"

"So a risky ask, then? Also, I don't want to know what you're looking for. You help me with my thing, I'll get your plans." She wasn't asking.

I could request a private research space. Dr. Morbit was a pretty big deal on Exodus, and he seemed to like me. Maybe I had enough pull to make it happen. "Fine. I'll try to get you a spoke."

"Call me when you do." She hung up.

I slumped back on the bench seat, and my head thudded on the acoustic foam wall. If Dr. Morbit had me studying Pardus, he'd probably be more willing to give me my private space. But I had to *stumble* on his research before I'd be allowed to study Pardus, which meant I needed those plans.

A rap on the door told me my time in the booth was up. I gathered my screen and paper scrap with Pauli's number and slid the booth door open.

"There you are! I've been calling and calling!"

I nearly jumped out of my skin. Trix folded her hands in her robe and smiled sweetly.

After my heartbeat got back under control, we retired to the Creature Café. Thankfully, I already had my anti-spy system running on my screen, so no one would know we were meeting. Whoever was watching would think I was sitting in my room mindlessly merging dragons or whatever Pauli showed them.

"Where have you been? I was worried. I haven't seen you around, and the cards said you were cut off or something. It can be hard to get concrete information from them, especially about technology. Did your screen break? Is that why you were using the booth?"

"You could say that. How did you know I would be here? Cards again?"

"Not exactly. I met Jasper for coffee this morning." Her lavender cheeks darkened to violet. "I saw you go into the call booth."

"I'm not allowed to talk about that thing we were looking into before." Just because my screen was safe didn't mean Trix's was. Even a mention of Pardus could flag her screen to be watched for all I knew, now that Miller wasn't protecting us.

Trix's eyes narrowed. "*You're* not allowed, or *we* aren't?"

"I'm not allowed, and we probably shouldn't, just in case."

"So, no progress, then? Are you giving up?"

Sharing the pinch theory with Trix could yield awesome results, considering how knowledgeable she was about particulates. I described my team's research, which I considered beyond reproach, and she seemed to get the gist.

She steepled her hands. "Do you know anyone working on the practical side of Dr. Morbit's research? They can't fault you for chatting with your colleagues."

"You'd think, but apparently, it's just Dr. Morbit. Anyone he wants to bring in requires special clearance—clearance I'd never be able to get because of...you know." I drained the last sips of my tea and toyed with the mug handle. "I've been thinking of trying to get a private lab in one of the spokes. Just a quiet place to work, you know?"

Trix nodded. "You should be able to reserve one for the semester."

What? Could it really be that easy to get Pauli her spoke?

"Oh! While I have you here, let's do a reading." She pulled her cards out of her robe with a flourish and shuffled. She cut three times and spread the cards out in front of me.

Obviously, I wasn't afraid to choose a card. That would be silly. Still, my fingers hovered over three different cards before I finally tapped one, then another, then a third. Trix was already gathering up my three cards when I tapped two more and crossed my arms. Hopefully, she was happy now.

Trix laid out the three cards in a row and the last two below, crossed one over the other. She flipped them all and stared at them silently.

The blue furry weasel was awake today, scampering through a tube. It popped out and took a flying leap to its hammock, where it attacked a little stuffed mouse. I definitely couldn't keep it in my room. Besides, if I had to leave Exodus, who would take care of it?

"This one here," said Trix and stabbed the third card with her finger. "Is not what I'd like to see in a spread like this one. I'd much prefer a lighter card there, something more star based instead of planet based. Maybe a moon wouldn't be too bad. Of course, a nebula would be too much to hope for." She chuckled as though I had any clue what she was talking about. "But then again, we also have a planet in the anchor spot, which is actually really good news for us. We shouldn't have too many surprises."

She brushed her lace head covering back from her face absently. Trix tapped her lips with a card as she continued to survey her board. "But the really interesting part is this binary you couldn't resist."

The two crossed cards. Ship and unbroken field of stars. Was Trix going to tell me what they meant, or was I supposed to guess?

"This ship can mean home, safety, independence, or loneliness, depending on the spread."

"Why am I not surprised," I muttered. In other words, it could mean anything. How was that useful?

Trix glared at me and laid the star field over it. "Combined with the void card, I would say loneliness though, wouldn't you?"

Escape, whispered a little voice in the back of my head. *Leaving Exodus far behind me.* "You're the card reader." I shrugged.

Trix, for once, didn't respond, but her smile said she knew I was being curmudgeonly on purpose. She gathered up her cards. "Let me know when you get your spoke. Maybe we can meet up."

And put Trix in danger? No, thanks. A pang hit me right in the chest as Trix smiled at me. All the more reason I couldn't bring her into this again.

Chapter 10

I was almost certainly going to be refused a spoke, considering I already had a desk at the lab and an entire cabin to myself, but approval was granted immediately. When I actually went to check out my brand-new spoke, I realized why.

I ducked under the low bulkhead, through the entrance hatch. I straightened slowly; Yarrow wouldn't have been able to straighten at all. I waved my hand in the darkness, and lighting hummed, flickered, and reluctantly half turned on. That recess at the far end must be a viewport, somewhere under all the grime, but the scratched and dinged steel table and benches were functional, at least, if missing cushions. A rank, mouldy smell hit me, and I gagged. The reconstitutor was overflowing with black sludge. There would be no salvaging that.

I poked my head into the two stale office cabins—empty and dark. Why weren't the lights working? Pauli wanted to escape on this thing, which meant working life support, lights, at least one bunk, a working galley and head, and I'd have to clean everything. Exodus had given me the space, but they sure as hell weren't going to come clean it for me.

I started with inventory. No point in starting a project and realizing halfway through that I didn't have the right supplies. I catalogued everything that needed to be replaced and all the work to be done. And with that, I called it a day.

The next day, I came better prepared and cleared out everything I could by hand. The day after that, I borrowed a laser saw and hacked out the gross reconstitutor. Then it was scrubbing the steel plating on my hands and knees, which is where Frodli found me. I plopped the scrub brush in the bucket of grey water and wiped my hair off my sticky forehead with my sleeve.

"You've been away from the lab a lot the past few days." She crouched and stepped inside.

"How did you know I was coming here?"

She shrugged. "I followed you."

She'd followed me. As the team lead, she probably could've got security to tell her where I was going. Or she could have asked.

"I'm sure Dr. Morbit could find you another lab, if you want to avoid Margot looking over your shoulder." She smeared dirt over the floor with her toe. "This one isn't exactly..."

"Habitable?" And that's what made it such a good project. I'd fixed the lights, and now that the gross old reconstitutor was gone, it didn't smell so bad. The laser saw still sat where the new reconstitutor would go. I was on the wait list for the life support technician to come fix that, but I was trying to learn to fix it myself since the list was so long. They didn't need me at the lab anyway. My part in the project was done, and when I was there, I just hung around and reminded them how much trouble I'd caused.

"Do you want help?" Frodli beckoned, and a sheepish De-hua and determined Lami appeared. A lump swelled in my throat. They really wanted to be rid of me this badly?

"We've been treating you like crap," said De-hua. "It's the least we can do." But he grimaced at my bucket of nasty water.

"I'm a fair hand with a mop, and De-hua can work a sewing machine." Lami elbowed him in the ribs, and he yelped.

"And I'm not bad with a wrench," Frodli added. "Just tell us what you want done."

They had chased me down to help with my spoke? Why? "I can't make you do that." I scooped my brush out of the wash water and scrubbed, the scratchy sound filling the silence.

"You're right, you can't *make* us." Frodli raised her voice over my scrubbing. "And we can't *make* you accept our help."

"Looks like you could use some cushions for your benches," said De-hua. "There's this cool fabric that eats stains I've been looking for an excuse to buy." He rapped on one of the cold steel benches. Just the thought of trying to upholster them myself was exhausting. "And I know Lami wants to give her cleaning robot a go on something really gross." He grimaced. "Like that viewport? It *is* a viewport, right?"

"So you'd be doing us a favour, really." Frodli smirked.

Okay, fine. Having them there helping me was better than scrubbing all alone, swearing to myself. By the end of the week, I had comfy cushions at my kitchen table, the whole place was robot cleaned and lemony fresh, and the life support was mostly limping along. The tech would still need to tune it up, but it would keep someone alive for a bit. Probably.

The new reconstitutor arrived on the Friday, and Frodli helped me install it. Once the thing was set up to Pauli's specs, we sat at the table and admired the place.

The viewport was actually bigger than I'd first thought, and the curtains De-hua had made were perfect. Florals in space never got old. Shuttles blinked by outside, the starry backdrop ever-changing as the huge station rotated.

"We have one last thing for you," said Frodli. "Something to remember us by, wherever you're going." She slid a data stick across the table. "All of our research on the pinches."

They'd been compiling this for me to take? To take. They thought I was the one leaving. And maybe I had started to think that, too. This wasn't even my spoke, it was Pauli's. But maybe it would be best if I did leave. All this sneaking around was exhausting. But if I could help Dr. Morbit get Pardus free, then I would. Once I joined Dr. Morbit with his experiments, I would be leaving the theoretical research group, but they didn't have to know where I was going. They'd be safer if they didn't. I put the stick in the locker next to the table.

I said goodbye to Frodli and detoured back to my cabin so it would look like I was there while I turned on Pauli's decoy game. I turned off network access and headed to a call booth to let Pauli know her spoke was ready and that she'd better have my plans.

Pauli sent them right away, over some circuitous route that I couldn't pretend to understand, but as soon as I got back to my cabin and turned on my network, there they were. Dr. Morbit's office, a lab across the hall, then a red line and a plain corridor and a maintenance closet. I scouted out the corridor, and it was publicly accessible. The closet was unlocked. It wouldn't be hard to cut through the bulkhead with the laser saw and poke my head in, see what I needed to *stumble* on, and get out again.

The next night, I was ready to check it out. Before I left, I updated the "Question Marks" document with all the information I'd learned at Exodus about the pinches in space and the similarity between what we'd found at Pardus and our team's visualization. HGNT couldn't fault me for updating my own notes, surely, even if they could see that I was doing so.

I set Pauli's decoy running and turned off my network access, as usual. What was so secret about Dr. Morbit's research that all this was necessary for me to essentially blackmail my way into getting clearance? His lab was even marked with that red line.

I reached my spoke to pick up the laser saw, but the lights were already on, and someone was in there. Pauli lounged with her feet on the freshly cleaned table. She looked up from her screen. "This is my spoke now. Scram."

I snorted. Was that right? Just like that, the spoke was hers? Me and my team had fixed the place up from the dump I'd been assigned to a livable, dare I say cozy, space, and this little firecracker was kicking me out?

Pauli frowned. "Do you not know the word *scram*? I thought old-Earther people like you talked that way."

I couldn't hold back my chuckle. "I appreciate you getting me those schematics, Pauli, but not enough to let you just take over this spoke. When the time comes that you want to run"—I hefted the laser saw over my shoulder—"let me know. Until then, we share."

She frowned at the laser saw. "You're not going to kill someone are you? Those things can do serious damage to a person."

"I thought you didn't want to know? It's probably best that you don't anyway. See you around!"

Pauli called after me, but I was on a mission and out of time for her petulance.

As I'd hoped, the corridor and adjoining closet were empty. No one was guarding this area, unlike the actual entrance to Dr. Morbit's particle labs—I'd checked.

I shut myself in the closet and pulled up the schematics. How embarrassing would it be to cut through the wrong wall, after all this?

I turned, holding the map in front of me. Okay. It should be right on the other side of this bulkhead right here.

I pressed in the safety and squeezed the trigger on the laser saw. It hummed as it melted a hole the size of my finger in the steel. Awesome! This wouldn't take long at all. The light from the laser saw wouldn't be enough to penetrate the black that appeared on the other side as I cut a wobbly hole big enough for me to clamber through. I let off the saw, and it clunked on the ground. I wiped my sweaty palms on my pants. I'd tried to be careful to keep the beam on the bulkhead and not on the places I'd already cut through, and the safety shouldn't have let me damage anything on the other side. How pissed would Dr. Morbit be if I accidentally lasered some of his specialized equipment? Too late to worry about that now.

The light reaching through the hole made a glittering pattern on the floor, and I leaned in. Of course, my body blocked the light as soon as I did. I turned on my screen's flashlight and shone it in, but still, it was just glittering blackness. What was in there?

I leaned a little farther, and my stomach swooped as gravity *changed direction* and pulled me *across* the room, falling toward the glittering surface. The substance cushioned my fall, but it popped and shuddered beneath me. That couldn't be good. What kind of equipment was this: squishy and tough and rubbery?

I scrambled off it and right into a puddle of oil on the floor. Except oil wasn't tacky like this. I poked at the dark mound with the toe of my boot. It gave and then sprang back. It wasn't a pile of something, it had structure; after all, it had done a good job of breaking my fall. A huge container of some kind? Maybe there was an opening. I ran my flashlight's beam up and down the side of the blob as I paced around it. The thing was as big as a whale, taller than me, even deflated as it seemed to be.

I rounded the end of the blob, the light from my flashlight still glittering off it. There on the floor was a big puddle of that oily, tacky, black ooze. It leaked from a rupture in the blob's side, probably the source of the pop when I landed on it. Maybe the black stuff was a material Dr. Morbit was using for his research? Hopefully, he wouldn't be too upset that I'd wasted some.

Touching some mystery substance was a terrible idea, but I bent to bring my screen closer and played the beam over the little stream of liquid. The blob still glittered out of the corner of my eye...but the light from my flashlight wasn't even hitting it. Was it a light source as opposed to just reflecting?

I bopped the Off button for my flashlight. The only illumination now should have been coming from the hole I'd sliced in the wall-turned-ceiling. But still, the blob glittered. Right in front of me. Was it only here? It had been glittering around the other side when I was over there, hadn't it?

I set off to double-check, and the glittering pattern *followed* me.

And then the blob moved.

A shudder seemed to ripple through its skin, a tremor, from one end to the other. The rupture burped a stream of dark liquid. Was it possible that the blob was alive? If so, it was like no creature I'd ever seen. Its glistening black body was the size of a small spaceship but acted more like a blobfish with its boneless, oozing quality. If it had sensory organs, I wasn't up to identifying them, or orifices, for that matter.

Okay, I had popped a living thing, and its fluids were gushing all over the floor. I turned my light back on. Maybe there was a first aid kit somewhere in here?

It didn't take me long to determine that the room was more of a cell. Totally bare, hardly big enough to walk around the blob creature, no furnishings, no viewports, definitely no first aid kit. Could I at least plug the hole to staunch the...bleeding? It likely wasn't blood, probably more of an interstitial fluid—not important. I took off my coveralls and balled them up.

"This will probably hurt," I muttered to the no-doubt uncomprehending blob.

I took a deep breath and reached my bare fingers toward the creature's skin. Just because it was alive didn't make it sentient. Perhaps this was just some unfortunate creature that had been in the wrong place at the wrong time, and Exodus had picked it up by accident; it might lash out if I hurt it.

When my fingers made contact, the blob's skin shuddered, and spidery veins seemed to glisten more brightly under it. The blob was cool and smooth, perhaps not homeothermic as it didn't seem to radiate heat into my fingers. A rumble juddered through the soles of my boots up through my feet and reverberated into my chest. I snatched my hand away.

Okay, so no touching. Fair enough. What had looked like a puddle beneath the creature was, upon closer inspection, the creature's squashed flesh. Maybe it wasn't used to this level of gravity. Either way, I needed to stop the creature's bleeding. I left my screen on the floor and brought my coverall closer. The glittering intensified, definitely directed at me.

"If you didn't like me touching you, this is going to be worse. I'm really sorry." I shoved my coverall into the rupture, and the black gunk seeped into the fabric, practically gluing it there. I peeled my sticky hands away, dark with the creature's fluids, and my weird bandage held.

"Hopefully, you haven't lost too much already." I wiped my hands on my pants. I had to get this creature some help.

I found the single door to the lab and smacked the palm pad. Nothing happened. I smacked it again, harder. A red light blinked. The door was locked from the outside. Maybe that was why the lab seemed so much like a cell. Maybe it was one.

Oh shit. My laser saw hole taunted me from the ten-foot ceiling. If this was a cell, I was a prisoner now, too. I sank to the floor in a spot not covered in bodily fluids.

The organism was beautiful. The switch from weird alien puddle to lovely wonder of nature was gradual over the next quarter of an hour, but something about the glittering on the deep black background evoked a field of stars. An ever-changing field of stars, controlled by this fascinating being.

I pulled out my screen, pointed it at the glittering patch, and pressed Record. Would my camera be high enough resolution to capture the sparkles? It might be nothing, just a random assortment of lights. But it might be conscious; it might be trying to communicate with me.

I wouldn't be able to send this video to anyone with my network access turned off, and turning it on would immediately alert HGNT to my activities here. Which was what I had wanted until I accidentally assaulted their prisoner. What would they do with me now? Lock me up like this poor creature?

Either way, I couldn't just let the blob die. I stopped recording, flicked over to my network settings, and turned them back on. Fingers crossed someone at HGNT would know how to doctor a blob. The network showed *Connecting... Connecting... No signal.*

Wait, did that mean I was trapped in here with a dying creature? How often did they check on this thing? No orifices could mean that it didn't eat. There were some species that consumed all their food in the larval stages and didn't eat as adults. What if they didn't check this cell for days or *weeks*? They'd come for their monthly check and find both our corpses.

I slumped forward over my knees. Who would come looking for me? My team here already thought I was leaving; Yarrow had abandoned me; I'd told Trix to stay away; Pauli would be happier with the spoke all to herself; even my parents wouldn't notice I hadn't called in a while until after I'd already succumbed to thirst.

I started another video running so that at least when someone found our bodies, they would have some idea what had happened.

"Just you and me in the dark," I said. "If this is your way of talking, I'm guessing the dark doesn't bother you. It would be like silence for me and my air compression patterns."

A vibration jolted through my butt and up my spine into my chest, the same way it had when I'd touched the blob.

"You know, I don't understand your sparkles, but I definitely feel that." My eyes prickled, and I wiped away a tear before it could fall. No one was around; the sparkly being probably didn't know what tears were.

"Hey, if we're going to die together, I need to call you something. You look so much like stars. Starblink. That'll do. I'm sorry I landed on you, Starblink." The creature kept humming.

I realized I'd picked up the hum in my chest when the first few notes of a lament tumbled from my lips. I held the camera steady, and my breath carried the low dirge my grandmother had passed down to me, rising and falling like ocean waves, droning like a ship's engine, carrying the creature far from its home on its last journey to the stars.

❖

I must have fallen asleep and dropped my screen, because I jolted awake to a rapping on the door. Why knock on a cell?

The door slid open, burning my retinas with glare, and I squeezed my eyes shut.

"Carolina Dawn! I must admit, I didn't expect your stumble to be quite so dramatic."

I prised my eyes open. Dr. Morbit was silhouetted in the doorway, flanked by his security guards. My stomach rumbled, and my mouth stuck together. He'd come to find me. His tone had been playful, but when he spoke next, it was anything but.

"What have you done to my AVDO, Carolina?"

AVDO? The blob? "I'm really sorry, Dr. Morbit. I fell when the gravity changed—"

"I don't require your excuses."

The creature had ceased glittering and thrumming sometime while I'd slept.

"It's dead."

Fuck. Not only had I killed a living thing, but Dr. Morbit was not going to take this lightly. Was it worse than disappearing Lancaster's ship? I scrambled to my feet, bracing myself on the wall.

"Do you know how long I worked to capture that specimen, Carolina?"

"No, Dr. Morbit." The puddle of ooze on the floor had dried.

"Come."

My ass was still asleep from spending—I checked my screen—pretty much all night on a steel floor, and my feet stuck to the deck as I crossed the dried fluid. On the bright side, I had a network signal now that I was out of the cell.

Dr. Morbit ushered me into his office across the hall and shut the door on the guards.

"What shall we do about this, Carolina?" he said as he motioned me to a seat covered in a stack of papers.

I moved the stack to the floor and took the seat.

He didn't wait for my answer. "I said *stumble* on my research, not set me back by a decade."

"I *am* sorry."

"Your apologies won't bring my AVDO back to life, you know."

What was I supposed to say to that?

"They're extremely wily. They always know somehow when I'm coming. Catching one alone... Well, it doesn't happen often."

Wily? That must mean they were at least aware. And if the AVDO I'd met *had* been trying to speak to me...

"Dr. Morbit, I think the AVDO might be sentient."

He chortled. "Don't change the subject, Carolina. HGNT has been very lenient with you, at my request. After this, I will be far less inclined to defend you to them. It's possible you're more trouble than you're worth." He wagged his finger at me.

Was he going to fire me? Disappear me? Hand me over to HGNT?

"Of course, we can't have you telling anyone about the AVDO. We've kept our secret for a century, and we're pretty darn good at it by now." He leered at me. Had his teeth always been that sharp?

He pressed a button on his desk, and his door swished open. The two security guards stood on either side, peering in at me.

"Put Carolina somewhere safe while I decide what should be done with her."

Shit. I couldn't let them lock me in a cell and forget about me. Been there, done that. Now would be my best chance. The guards were waiting for me to come out to them, and Dr. Morbit was leaning back in his chair, not prepared to jump up and grab me.

I hefted a huge stack of paper and lunged for the door, leaped into the corridor, and tossed the stack over my shoulder. The hiss of paper tumbling across the deck followed me as I broke into a run, and the thump and swearing of one of the guards going down faded as I rounded the corner.

I pictured the station schematic. I'd have to go all the way up to get on a shuttle, and besides, they could just bar my access. There had to be another way off the station.

I might be free of those two guards, but getting in an elevator would be like crawling into a cage.

I pulled out my screen as I ran, taking random turns, moving away from the shuttles. My screen shook as I tried to read the schematic. Where else would decks connect, besides the elevators? That red line around the AVDO's room. Maybe it hadn't been security, but gravity.

I frantically scanned for a useful gravity marking on the schematic... *There!* Gravity switched directions right at the bottom of the concourse, no doubt for safety reasons. The galleries that spanned ten decks were not *intended* to provide access, but that didn't mean I couldn't make it work.

Where would I go from the bottom, even if I survived the fall? Maintenance hallways, unused offices, accommodations, and spokes. *My* spoke.

My lungs burned. I couldn't outrun security. I would head for the concourse.

I skidded around a corner and down a narrow hallway, still going in the right direction, or if I wasn't, signs for the concourse were plastered all over the station. I followed the arrow right. Just as long as security didn't cut me off before I got there...but they expected me to run for the shuttles.

I rounded another corner into a narrow tunnel to the concourse. It had to be easy to cut off a space like this completely. An open column between decks could become a liability very quickly in an emergency. They wouldn't let me back out this way.

I burst into the open space, knocking someone into the wall, but I didn't stop. My spoke would be...that way. I dodged an oblivious security guard, who shouted after me. Almost there...the end of the concourse closest to my spoke, six decks below. I pulled back from the edge, head spinning.

Security barrelled through the corridor about six metres away. Was I really going to trust my life to a schematic I couldn't accurately read? Security was not playing around anymore; the grim faces hustling toward me made that clear.

I leaned over the railing and tipped sickeningly forward—fingers dug into my shoulder hard enough to bruise and slammed me back onto the deck. I tried to gasp, but air wouldn't come. *I'm not dying, just had the wind knocked out of me, that's all.* I scrambled up, finally pulling in a gasp of air, spots dancing in front of my eyes, the railing digging into my back.

The guards surrounded me in a loose half circle, with the one who grabbed me the closest.

"Just hand over your screen."

My screen? Why? I clutched the pocket it was zipped into. What could possibly be on my screen? The video I'd taken.

As soon as I'd connected to the network, they had been able to search my screen. They must have found my video of the AVDO. If they didn't want it getting out, then clearly it was essential that I upload it immediately. Or as soon as security wasn't waiting to rip my screen out of my hand, looking as if they might take the hand with it if necessary.

"I wouldn't get on our bad side," said the security guard. "Just follow me."

I couldn't retreat anywhere as he reached for me again. Nowhere except a leap into the chasm behind me. But it was that or go with these very nice gentlemen to visit Kronenberg, and I'd been assured I didn't want to do that.

The cold metal railing bit into my palms as I hauled myself up, got a foot on it, and vaulted over. Shouting chased me down past deck five, then four, then... Yes...the air almost felt thicker, as though something was repelling my body. I pried my eyes open, past deck two, and—

I crashed into the floor. My head spun, but I climbed to my feet.

The narrow exit corridor yawned in front of me, and I ignored a throb in my shoulder, which had taken the brunt of the impact. A light flashed in the tunnel. They were going to close it off. I sprinted for the exit before it could slam shut. If they closed it while I was in here...No point in imagining my cracked and smooshed remains; I would be too dead to care if that happened.

My footsteps echoed in the empty corridor until I slipped out the other side, the slam of the safety door behind me making me jump.

Okay. My spoke. Shit, what if Pauli was still there? I'd have to boot her out before I launched. No way was I bringing a kid into this ill-advised escape with me.

Two more turns, and I'd be at my spoke. A stitch bloomed in my side, and I slowed a little, my gasps filled with knives. Footsteps echoed up the corridor behind me, and I took the last turn to my escape at what could only be termed a hobble.

Pauli stuck her head out the hatch as I came level with her. She tucked herself aside while I stumbled through and slammed the hatch after me. My knees hit the deck as I tried to recover enough breath to tell her to get out. My throat tasted like blood.

"You really were up to no good with that saw. Kill someone for real?"

She was joking, but I *had* killed someone. Not now. I shook my head, still gasping and incapable of intelligible speech.

"Seems like we should get going."

"Not...*we*..."

"After all I did to get this spoke, you think I'll let you take it?" The little pipsqueak popped her gum as she keyed in the launch passcode. How did she even *have* the passcode?

I clambered back to my feet and staggered to the viewport in time to see Exodus Labs retreating. So, good. I'd escaped. With the video. Which I should probably post publicly while we were still in network range of Exodus. I pulled up the video on my screen and typed in some quick metadata. I could always fix it later. Getting it posted before I lost network signal was most important. I tapped Upload and leaned against the frame of the viewport.

The upload bar filled steadily as Exodus receded, bit by bit, in the viewport. Would they come after us? What would they use? Another spoke? A shuttle? No other spokes were launching, and the shuttles were holding course so far.

I blinked, and Exodus was gone.

"What the fuck?" said Pauli. "Did we just speed up or something?"

We hadn't. Spokes were designed to piggyback on other ships, not speed anywhere. We hadn't left Exodus behind; Exodus had left us for another sector of space.

My upload bar stayed frozen. And Exodus Labs had been teleported.

Chapter 11

Miller got the call as he was walking out the door of
his office. His shoulders had just started to drop, and
he'd let himself ponder what he wanted for dinner.
Too early. Should have waited until the door was shut.

He trudged back past his security and picked up.

"Your little troublemaker is quite the handful."

*I should never have claimed her as a contractor. It
seemed like a good idea at the time.*

He closed the door. Maybe it would be a short call?

"Get me her supervisor."

"Isn't she HGNT's problem now? I heard she's
working for you guys."

"The one whose ship she stole."

"She didn't exactly—" Why was he defending her? "Fine. I'll send you Lancaster's details. You already have eyes on him, as I understand it."

"We work well together, Miller. We always seem to be on the same page."

Kronenberg's lackey. She was a fucking wet dream, but not a moral bone in her body. Unless he was boning her. Then there would be one.

She was going to eat Dawn alive, and it would never cross her mind again. He'd tried to shield Dawn, and he'd done the best he could. She was the one who'd broken all the rules, commandeered her supervisor's custom ship, kept digging no matter how many times he warned her off. Now she could handle the consequences. His career wouldn't survive protecting her again.

"It's not my problem that you can't control your staff. I don't know what you expect me to do."

"Dawn was your responsibility, Miller. She's infected my staff because of your ineptitude."

He shrugged. Not his problem. "One, I don't answer to you. Two, protecting HGNT's interests isn't actually part of my job description."

"You've done it plenty in the past," she snapped. She clearly wasn't used to conversations not going her way.

"Consider them favours. And hope I never call them in," he said.

She looked as if she wanted to smack the smile off his face. Or hand him over to Kronenberg. His heart pounded. This was fine. He wouldn't be here when she brought the hammer down on him.

"Perhaps you can keep me informed of Dawn's movements, in that case? As another favour?" She couldn't keep the venom out of her voice, or maybe she wasn't even trying.

"I thought your network would keep you informed? Doesn't HGNT keep tabs on these types of loose ends?"

"I'm not sure what you're referring to. HGNT operates within the law. Spying on a former employee would most certainly be an invasion of privacy."

He smirked. "Yeah, okay. If something comes up, I'll let you know."

She nodded. Her eye twitched.

"If you're sure you want to owe me two more favours?" He couldn't resist getting in another jab.

"You're keeping track?"

"I am now." It would be his only recourse if they tried to blackmail him. Though she wouldn't honour favours to him over Kronenberg if it came to that. And that's why he had to get out of here. And he would. Soon.

I kicked at the hissing condenser, and it gurgled, but the steam shooting from the side abated. I swiped at the sweat running into my eyes. This was going to be okay. Frodli had done a good job with the life support under the circumstances.

Frodli. She'd given me this life support system as a gift, along with the simulation. I'd gone for the data stick she'd left me while Pauli was shut in her cabin, and found it missing. Without that, my plan to match our simulation with physical data and prove that Dr. Morbit was involved in the disappearances was quickly falling apart.

I slouched back into the living space.

"So, are you going to tell me what HGNT has on you?" Pauli didn't even look up from her screen.

"I think it's more what I have on them," I grumbled.

Pauli's screen was forgotten in an instant. "What?"

No way was I sharing the deadly AVDO secret with a literal child. "Never mind."

"Not going to happen. I'm in this shit with you now. I deserve to know."

"Absolutely not." One of us had to be responsible.

"Fine." She went back to her screen.

I slid a packet into the reconstitutor and tapped the button. Finally, food, after being locked in that cell with no breakfast.

"Shit," said Pauli.

I sidled closer to look over her shoulder..."Dammit!" The AVDO video I'd taken in the cell was playing on her screen.

A dark room, something sparkling in the middle distance. Too flickery to be stars, and they changed sequence in a way that didn't seem at all random. My voice, talking about how we were both going to die, then that low dirge. I watched the whole video over her shoulder. The sparkling went on for five minutes and then dimmed and faded to black.

The reconstitutor beeped.

"What the hell was that video?" said Pauli.

"I'm not exactly sure."

"Give me the broad strokes."

"A creature HGNT was holding hostage." I grabbed my food and slapped it on the table.

"No fucking wonder they were after you with this on your screen. I hope it's backed up?"

"I didn't have time to upload it anywhere, but I will." I opened my pad thai breakfast and slurped in a big bite of noodles.

Pauli, for once, turned pale. "Do you have any idea what they'll do to you if you share this?"

I swallowed my bite. "I'm pretty sure it can't be worse than what they're doing to the AVDO."

Pauli finally looked as though she regretted coming with me. Exodus disappearing without a trace was nothing compared to the possibility of sharing this video, apparently. But we couldn't do that until we reached the port and found a network anyway.

"Just don't, okay? Let me figure out how to do it without killing us in the process."

Let the teen keep us safe? I nodded. I wouldn't leave it up to her to figure out a safe way to share the video, but I would keep her out of it.

It only took a day or so to get to the port by spoke, a trip that had taken ten minutes on a shuttle. We were picked up and towed into a station in chaos. The place was packed with folks trying to get to Exodus Labs, which was no longer there.

The people who towed us in said it was probably invisible, something about an experiment gone wrong, but when we got into the port proper, everyone was saying how a rival corporation had blown the station up.

I made a beeline for a call booth. I'd have to tell my parents I'd been fired (probably true) and beg them to let me stay with them for a while, just until I figured out where I could live, how to survive, and what to do with the rest of my life. And I guess now I was responsible for Pauli. She'd already slammed into another call booth.

A giant invisible hand squeezed my middle and almost stole my breath, but I dialled in the call before I could chicken out and waited for it to ring through. My parents picked up together, which saved me from having to repeat what I was about to say. I went through the *Hi how are yous* on autopilot.

"I actually need somewhere to stay," I said and rushed on before they could ask me what happened. "I've lost my HGNT job." Along with the entire lab complex.

Two blank faces stared at me through the screen. My mom pursed her lips.

"So I just need a little time to figure something else out, and I was wondering if I could come and stay with you, just for a few weeks." And plan my next move.

My dad leaned back and crossed his arms. "Wow. What was that, a month?"

"I know, I—"

"And after your mom and I pulled strings to get you that job."

A pit opened up in my stomach, and the giant hand squeezed tighter.

"And now you're planning to, what, come home and live in our basement rent-free?"

"I can pay rent if you want—"

"From your month of savings?" He waved dismissively. "We've really helped you all we can, Carolina."

"Your dad called in a favour to get you that job," my mom chimed in.

My parents got me the HGNT job? *I never asked for your help getting that job. I'm asking for it now...* But I didn't say that. The conversation was only going to go one way. I could go home; they wouldn't turn me away, but if I did, I'd suffer for it. HGNT hadn't wanted me there at all; they just wanted to keep rich shareholders like my dad happy. The only reason they'd kept me on was that Dr. Morbit made them, and there was no way he would stand up for me now. Once Exodus was found.

Shit. What if Exodus was in a pinch in space like Pardus? I'd take some time with my parents, get my bearings, and then I'd fix all this. But Exodus wasn't self-sufficient like Pardus. Without supplies, people would start dying within weeks if not days. I didn't have time to waste getting my bearings. Exodus didn't have time.

"Okay," I said.

"Okay? Don't you mean thank you?" said my mom.

"I'll figure something else out," I said.

"Now that's an overreaction," said my dad. But he didn't say Come on home, and we'll figure this out together. He didn't say You know you're always welcome here. Take as long as you need. "But if you're sure you have somewhere else to land."

"Make sure you let us know where to find you," said my mom. But she didn't say she was sorry I'd lost my job. She didn't tell me she was sure I'd find something else soon.

"I will," I said.

I ended the call.

I absolutely did not have anywhere else to land. But I did have the privacy of this booth for a few more minutes, so no one would see me cry.

Once I'd scrubbed the tear streaks off, I peeked out to make sure there wasn't a line of people waiting and pulled out my screen. I filled out the video description:

Video footage taken at Exodus Labs of an unknown creature that I named Starblink. The light patterns are presumed to be a form of communication. Anyone with the ability to translate/caption please do so below or contact me. Starblink is, unfortunately, deceased.

But if I uploaded it, HGNT would be on me in a second, and with good reason. Taking the video was one thing, but sharing it would mean retribution for breaking my agreements with HGNT. Pauli had warned me not to share it, and I'd kinda agreed to at least wait.

But what else could I do? I wasn't allowed to contact anyone at Exodus, even if they were somehow able to receive messages wherever they were, and Miller had made it very clear that trying to talk to the council was only making things worse. Lancaster did not want to hear from me, nor did Dr. Sycamore. HGNT had well and truly cut me off from this project at every turn. But I couldn't just sit here.

Was there anything at all that I could do? I scrolled up the "Question Marks" document a bit too aggressively and ended up at the top.

I paused. I'd sworn I wasn't going to use this lead unless I was desperate. Hounding tragically deceased people's families was the absolute bottom of the barrel. But there it was, a note from my past self:

Miner's obituaries—suspicious circumstances; families know more?

❖

I had enough money left to rent a ship. I was banking on the fact that HGNT could see that I'd charged a call to a booth but not monitor that call. I had no control over whether the other end was monitored, and after my experience with Dr. Sycamore, I was fairly sure it would be. I left my camera off, but it didn't end up mattering. I got dumped to voicemail.

"This is Fiona Klein of FiOREna Limited. I'm on a job right now, in the asteroid belt. Shouldn't take too long, so go ahead and leave a message. My wait times remain at six months, so keep that in mind, but I'll be back by then for sure."

I ended the call. If I left a message, what would I even say? *I want to talk about your dead husband, so call me back?* In the asteroid belt, there should at least be some kind of network coverage. Maybe I could get her to call me back; waiting months for a call with her wasn't an option.

FiOREna Ltd. was an independent mining company that mostly worked in collaboration with larger firms or on more delicate tasks.

If they were in the asteroid belt, it was probably a delicate task. No one wanted to make a mistake so close to Earth. I did a quick search for active mining operations in the asteroid belt, and only a handful appeared. Few enough that, with a ship, I could check them out myself and I wouldn't have to tip HGNT off that I was doing so. As long as I was careful.

I'd take an express star liner back to the Solar System and, hopefully, have a ship waiting for me there. Ship rentals were a disaster ever since some start-up had tried to implement a ship-sharing scheme that had wiped most of the big rental companies out completely. There was still a small one operating in the Solar System though, so it shouldn't be a problem to get a ship.

I threw together a quick budget. As long as I wasn't expecting a room to myself on the star liner or a huge fancy rental ship, I could just afford all my plan's expenses.

I contacted the ship rental company next. They had a counter in the Solar System port, and that's where I would pick up my ship. The call rang through, and I let the rep know what I'd need. The trip back to the Solar System would only take a couple days on an express star liner, and the rep let me know that a ship would be ready for me when I got there. They took my information and then hesitated.

"Can you scan your fob, please? I think I might have the wrong Carolina Dawn."

A pop-up covered their face, warning me that they'd requested a fob scan and only to comply if I trusted the caller. I punched the Scan button and held my fob up to the reader. The warning disappeared, leaving just the person's frowning face in the frame.

"Um, I'm sorry, Miss Dawn, I don't think we'll be able to offer you a rental."

"Is there something wrong? I have the currency—"

"It's not that..." They glanced at the camera.

"What else could it possibly be?"

"It's probably a mistake, which you can clear up and get right back to me."

"What's the mistake?" I picked at my fingernail.

"It says here that a ship you were operating was reported missing, probably stolen. But it must be some mistake. I'm sure that never happened. Just put in a call to your fob company and sort it out. You can even call from the star liner, and it'll be sorted out before you arrive. I'm sure there will be a ship available for you by then. Thanks very much for calling, and best of luck sorting out that mistake!"

The screen went dark. A ship that I was operating went missing. *Lepton*. Had Lancaster reported it stolen, after we'd told him what happened? Did he really think we'd stolen his ship and, what, sold it for parts? I'd thought we had an understanding, that the ship had disappeared, nearly killing us, and it was water under the bridge. Lancaster being angry, I could understand; Lancaster making it so that my history was wrecked—maybe for the rest of my life with a ship that expensive—without even telling me about it?

Last I'd talked to him, he'd been furtive, as though he was being watched. So maybe it hadn't been Lancaster who made sure the *Lepton* debacle appeared on my history. Maybe it had been HGNT. Either way, I couldn't clear it up with a call.

I could get to the Solar System, and I would. But without a ship, I couldn't get to Fiona in the asteroid belt. It's not as if there were shuttles to the middle of nowhere. Was there any point to going back to the Solar System, in that case?

The last of my determination and purpose was slipping through my fingers. Going home would be torture, and I couldn't go back to the Oort Research Centre or Exodus. Getting a new position somewhere more relevant to my thesis was probably a dead end, with my short tenure at Exodus being the nail in that particular coffin.

Someone tapped on the door to the video booth, and I jumped. The screen was flashing that my time was up. I put my screen away. I had to leave the booth. One thing at a time. Leave the booth and find myself and—*crap*—Pauli some dinner, then a place to sleep. I wasn't totally out of currency yet.

When I slid the door back, Pauli beckoned from the bar across the way.

"They wouldn't serve me booze. Can you get me a real drink?" She waved at her bright-pink fizzy thing. "Just a shot of starshine would be great."

"Uh, no, I'm not going to buy a minor alcohol."

"I'm eighteen. Some places that's legal age for humans."

"Some places that aren't here. I'm surprised you don't have a fake ID."

"Who says I don't, but I'm saving that for a special occasion. I figured you'd be a good sport and help me out."

If anyone needed a drink here, it was me, for having to deal with this hooligan. "There are way more important things to deal with than getting you contraband."

"Fuck. Please tell me you didn't upload that video. Speaking of which, you're going to need to torch your bugged screen."

Surely she didn't mean with a literal torch. How did kids even keep up with all their slang? "I'm not planning to post the video." Not unless I'm completely out of options. "Things are a little complicated, but I still have other options. Do you have anywhere to go?"

"Not really." She fidgeted with her straw.

"You wanted to take my spoke and go somewhere. What was your plan?"

"Travel the Galaxy?" She winced.

I picked at my thumbnail. Where could I leave her that she would be safe? Once I got Exodus back, I could send her home, but I didn't have anywhere near enough currency to put her up here at the port, not indefinitely, and not with all the crowding here since Exodus disappeared. *Okay. This is fine.* She could stay with me, at least for a while.

"Then I have good news for you. We're going to the Solar System."

She didn't smile at me or anything, but she didn't roll her eyes, either. We would somehow hunt down accommodations for tonight and then grab a star liner home in the morning. We only found a small room, but it was clean, and, anyway, we wouldn't need much space just to sleep.

Pauli was still snoring away in the morning when I scribbled a note on paper, tore it out of my notebook, and left it for her. I just had time to get rid of my screen before the star liner boarded. Every port had a tech pawn shop, so I went in search of the one here.

Its dingy storefront meant that this place's wares were probably not completely on the up and up. No big deal. In fact, that was probably an asset. I'd walk out of here with a clean screen and maybe a little untraceable currency.

The attendant glared when I walked in. This hole in the wall had just enough room for the attendant to sit behind the counter, and just enough room for me to stand, the walls stacked with shelves of old electronics. Some of the antiques would probably fetch a decent price at auction. If auctions dealt in less than legitimate goods.

"What can I help you with?" said the attendant. A small person, oily black, antennae and four arms like Yarrow, but insectoid rather than humanoid. Their faceted eyes gave me no clue as to their opinion of me, but the translator was doing a good job of communicating their desire for me to get the hell out without them having to say it.

"I'd like to trade in my screen," I said as I laid it on the counter.

The attendant snatched it and put it on a cradle beside them. The screen lit up, and they scrolled and tapped around too fast for me to see what they were doing. They woke a secondary screen attached to the cradle and made a whistling sound. "You're in trouble, I guess."

So they'd noticed the tracking software.

"Want something less traceable," they said.

It wasn't a question, but I nodded anyway.

"The second you log in, they'll have you again. Any messages you send and all the rest."

Shit. Of course it wasn't going to be that easy. It would be a shame to lose my connection to the others, my access to the shared document with Yarrow that I was 90 percent sure was under their radar. But what use was having messaging and call access when I couldn't use it anyway because of the surveillance?

If I told this attendant about my situation, would they be able to help me? Would they even be inclined to try? And what was to stop them from lying and telling me they'd fixed me up and then passing my new information back to HGNT?

"You can ask around. We're discreet," said the attendant. They rubbed a claw over their antenna and then licked it with their mandibles. "You want to get out from under HGNT. I'll get you a new screen, untraced. But if you log into your accounts, like I said, they'll have you again."

I couldn't afford to lose access to the AVDO video, my only weapon against HGNT. "Would it be possible to access a shared document from the new screen?" I could save the video there.

They clicked their mandibles. "Clever. Yes, under a guest or another account login. You'd have to invite the new account, though."

"Would they be able to see that if I did it from my old screen over there?"

"Depends." They tapped around on my screen and the secondary one. "I can grab a link for you and type it over onto the new screen. No traceable elements."

I drummed my fingers on the counter.

"Except me, you're thinking. I can tell." They made the clicking sound again and motioned around to their shop. "You think I want HGNT checking up on me?"

"No, that's exactly why you'd give them information if they came around asking for it."

"As I said, ask around. We're discreet." They laid my screen gently on the counter and slid it toward me.

What choice did I really have? I would need a new screen if I was going to do literally anything or go anywhere. And the star liner was leaving...like, right now. *Dammit.*

I saved the video to "Question Marks," had the attendant grant a clean screen access, and bounced on the balls of my feet as they wiped my HGNT bugged screen.

I hustled to the gate and met up with a yawning Pauli.

"Finally. I thought you weren't going to make it."

I wasn't cutting it that close, was I? I checked the time. A cool five minutes to spare.

"What's *that*?" said Pauli, as though I were holding a dead rat.

"New screen." I wiggled it. "Untraced."

"What the actual fuck did you do?"

I recoiled. We'd talked about getting me an unbugged screen. Where was this coming from?

"Did you dump your old one down an incinerator, at least? Please tell me you torched it. As in, destroyed it completely."

"What? No! Who does that? I traded it in like a normal person." Who was this kid to be scolding me like I was the child?

"Okay, whatever. Let's just get on the star liner and the fuck out of here."

We boarded the star liner, Pauli not even deigning to look at me. HGNT might be able to keep me from renting a ship, but no ID was necessary to book a star liner ticket. Plus, we'd managed to sell our spoke for untraceable currency—Pauli had insisted we split the take on *her* spoke, probably to keep me from buying things with my fob and alerting HGNT to my every move again.

I claimed a video booth before we'd even left port. Most numbers would not be accessible to me. Since my screen wasn't signed in to my account, I didn't have access to my contacts. It would be publicly available numbers only. If I'd been thinking ahead, I would have copied some numbers into my notebook before trading in my screen. Not that Exodus numbers would have helped me, since it was impossible to call a closed space pocket, apparently.

None of that mattered because my goal was to get myself a ship. Since I wouldn't be able to rent one, I'd have to charter something from the port in the Solar System, when we arrived. And it would have to be under the radar since any licensed captain would look me up and immediately see the missing ship notice when they scanned my ID. I didn't have any contacts with that kind of business, but maybe I knew someone with contacts like that? In the meantime, I did know one person with a public account at CHUSI that might be able to sort this out for me. Probably not, but it was worth a go.

The call rang through, and the timer at the bottom of the screen started ticking up. The screen remained black. But he'd picked up, so I took that as a good sign.

"There's a notice on my account that I maybe, possibly stole a ship. They won't let me rent one while it's active."

"And that's my problem because?" But what was that note in his voice...guilt?

"Lancaster knows we didn't steal the ship. He never would have reported it. He knows we were almost killed. It's a funny coincidence that the moment HGNT wants to keep me grounded I get this notice attached to me."

"It wasn't me. Are we done, Ms. Dawn?"

"I actually have a bunch of free time now that I lost my job. How's the council right now? Any fun drama I should know about? Oh yeah! I meant to ask you: Do you know where Dr. Morbit hopped off to last week?"

"Wonderful. Now we're old friends catching up about our mutual acquaintance. Ms. Dawn—"

"Or maybe where Exodus disappeared to? It was the funniest thing. A whole lab complex vanished right in front of me. *Technical malfunction* is one way of putting it, I guess. That's what HGNT landed on in their press release."

"How would I know? I'm not actually aware of what every lab is working on at any given moment, though I'm flattered that you think I'm that powerful."

"Ooh, have you heard about the alien blob species that sparkles? So pretty!"

The clock at the bottom of the screen ticked up slowly. I picked at my fingernail. He was going to hang up on me. I'd gone too far with my flighty-young-woman shtick. He wasn't going to risk himself to give me answers. He'd been clear on that from the beginning; I was the one who couldn't take no for an answer. I'd wasted enough time with Miller. He'd said he wasn't going to help us, and he wasn't going to.

He cleared his throat. "I've told you before that you're in over your head, and I'm not going to tell you again. But if you were over your head then, you're at sea being circled by sharks now."

"I know, I know, back out now, save myself."

"I'm not sure you could back out if you tried anymore."

That did something to me. Knowing that I was caught up in this, maybe this thing with my screen wasn't as temporary as I'd thought, maybe it was permanent. Maybe I would be flying under the radar for the rest of my life. After all, it wasn't as though a person was sitting there waiting for me to pop up. All they had to do, and they definitely already had, was set their system to watch for me and flag any activity or contacts that they deemed suspicious. If any of their flags came up, the system would crawl through everything again and put together a report on how to bring me down. No human intervention required. And by *bring me down*, I mean kill me and make it look like an accident.

And now I'd called Miller. They might not be watching me at this exact moment, but the trail would be clear enough in retrospect: who I'd called, how long we'd spoken. Guilt choked me. He'd told me not to call him, not to get him involved, and I kept on pulling him back into my crusade.

"Hey, I probably shouldn't have called you. I'm...sorry."

"Don't worry about me, Carolina," said Miller seriously. "Unlike some people, I have self-preservation instincts. It's my job to handle the cases that no one else will touch, and with good reason. Like Exodus Labs! Were you aware that the entire station got teleported halfway across the Galaxy?" Was he doing my own small-talk bit back to me? Jerk. "And since the whole project is so touchy, that's one of my new files. I get to assign the project to someone."

"Are you...offering it to me?"

Miller actually laughed. "You don't even have a ship, an affiliation, any instruments or tools."

"Who got the project?"

"Oort Research Centre, of course. They're the best interstellar research institution in human-dominated space."

Something had finally disappeared that couldn't be ignored...but it had reappeared. Even if Dr. Morbit had cracked teleportation and not told his own team, why would he have wanted to teleport his lab?

"Do you think I want to be on this project? HGNT has it out for me permanently, and I pissed Dr. Morbit off personally, too."

"Maybe, but you might be the only one not currently on Exodus with the expertise to really help. And whoever works on the project will also get authorship on a very prestigious paper and have exclusive access to the research site."

"A prestigious paper full of fudged data and omissions, screened by HGNT?"

Miller didn't answer. We both knew it was true. Even if working with them was enough to make them forgive my AVDO murder, I couldn't forget the way HGNT and Dr. Morbit had treated me.

"I wish I could say yes," I said. "A month or two ago, I would have. But we both know the AVDO change everything."

"We do?"

"It's not about a few ships disappearing or even a station disappearing anymore. I worked there for long enough to know they don't have the technology to make that happen. Or if they do, it's not in production. They don't understand the systems they're trying to bend to their will."

"You're sure?"

"I'm sure. I'm going to find my own way. It would be easier without that alert on my fob."

"There really is nothing I can do about that. But a call to Sparks at the Solar System port might be worth your while."

A call to Sparks? Was Miller...helping me? Had that whole research voyage offer been a test? Either way, he might really have given me a lead on a ship. I grinned. "Just mention your name for a discount?"

"You are under no circumstances to mention my name to anyone, ever. Especially not Sparks."

Call Ended flashed on the screen.

Chapter 12

I found Sparks in a buried directory and put a call through next. He wasn't interested in talking details over video call, but I was confident that he'd at least hear me out when I got to the port in the Solar System.

When I popped open the door of the call booth, Pauli waved her screen in my face.

"You said you didn't upload it," she hissed.

I grabbed her arm and steered her to a lounge with our backs to the wall, then peered at her screen. The black background, the flickering sparkles...

"Why are you watching this again?" Why had she even kept the copy on her screen if she was so worried about—

She swiped at the video, revealing the streaming interface.

"You uploaded it? After you gave me so much crap about it?"

"It wasn't you." She closed her eyes. "I'm not the one who uploaded it. Did I or did I not warn you about destroying your old screen?"

Sure, blame me for not knowing every random slang word. "I didn't just hand it to HGNT. I watched the attendant wipe it. Besides, it wasn't actually me, so HGNT can't—"

"They can. They'll see that it was uploaded from *your* profile on *your* device, which they are tracking ever so carefully, in case you forgot."

I'd wanted to wait until I had enough corroborating evidence to protect me with whistleblower status before I shared the bombshell video. Without the simulation, I didn't have that evidence.

Shit. In the meantime, there was no way to prove it *hadn't* been me. But why would a junk dealer want to post an AVDO video? HGNT certainly wouldn't want it posted, right?

"I can tell by your dopey expression that you don't know what's going on here." Pauli jabbed at the description.

> Alien that STOLE Exodus: This strange blob, known by the code AVDO, might look harmless, even beautiful. You'd never think it could pose a risk, but what if I told you that this creature KIDNAPPED an entire research complex, AND THERE'S NOTHING WE CAN DO ABOUT IT. This power is TOO DANGEROUS to run free. These beings should be REGULATED! Or better yet, KICKED OUT OF HUMAN SPACE!

It was a far cry from the description I'd written.

"It gets worse." She tossed the video over to my screen somehow so I could hear the sound.

The track that I'd recorded along with the video of myself and my dirge was gone, replaced with some kind of inhuman growling wail. It was even in time with the sparkles. Whoever had put this together had totally made it seem like an authentic soundtrack—credit where it was due. Not enough of the room was visible to make it obvious that the AVDO was trapped, and the wound was out of frame as well...but the video metadata showed that the video had been taken at Exodus Labs not long before it got teleported.

I should have posted my version first. Why did I listen to Pauli? Now that this version was posted, everyone would naturally assume that it was the original, and with the view count already in the millions, anything that I uploaded would seem like an obvious remix.

The AVDO would have been dragged out of hiding either way, but now they'd been firmly cast as the villains in this narrative, when all the actual evidence pointed to their being victims. And the comments bore that out.

> These animals should be EXTERMINATED.

> That thing looks like a dying blobfish. I hope it died after what it did.

> Whoever took this video GET IN TOUCH WITH ME. I have a fast ship with lots of guns.

I swallowed down the bile crawling up my throat. A wall of text stopped my scroll. Someone had translated Starblink's final words.

Before reading through the translation, I tapped over to the poster's profile. Who was it that knew Starblink's language? Maybe someone I could contact for more information about the AVDO.

Damn. It was a burner account. "Starblink_8473" with only one comment on this video:

> —ever more fertile, roots reaching to the stars. We span generations, we span systems and galaxies[?] from the very beginning. These will be my last gasps

[lit. EM waves], and I am grateful to the being with the recording device. I hope the recording will seed the stars and echo [lit. reflect] to the corners of the Galaxy. Please know that my death was no accident.

I recoiled. The pain of Starblink's death washed over me again. I already felt like shit about it without the AVDO accusing me from beyond the grave. But I pressed on.

The culpable party, however, is not the being present at my death [lit. disintegration] but the societal structures [lit. groups of beings] who profit from the destruction of my kind. My time grows short, and though I cannot be sure that anyone will hear these words [lit. integrate my radiation], I would urge those remaining not to give up hope. It is not too late to diverge from this path [lit. enter a different orbit]. Keep fighting, keep resisting. May your light shine brightly through the darkness [lit. radiation travel far in vacuum].

Then, at the end of the comment:

Please note that I am not a native speaker. I have done my best to present both connotative and literal translations of idiomatic phrases. Feel free to correct below.

I grabbed the comment and pasted it into my "Question Marks" document.

There was no doubt now that they wanted their words spread through the Galaxy.

"Did you see the translation?"

Pauli jumped as though she'd forgotten I was there, and tilted her screen away. What was she doing on there?

"Starblink…" That was the name I'd given to the AVDO in the video, but how did the translator know that? They must have had the original audio, which meant access to my unaltered video file. Was that why Pauli was so nervous? "Did you translate this?"

"What? No! I sure as shit didn't know about these AVDO teleporting blob creatures before you dragged me into this mess."

So defensive. Apparently, that wasn't what she was hiding. "Who else had access to the original video?"

"Are you fucking kidding me right now? HGNT security, the higher-ups, whoever you gave your old screen to, and anyone *they* gave it to. Why do you think I fucking *told* you to torch your old screen? Wiping does fuck-all to destroy data. Do they not teach you that in stuck up Earther kindergarten?"

Still harping on that, I guess. Deep breaths. "Fine, let me rephrase. Who, of all those people, would both be capable of translating Starblink's message and want to undermine this bigoted spin?"

That, at least, earned me a blank look. Not such a *fucking moron* now, was I? Not that that got me any closer to an answer; Pauli was right that it might have been better to destroy my old screen. Anyone could access it now, and I would never know.

Lucky for me, the star liner trip home was a few days long, so I had a few days to really think about what the hell I was doing. In fact, there wasn't much to do besides that. I had no research to look into, no literature to review, and no one to contact for more information or collaboration possibilities. No supervisor to update.

So I picked at what little we had: records of the ship those miners had died on, Moritz distribution, entangled neutrino generators, and any mention of AVDO I could find (which was currently one, if you counted my mangled video).

I settled myself on the bench facing a huge viewport scattered with stars, Pauli still shielding her screen from my view. Time to make that total much higher.

After twenty minutes of searching, I had found nothing. Not *nothing interesting—nothing at all.* Searching for *AVDO* gave about fifty unrelated results and the video. Very much like when I'd tried to track down that paper by Sycamore and Proust. But someone had come up with a translation for the light show in my video, which meant that someone was familiar enough with the AVDO to have translated their language. The account from which the translation was posted seemed to have been created for the sole purpose of posting it; no other comments either before or since, no videos of their own, and no accounts at other services associated with the name.

I pulled up the video again and refreshed the page to make sure there were no new posts from Starblink_8473...and it was gone. The translation, I mean. Under their history, it said: *This account hasn't posted yet.* That was all. Either they had changed their mind and deleted it, or someone else had done it for them.

"Shit, that was fast," I muttered.

"What was that?" Pauli glanced around as though she'd spot security coming right for us.

"The translation is gone."

"I fucking told you," said Pauli, shaking her head. "They're not playing. I hope you have a hell of a plan."

Absolutely. Get a ship, find the spouse of a dead miner, badger them for information, and cross my fingers that it led to a better plan than that. "Yep."

"Great." But Pauli didn't have a plan at all, so we were doing mine. She was still hiding her screen from me.

"Time to show me what you're working on."

"Nothing."

"Yeah, right." I grabbed her wrist and twisted her screen to me. Familiar visualizations stared back at me. Very familiar visualizations. "Where the heck did you get my team's research report?" She'd got it from the damn data stick I'd left in the spoke. She'd stolen it and hidden it from me. I let go of her wrist, and she scrambled away, glaring.

"Your team?"

"Yes, *my team*. Working on creating a simulation, *that* simulation. Why did you hide it from me?"

"I found it on *my* spoke. Why would I tell you about it?"

"You didn't think maybe I left it there?" With that simulation recovered, I could go through with my original plan: compare with practical data and prove that someone was causing these pinches in space that were trapping ships and stations.

Pauli rubbed her wrist, the skin already darkening. "Why would you leave something on *my* spoke?"

"Maybe because I put a lot of work into that space. Besides, we're working together on this."

"Seems like we're only working together when you say so. You won't tell me why we're going to the Solar System. You never told me what you were even doing on Exodus, and I seem to recall having to steal your little video from you after you told me it's probably best that I don't know what you're up to."

This was all so unfair. Pauli was making it sound as if I was hiding things from her out of spite. "That's all to keep you safe."

"Uh-huh. Okay." She didn't apologize for keeping the simulation data from me, but she did pull the stick out of an inside pocket and toss it at me. I caught it and plugged it into my screen. A note from Frodli popped up in the ReadMe file.

> I really hope this helps. Your plan is a good one, and I know you can get those readings to make your point to HGNT. We're all sorry to see you go.
> Frodli

No way they were sorry to see the back of me after the trouble I'd caused them, but it was kind of her to say that anyway. Now my plan didn't seem so bad. Get some readings, compare to the simulation, show that they were identical. Somewhere in there, I'd also have to keep Pauli from killing me, which she was currently attempting with her mind.

❖

Luckily, that last part ended up being easy since we barely saw each other the rest of the trip, despite sharing a room.

When we got to the Solar System, we slid easily through the port and hoofed it to Sparks's meeting place of choice, which was, of course, a seedy pub on the lowest level. As if uptight, rule-abiding Miller had directed me to this person. I recognized him from our video call: a skinny brown-skinned man with one knee poking above the table, his elbow resting on it.

Sparks sat alone in a booth, a solo game built into the table in front of him. He moved a round piece from one spot on the board to another and didn't look up when I loomed over him.

I dumped my pack on the bench across from him since I'd probably need a crowbar to pry it off the sticky floor if I put it down there.

"Carolina, you made it," he said without looking up from his game board.

"I made it," I sank onto the padded bench seat next to my luggage.

"And who's this?" His sharp gaze flicked to Pauli.

"I'm no one. You never saw me. Can one of you get me a fucking drink?"

Sparks lifted a brow at me.

"Get your own. Either put that fake ID to good use or stop whining." She might be my responsibility, but I wasn't her mom.

Pauli grumbled and stomped away.

Sparks's attention was already back on his game.

"Go ahead," he said, still not looking up. Did he want me to play?

"I don't know the game."

He laughed. "As if I'd let you touch it. No, make your pitch. You need something from me."

My pitch? I hadn't exactly prepared to convince Sparks. Wasn't I supposed to be hiring him? "Yes, I need a ship to meet up with someone in the asteroid belt."

"Asteroid belt is big, someone is small."

"I have three locations I'd like to survey—"

"Survey? You make it sound like you're a resource hunter," said Sparks. Finally, he sat back and took my measure. "You don't look like a resource hunter." He said it as though I was not only not a resource hunter, I was also not worth the few minutes of his time I'd already taken up.

"Why? What makes you say that?"

He waved away my question. "You want to meet up with your friend. You gonna pay me, or you think you're getting this as a favour?"

"Yes, of course, I'll pay the going rate."

He smirked. "Going rate for an under-the-radar trip to the asteroid belt? You're funny, Carolina." His eyes narrowed. "Oh, no... No, no, don't tell me. Goddamn it! Miller sent you!"

"I don't—"

"Shut up. It's stamped all over you. You're one of Miller's little intellectuals. I told him, no more little students who don't know what they're getting into. I guess I'll need to tell him again." He pulled out his screen. Shit! Was he calling Miller? The same Miller who had emphatically told me that I wasn't to mention his name?

"No, Miller didn't send me. He specifically said—" *Shit.* I should have told him I didn't know who Miller was. "I mean, you can call him, but I don't know who you're talking about."

Sparks laughed so loudly that heads turned in our direction, and it triggered a coughing fit that had him doubled over. "Hush, little schoolchild. I'm playing with you. Don't you worry, I'll take care of you. I know Miller, and if he sent you to me, he wants you in good hands."

Was that...threatening? Comforting? Miller had been a good friend to me, despite the open hostility and the requests to stop asking him for help—which I guess I'd completely ignored. Maybe he was finally giving in and helping me just to get me out of his hair? I was shit at this game, whatever it was.

"Ugh. Fine. Miller sent me here to ask for your help, okay?"

"Why are you telling me what I already know?" He grinned again. Good thing he found me amusing and not offensive. "If you can pay me, all the better. Just tell me what you're looking for, Carolina."

"Do you want the long version? I sort of already gave you the short version. Friend in the asteroid belt and all that."

"How about we go with the medium version, and I'll tell you when to stop yammering?"

By the time Pauli stomped back to the table, Sparks had hushed me, finished his game, and upended his drink.

"Let's get going. The less time we spend here, the fewer people see you with me."

Another sign that my paranoia was utterly warranted. We followed Sparks to an even lower deck. Pauli had her bored face on, but she had to be a little nervous, right? Once we were on Sparks's ship, he could take us wherever he wanted, and she had no reason to trust him.

"It's okay," I said, laying a comforting hand on her arm.

She shook me off. "I'm not trapped with my dear dad anymore, so yeah, it's fuckin' okay. Keep your hands and your maternal bullshit to yourself."

Hopefully, I'd comforted her anyway?

Sparks stopped in front of a viewport with a flourish.

That was his ship?

Sparks watched me very carefully. Was he worried that I wouldn't like his ship? The strange craft didn't look like it would make it through re-entry without losing a few pieces. Important pieces. Like the cockpit.

The sleek body of the ship was reminiscent of Lepton, but the cockpit on top had been replaced with a narrow old shipping-style nose, patched over and stuck on. Another expanse of pockmarked steel was just visible over the top of the ship, maybe another scrappy section attached to the port on the other side?

"Deal's off if you don't like the look of her," said Sparks, his hands in his pockets.

"I've never seen a ship like her," I said.

Sparks grinned as if the joke was on me. "She looks like shit, but that wouldn't be polite to say out loud. Wait till you see the inside. She'll win you over." He strode toward the gate, leaving me to follow, still trying to parse what I'd just seen.

"Let's hope we survive this," Pauli snapped. Not brave enough to say that to Sparks's face, apparently.

It was space-worthy; Miller had recommended this pilot. Then again, if the ship fell apart and we were lost to the endless void, I'd be out of his hair. By now, he might actually hate me that much. But I'd spent the last of my money paying Sparks and stocking up for our trip, so it was this or go home to my parents.

I stepped through the gate.

"Wipe your shoes," called Sparks from further aft, and I did.

I could see myself in the floor, a dark wood that matched the eyebrow around the bulkheads. The vase of flowers in the nook opposite was not a projection, though real flowers didn't go in vases, did they?

Sparks wiped his hands on his coverall as he came through from the other port—from the steel section I'd glimpsed stuck onto the other side of the ship. He grinned.

"She's a beauty. Space for about five, so pick your cabins. Galley's right beside you. You might have guessed that upstairs is the cockpit." He pointed at a set of actual stairs—not a ladder—with his thumb. "Now come with me." He turned back to the other hatch. "I want to be clear from the outset. You touch my bench, I throw you off the ship. Yes, even in empty space."

Pauli cursed and stormed into a cabin, slamming the automatic door somehow.

I'd been right about the steel section: It was almost as big as the rest of the ship. A workshop with a gleaming bench.

I stepped from the pristine corridor into the battered workshop bay. The corridor, like most of Sparks's ship, was from a state-of-the-art cruiser, while the workshop was stuck on, transferred over, complete with tools and scrap, probably from his previous vessel, and maybe a few before that. Surface grime caked the corners, and there were more than a few dents in the floor, presumably from hauling heavy—maybe hazardous—salvage and scrap.

The smooth workbench was clear and unmarked, made of the same stuff as most lab benches: heat-proof, fire-proof, acid-proof, scratch-resistant—pretty well indestructible. So there was really no reason why he wouldn't let me touch it. Whatever.

"You want to work in there, fine. Here's a bench you can use." He pointed to a slab of countertop balanced on two sawhorses. Sturdy, sure, but it wouldn't stand up to flame or acid. A long scratch across it ended in a melted section.

"Do your passengers usually need a workshop?" I said.

He shrugged and led me toward the galley. "Got the usual re-constitutor. Laid in some rations, and I think you brought more. Should be more than enough for our week together. If you want to eat together, I'm fine with that. You'll usually find me in the cockpit or the workshop, when I'm not sleeping."

"Do you want me to take shifts on watch?"

He laughed. "I've got it covered, Captain. Focus on your own problems. By the sounds of it, you've got enough to worry about."

He'd talked to Miller. He must have, since I hadn't told him anything about my problems.

"So you know that I'm...blacklisted...by HGNT? I don't know if working with me is enough to get you on their list—"

Sparks lifted his hand to stop me. He didn't interrupt because he couldn't; he was laughing too hard. I had to keep from rolling my eyes like a teenager. I was just trying to be honest and help him out.

Once he caught his breath, he tried to look at me seriously, but a smile still pulled at his mouth. "I'm up for the risk. Want to make way?"

"That would be good, yes," I said. I'd been expecting him to make fun of me, talk down to me, something.

"You choose a cabin and stow your stuff. I'll meet you in the cockpit, Captain."

❖

The cockpit was the only part of Conquest besides the workshop that was built for utility rather than luxury. It was stuck on top of the rest of the ship, where a cruiser would have had it, but the entire thing had clearly been ripped from the front of an older (crappier, but I wouldn't let Sparks catch me saying that, or I'd be tossed out without an air tank) ship. Usually, the modular design of modern ships would let them connect together, but the rear-entry cockpit of a working ship was incompatible with the bottom-entry cockpit necessary for a luxury cruiser. So Sparks had slapped a plate on the back of the cockpit he wanted and sliced a hole in the floor for the ingress.

I paused at the top of the stairs to let the disorientation pass. It was as though gravity had shifted, expecting a Plexiglas cruiser cockpit and ending up in a dingy steel scrapper control room. But Sparks looked so cozy in here, curled in his worn old chair with the switches laid out in front of him.

Sparks helped me find the FiOREna ship. Something about a registry and transponder. Whatever it was didn't sound very legal to me, so I didn't ask for any more details. I sat next to him in the narrow cockpit, looking down at a meteor. The huge FiOREna ship looked like a moth crouched on it, wings spread wide, presumably in its mining formation.

"How are we going to message them? I don't want to get them involved with me, at least not on the record."

"It's secure, don't you worry. Out here, we use VHF."

"Like…ships on Earth's oceans?" How could ancient mariner technology possibly be secure?

He grinned. "Travels at the speed of light. Takes half an hour to reach the sun from here, diffusing all the way."

"So it's not secure."

"Is a needle secure hiding in a haystack? Sure, they could dig it out if they knew where to look—"

"Or they have a metal detector," I said.

"Hush, Dr. Dawn. If they knew where to look and their timing was perfect, but this low power? It'll blend into the CMB in no time."

CMB, cosmic microwave background radiation. Totally analogue. No record. Okay, yes, this could work. "All right, proceed."

"I'm honoured by your patronage, Dr. Dawn." He fiddled with the knob on his radio and put the handset up to his mouth. He pressed the button on the side and spoke into it in a voice I'd never heard before. Totally serious, totally professional. "FiOREna, FiOREna, *Conquest*, over."

"*Conquest*, go one-six, over," crackled through the tinny speaker on the side of the radio.

Sparks beeped the channel button until it displayed 16. "*Conquest* on one-six."

"Our ship's name isn't FiOREna, genius." Was that a kid manning their radio?

"Got your attention though, didn't it? I have a passenger that wants to talk to Fiona Klein, if you'd be so kind."

"She's busy. What does your passenger want?"

He looked at me. He didn't press the button. "What do you want?"

What did I want? I couldn't very well tell her I wanted to talk about her dead husband over the radio. "I, um, I need her help with a project."

Sparks gave me a look but relayed my message.

"You'll have to give me more than that, *Conquest*. If you're trying to boot us off this claim, you can forget it."

"Nope, no interest in your claim." He let go of the button. "Right?"

"Of course not."

His piercing look made it clear that he wished he had grilled me about this a lot sooner. But we were still in the middle of a conversation.

"Look, *Conquest*. I don't know why you're after my captain, but we don't have anything to discuss. Just go back where you came from and tell your boss—" The speaker popped as if the handset on their end had fallen on a soft surface.

Another voice cut in. "This is Fiona Klein, Captain of *Gracious*. Enough of this. Put your passenger on, and we'll clear it up right now."

My stomach fluttered as I took the handset from Sparks, the coiled cord stretching across the aisle between us. I cleared my throat. "Hello, Fiona, thanks for agreeing to speak with me." Which was a totally inappropriate tone for the tenor of this conversation. I plowed on. "My name is Carolina Dawn, and I'd like to discuss"—*your husband's death*—"an incident that took place ten years ago, involving a large mining ship—"

"You want to know about Graham?" Her tone was a bit softer but probably only because she was thinking of her beloved husband, whom I had no right to ask about.

"Yes, that's right. I have a few questions, and it would really help me if you—"

"Who raised you that you think you can call up a stranger and badger them about their dead loved ones? Get the fuck off my radio."

This was it. If I lost her now, I'd be truly out of options. The missing mining ship was my very last thread that I could follow to Pardus. If I screwed this up, everything I'd done so far, all the danger I'd put my friends in, would have been for nothing. "Before you hang up on me, at least tell me this: Have you ever suspected HGNT isn't telling you the whole story? That they're hiding something about your husband's death?"

Sparks flicked a tattoo on the edge of the controls. "Where to next? Any more grieving widows you want to—"

"Yes, Dawn. I have suspected that. Raft in twenty."

Was it still rafting if there was a giant asteroid rafted with you? Sparks had no trouble docking one of the five ports on the mining ship with the open port on *Conquest*. He slouched to the release lever and rolled aside the big airlock door. The empty airlock on the other side was bare steel, in contrast to *Conquest*'s wood and form-fitted manu- factured material living quarters. Sparks headed back to the stairs.

"Aren't you coming?" I called after him.

"I'm just the pilot. This is your show." He disappeared.

My show. I was alone. Was I supposed to go in? Wait for them? They hadn't mentioned. They just said raft. I crept through the airlock, and my footsteps echoed over the steel floor of *Gracious*. If she was a moth, *Conquest* was an ant. Though most of that space was for storing the ore that she mined from asteroids. The air itself seemed to sparkle with ore dust, and I sneezed as I followed the corridor up three steps into the main cabin of the ship. Four people sat around a table, two humans and two aliens. All four watched me cross the cabin and take the seat at the end of the table. This would be the body of the moth, set between the two mining wings. Dots of space in the ceiling, occasionally crossed by asteroids, peeked through between the wings, but this space needed protection from the asteroid field, and that crack a mere few feet wide was the only concession to comfort.

My seat had a cushion embroidered with sunflowers. So I guess there were a few more concessions to comfort in here as well.

One of the aliens looked almost human, her translucent white skin and lack of ears or hair the only indications that she wasn't. The other was green, maybe from the same area as Dr. Morbit, but the much darker green of moss on a forest floor.

A tall white woman slid a cup of water across the table to me, the surface of which juddered and never settled. The mining equip-ment's vibration was almost imperceptible, but they hadn't turned it off for our meeting. I wrapped my hands around the cup and stared into it.

"I'm sorry to bring up such a sensitive subject," I said.

"But not that sorry," said the woman. Fiona. Her voice had more depth in person, but it was still recognizable.

"I've been researching something for months, and I...haven't got very far. I think you can help me. But you should know up front that helping me won't make you any friends. If you want to tell me to fuck off, I understand."

"I think we're past that now. Just tell me what you want."

"I'm looking into the disappearance of a mining and colonization outpost, Pardus Station."

"Sadiq was on Pardus," said the green alien to Fiona.

She nodded. To me, she said, "What does this have to do with Graham?"

"I want to investigate whether they met the same fate, whether their disappearances were due to related mechanisms."

"And you think I can help because?"

"I don't know anything about the ship or the station or where he was located. I need that information from you so that I can go and take some measurements." But how would I actually take measurements? I had no access to a probe, not without begging one off of CHUSI or another research team. And to do that, I'd have to reveal my location to HGNT, and they would quickly figure out that I wanted to gather more measurements with the probe, measurements that would never be approved by CHUSI.

"I know the rough area they were in, yes. But mining accidents happen, and that's all it was in this case. They had just reached the surveyed system. Setting up the mining equipment is by far the most dangerous part of the operation. They dropped out of contact and were declared lost not long after that." She shrugged. "I don't see what going there will do."

"Pardus was still light years away from their planned operation," said the green alien. "What do they have in common?"

"I guess...I don't really know." A sob welled up in my chest, and I pushed it down, but it overflowed up my throat, and my eyes welled over. I was grasping at straws, and these people who, let's be honest, were being overly kind to some stranger who was badgering them, had called me on it. Albeit in the nicest possible way. Why had Yarrow thought that these deaths were related to Pardus? As the miners had pointed out, mining accidents happened all the time.

"Here," said Fiona, graciously ignoring my tears, "I can show you where they were headed." She scrolled on her screen, then turned it to me.

My arms prickled. A familiar patch of empty space looked back at me. Dr. Sycamore's coordinates. No, not empty, not really. I'd discovered an ablated Dyson ring there. Maybe they hadn't run out of money to finish the project, maybe something else stood in their way, a blobby, sparkling something.

Maybe Graham and his crew were somehow still alive, trapped in a pinch in space. We had to go find out. I told *Gracious*'s crew my theory.

"This doesn't mean it's a huge conspiracy," said the other human, the one Sparks had spoken to on the radio. "Projects get canned all the time. They can't get the permits or they run out of money—"

"But there's a chance," said Fiona. "We could find out what happened."

I nodded. "A small one. Even if we find a pinch, they might still be..."

"Dead. Yes, after all this time...I know. But the truth is worth the trip."

Janella grabbed her arm. "Fiona, no, we're not going to the ass-end of the Orion Arm just to find—"

"You can get off when we deliver the ore to Earth if you like," said Fiona.

"Fuck that. You're kicking me off?" She slammed her chair back as she stood and stalked out the forward doorway.

"Don't mind Janella," said the white alien, who could apparently follow the conversation without ears. "She'll come around."

"Probably in the next five minutes," said the green alien and grinned.

"Frall," said Fiona, pointing to the green alien, "and Bez." She pointed to the white alien.

"Bezixtralitasin," said the white alien, including several sounds that the human voice box was incapable of making. "But Bez translates fine, too."

"I'm Carolina Dawn, an interstellar researcher." But was I even that anymore? I was more of a fugitive, if anything. No, as long as I was doing research, I was a researcher, and cracking what had happened to Pardus Station was vital research.

"Nice to meet you, Carolina. We have a few days more to mine here, and we have to drop the ore on Earth, but then we can travel much faster out to the 'ass-end of the Orion Arm.'" She half smiled and put her hand on my shoulder.

I smiled back.

Chapter 13

To seize this opportunity to study the site of another disappearance, I'd need some way to gather data. Neither Sparks's ship nor the mining vessel had much in the way of sensors, so I'd have to use some kind of probe. In general, CHUSI handed out probes to applicants they approved. Expensive equipment wasn't generally purchased by individuals, particularly individuals who were broke: me.

The data that Yarrow and I had gathered at the Pardus site indicated that particulates and neutrinos would be the most crucial to study, and I wouldn't say no to a gravitational wave measurement...but that was absolutely out of the question. The only mobile gravitational wave sensor I knew of was built into the Oort Centre's research vessel, which, again, was assigned by CHUSI, at the end of the day, since they provided the funding to the centre.

All this to say that if I wanted to get my hands on the sensors I needed, I'd have to go through CHUSI, and I wouldn't be able to hide it from HGNT...

I was mulling all this over breakfast on *Conquest* when Sparks swung into the galley and threw himself onto the bench opposite.

"Something wrong? You look like you're trying to plot a course to Fiona's coordinates with your mind."

"Plotting the course won't be my biggest problem. What exactly do you do with your workshop?"

"That would be giving away what I do when you're not around."

"Which is highly illegal and secret?"

"I'd never admit to that."

"Hey, you know Miller. Any chance he could get us—me—a probe without asking CHUSI?"

Sparks laughed. "Yeah, right. Harlan? Break the rules?"

He had broken the rules for me, but I wasn't going to tell anyone that, even Sparks.

"You need a probe. Can't say I have one just lying around, but some of those mining ships have machine shops on board. If you know what you need, might be they can hook you up. My workshop has the tools to assemble such a thing. On your side."

"And we're swinging by Earth, so we might be able to pick up anything we can't make." And Miller was on Luna. If he could help us out, maybe I could convince Sparks to land there while *Gracious* was unloading. "Thanks, Sparks," I said.

"Yeah, well, you're such an adorable, pathetic little academic. I can't help but try to save you from yourself."

Hopefully, Miller would think that too and help me out with the parts I'd need.

We agreed to meet Fiona and the mining ship just north of Earth when they were finished unloading. Once the mining ship was empty, they would be able to match *Conquest*'s speed.

Gracious headed into Earth orbit, Sparks watching beside me in the narrow cockpit.

"You could have gone with them," said Sparks. "Then you wouldn't have to pay me."

"We're going to Luna."

"You are trying to get to Harlan again."

"Maybe he'll help me if I show up at his office."

"And you don't think HGNT will notice that?"

Sparks knew I was avoiding them? Had I mentioned it? He had heard my story, yeah, but he hadn't seemed interested in it. "Miller will report back to them, I'm sure."

Sparks grunted and punched in a course for Luna.

The bright edge of the moon crested Earth as we neared, and Sparks took us well away from the high Earth orbits crowded with ships. Earth's port trickled a steady shower of shuttles to the surface and back, and we flew directly over a half-built ship in dry dock.

Luna didn't have its own port; landing on the surface wasn't a strain for most ships because of its low gravity.

Once we were safely parked, Sparks crossed his arms and turned to me. "You going or what?"

"Going where...?"

He raised his eyebrows. "To beg parts off Harlan?"

"I don't even know where on Luna CHUSI's building is located, let alone his office."

Sparks sighed and tapped a few buttons on the dashboard. "Come on, then."

"You're coming?"

"I can't very well let you wander the surface of Luna aimlessly until you find Harlan. Don't have time for that. Let's go."

I trailed after him as he locked up the ship's systems, hollered to Pauli that we'd be right back, and exited the airlock into the moon's viewing corridors.

The moon base's primary revenue stream had always been tourism. Like with the CN Tower, people wanted to come up here and gape back at the Earth, and I was no different, even though I'd been here dozens of times with my parents. That thin blue atmosphere never ceased to make my heart pound at the fragility of humans' existence. Even after a century of interstellar exploration, Earth was the only planet upon which we could survive without intervention. Even terraformed planets like Mars needed constant upkeep to maintain the perfect conditions that could be found naturally on our pale-blue dot.

The AVDO could live anywhere. Maybe. But maybe their survival conditions were just as restrictive as ours, in a completely different way. In a way that impeded HGNT's progress, no doubt.

"Gonna stand around taking in the sights, or do you want to go blackmail Harlan?"

"I'm not planning any blackmail."

"Whatever you are planning, it had better be good." He jerked his head down the corridor, and I followed. "Harlan doesn't stick his neck out for people."

This was about more than just me at this point, even I could hear that in Sparks's tone. Maybe it would be good for me to know their history before I showed up with Sparks in tow. "Not even for you?"

"Especially not for me, schoolchild." We reached an intersection in the corridors, and Sparks swung right without pausing. "I guess that's not fair. He's no worse with me than with anyone else. Doesn't treat me any different."

"Should he?"

Sparks shrugged and pointed me to a door in the white formed-plastic wall. The plate by the door read *Dr. Miller*. A pang of guilt dragged at me; I hadn't even known Miller had a PhD. But if he was running a bunch of research projects, I guess it should have been obvious. I turned back to see whether Sparks was going to stay, but he was already retreating the way we'd come, shoulders slumped.

I took a shaky breath and knocked on the door. Alone again.

"Ms. Dawn."

I jumped as Miller's voice came from behind me instead of through the door. He was holding a steaming coffee I could smell at ten paces and wearing a very intolerant expression.

"Tell me why I should even consider letting you into my office, from which I have no doubt it will be an extensive ordeal to extract you."

"I need your help...?"

"Of course you do. I suppose since you've come all this way," he said dryly, waved the door open, and barged past me into his office. But he didn't close the door behind him, so I slipped through.

"Where's your security?" I said as the door slid shut. He'd always been flanked by two sunglassed toadies before.

"Why would I need them in my own office?"

The office was strikingly similar to our tiny boardroom at HGNT, where Frodli and the others were hopefully still hanging out—wherever in the Galaxy they had ended up—and working on important research. Like the research currently being hoarded by Miller, who had slumped into a patched leather chair behind his preformed-plastic desk. Luna had been colonized at the height of the futurism frenzy, when all the furniture was moulded into the walls and a room could never just be a plain box. Miller's chair bumped over a seam in the floor, probably where the "ergonomic" plastic version had been ripped out. There was no chair across from him, just a small table that took up the other half of his office below a pristine whiteboard—built into the wall, of course. As were the chairs, so I couldn't even pull one up. I stood.

Miller sipped his coffee.

Everything I'd thought to say to him seemed juvenile and pointless. I was asking him to risk his position for me, again, for absolutely nothing in exchange. Why had I even bothered to come here? The best-case scenario was that Miller waited to report it to HGNT until I was safely off Luna.

"Just tell me what you want, Dawn." His voice was surprisingly gentle. I'd take the pity at this point.

"I just need one more probe," I said. "There's this site out near—"

"I don't want to know. I hope it's far from here."

I nodded and kept my mouth shut.

"I don't have the power to hand you a probe."

"I understand." *Shit.*

"But there is a reclamation and recycling facility that CHUSI uses here on Luna. It's mostly unmonitored, but the probes you find there will be past the end of their useful life."

Not a problem Fiona's machine shop and a little creative welding couldn't fix. "Thank you for helping me."

He looked at me askance and put down his coffee. "Now that we're speaking in person, let me make something clear to you, Carolina." He brushed invisible dust off his desk. "I neither like nor do I condone what CHUSI and HGNT are doing. I don't condone CHUSI working with a large corporation, for that matter, but we don't have any control over that. I told you that it's too late for you to get out, and I stand by that, but if you go down this path, and trust me, there is much more that you could discover that would put you in greater danger..." He ran a hand across his mouth. "I'm helping you, as you put it, because I don't want this to drag down the rest of your life. It will already follow you forever, but you can still put it behind you. One call to HGNT, and they would nail you to the wall." Did he mean that literally? *Yikes.* "If I told CHUSI you came to me asking for an unauthorized probe, you would be barred from receiving project grants for the rest of your very short life.

"So my question for you, Carolina, and I want you to give me your honest answer this time, is this: Why are you doing this? What makes this so important to you?"

I reeled back and crumpled into a preformed-plastic chair. I'd started out wanting to make a discovery, make my career by studying how Pardus Station had simply disappeared without a trace. Then I'd wanted justice for the people who had been snatched away by a greedy corporation. Now I wanted to get them back and find out how HGNT was doing this to keep it from happening to anyone else. But was it really just academic curiosity? I didn't want HGNT to keep such a potentially huge discovery under wraps and keep full control of the information. That was still true. Then my mouth started talking.

"Everywhere I go, things keep falling apart. I had a good career at the Oort Research Centre. I was on track to have my own project. Then HGNT got involved, and now my mentor can barely look at me. At every turn, they make my life harder, worse.

"I've always wanted to make life better. I thought that's what academia was about." The way Dr. Morbit had talked about Starblink had been academic, and it had turned my stomach. "And that's nothing compared to what they've done to the people on Pardus Station and many others." The AVDO, Graham and his crew, and who knew how many folks, their lives ripped apart by HGNT's greed and some researchers' quest for progress at any cost.

Miller sighed. "Idealist."

And maybe I was an idealist to think that I could single-handedly take down a corporation like HGNT, make them suddenly have ethics, but maybe I wasn't for thinking that I could help the people of Pardus, the entire species of AVDO. What was my career—my insignificant life—next to that? I just shrugged.

Miller smirked. "What, no more rambling idealist rant for me?"

"Would it change anything?"

"Unequivocally not. Now, get out of here before someone sees you. HGNT will no doubt be breathing down my neck again before I've even had a chance to finish my damn coffee. Give me your screen, and I'll drop you a salvaging permit so you can fu— bug off." With a tap, it was done.

"They won't know you gave this to me?"

"Please. Give me some credit, Ms. Dawn. They've been watching me a long time."

I nodded. Of course they had. "Well, thanks again. I don't suppose you'd tell me why you keep helping me?"

"Miller grinned. "Must be my latent idealism flaring up."

Even though Miller knew a lot more about the AVDO, he still refused to tell me. "You require survival instincts, and since you have none, I'll substitute for the moment."

He didn't ask about Sparks, and I didn't mention him, but he must have guessed that he was my pilot. Because he also said to take good care of my crew.

Sparks lit up when he heard we were going to Luna's junkyard. He bounded up to the cockpit and was taking off before I'd even had a chance to strap myself in. Luna's gravity was low, so I only stumbled once on my way upstairs to join him and caught myself easily on the rail. I buckled into my seat while Sparks hummed to himself.

He used the conventional communications to get clearance to land in the junkyard. The fields of debris, tucked on the far side of the moon, safely out of sight of both rich Earth travellers and Earth telescopes, stretched in a dark blotch before us on the shining white moon dust. Sparks craned his neck to peer out the viewscreen, tapped on the dashboard, muttered to himself, and then set *Conquest* down. Junk crunched under her belly, and I glanced nervously at Sparks, but he didn't seem concerned, already eagerly perusing the junk field.

I had to smile. "You've done this before."

"Done this before? Schoolchild, I was doing this before you were born. If I recall correctly," he said, "this will be a good place to get the academic junk you're after."

I followed him down the steps. Something thunked against the hull, and I jumped. Sparks pulled the lever to open the airlock and jerked his head at me to come through with him.

The tiny pod was glass, like a soap bubble floating over the junk. The low seats sat back to back in the small space, and each faced the controls of a pair of mech arms for transferring objects to the hovering basket that trailed the bubble.

"Never used a junk picker before, eh?"

I shook my head.

"We've got clearance to take whatever we want, with a limit of one basket, so go to town." He scrambled into the low seat and gripped the controls of the mech arms. "Close the hatch, will you?"

I shut the airlock and folded my legs under me to sit in the tiny seat. It was almost like sitting on the ground outside, which would be ideal for hunting down the relatively tiny parts I would need for the probe. Most of the junk here wouldn't be custom made, thankfully. Geometry made lots of the off-the-shelf detectors that I'd be looking for, so anything with their logo on it would warrant a closer look, but Q-rest, Magfree, and Zolt might get me somewhere as well.

The tapping and clanking of Sparks digging through the junk was punctuated by the rustle of something being set down on the hover. He didn't waste any time. I slid my hands into the control gloves sprouting from my armrests and flexed my hands, watching the mech claws flex outside. This was super old tech, but it remained super awesome and fun to use. I'd had a robot arm as a kid with a little glove to control it, but it only survived about a year of fetching me things across the room before its motor burned out.

These were far more sophisticated than that and provided slight resistance when the claws gripped something. I quickly got the hang of locating a promising component, gripping it, and moving it close enough to examine.

"It's the pedal on the right to put something in the basket," said Sparks. "If you try doing it manually, you'll just break our hover basket, and that's an expensive mistake." A mistake he'd clearly made before.

I squinted at the black case a little bigger than my screen clutched delicately in my mech claw. No logo on this one, so no way to tell what it could be except for the ports on the back.

"Is there any way to see this junk better?"

"Magnify pedal?" said Sparks.

"Thanks." I pressed it, and the floor in front of me warped and seemed to draw the box right up to my face. If I didn't hurry up, Sparks would have filled our whole basket before I could snag any good components.

Once the basket was full, Sparks and I transferred our haul to the workshop. The hover basket latched onto the bottom, and the hatch inside popped open. We moved our junk treasures into the workshop, me to the crappy old workbench on one side, him to the pristine, glowing workbench I was not allowed to touch.

I'd found everything except for the body of the probe and the software to run the thing once I put it together. When we checked in with Fiona's people, I'd hit them up for a case and any ideas on how to run the thing.

I sidled up to Sparks's workbench and tried to look over his shoulder.

"You are way too close to me," he said without looking up.

"I just wanted to know what you're making, that's all."

"Nope." He waved me away.

Whatever. I was hiring him to get me to the coordinates Dr. Sycamore had provided; we weren't a research team. Once this trip was over, I'd probably never see him again. His loss.

I knocked gently on Pauli's door, but like the last dozen times, I got no answer. Sparks assured me that her life signs were still fine, and his ship would alert us to any distressed lifeforms aboard, but still, could it be good for her to be shut in a cabin for days on end?

Once everything was squared away, we headed for the rendezvous point where *Gracious* was already waiting for us. It was going to take us a few days to get to the coordinates of the mining incident, but our two ships would still be travelling together.

Like last time, when I opened the airlock, no one was there to greet me, but better no one than a surprise visit from HGNT. I paused when I reached the entry to the big central room. The dining table was somehow standing vertically against the wall, and the chairs were pulled aside to clear the floor.

All four of *Gracious*'s crew were doing what looked like a silent dance, in time. None of them acknowledged me; they just kept flowing through the synchronized moves. Abruptly, they all dropped their final pose. Frall waved at me, and Fiona sauntered over. Bez and Janella linked arms and took another hallway off the big room.

"What was that?" I said. "Are you practicing for something?"

"It's called tai chi. I've done it since I was a kid, and my crew picked it up on those tedious mining missions. It's very relaxing once you learn the forms. I can teach you the first few if you want join us sometime."

I'd barely met this woman once and she was offering to teach me something that looked so personal, so intimate for her? My attempt at a smile probably came out more as a frown, because she shrugged and moved on.

"It's not for everyone. Is *Conquest* ready to get under way? We can be ready to cast off in half an hour over here."

"Yup, we're all ready as well. I suppose we could have radioed. I didn't have to interrupt your tai chi."

"Don't worry about it. We were almost done. Besides, I like speaking in person. Did you get what you were after?"

"What?"

"On Luna?"

"Oh, yes, mostly. You don't happen to have any spare parts lying around?" I explained to her what kind of component I needed for the body of my probe, and she took notes on her screen.

"I'm not familiar with our supplies in that respect anymore. When Bez took over machinery maintenance, she took over most of the on-board machine shop as well. We spend enough time out of touch that we need to be able to repair most of our equipment ourselves. I'll let her know what you're looking for. If she doesn't have anything, she can build something that will work. Let's get going, and we can manufacture on the way."

Just like that? Full confidence? No wondering whether we could build the probe? Questioning whether we should make sure before we leave? If we reached the coordinates, without a working probe or sensor array, we would have made the trip for nothing.

Fiona grabbed the edge of the dining table, and I joined her in pulling it back into place.

"You have a lot of faith in me for someone who just met me."

She shrugged and carried a pair of chairs back into place at the table. "You didn't even know my husband, but you're here, doing this for me."

I grabbed a couple chairs as well. And if this voyage all came to nothing? If it had just been a mining accident? What would Fiona think of me then, having dragged her halfway across the Orion Arm? I straightened the chairs at the table.

"Okay, let's get going." The dining room was back to being a dining room again. I drifted toward the hallway.

"Let's meet up for dinner. Janella will send over the speed and trajectory. As you can see, there's plenty of room for you and your pilot, if they want to join."

"I'll let him know," I said. Why was she being so friendly when she knew that associating with me could get her and her crew in trouble? Possibly killed? It was probably best to keep my distance so I wouldn't get burned too badly when that finally sank in and they turned on me.

I retreated to *Conquest*, and we got under way.

We travelled for a couple of hours, Sparks lounging at the helm, more watching the stars go by than actually steering the ship. I sat on the other side of the cockpit, more for the company than any actual job. Pauli still wasn't answering my knock, even though Sparks had seen her come out to eat, and I was still waiting for a probe body before I could start assembly.

A warning light came on, and then another. My gut twisted. Was another ship going to disappear out from under me? I shot to my feet and was five steps out of the cockpit before I realized that no other lights were coming on.

"Shit," said Sparks and followed it up with a stream of curses befitting a true sailor.

I hovered on the stairs. "What's up?"

"The fuckin' hatch is leaking."

"Which one?"

"The one we used for the damn junk basket."

"I thought you said they were designed to seal together. Did the basket damage the hatch?"

"We would have noticed that before now." He scowled at the dashboard. He ran a hand over his face and chuckled sardonically. "The basket was assigned to us."

"So?"

"So whoever assigned it was trying to sabotage the ship, now that we're too far out to go for help."

The warning lights kept blinking. "What do we do?"

"I've sealed off the workshop, but"—he closed his eyes and shook his head slowly—"we're going to have to jettison it. If it bursts, the contents will turn into shrapnel, and the whole ship could become a colander."

"Jettison the entire workshop? We can't do that, all my parts—"

"Your parts? Schoolchild, you think I want to jettison my workshop? That shit can't be replaced. It'll be forever. But it's not worth losing the whole ship, and us along with it."

"Okay, how long do we have?"

"It's a slow leak, but it could get bigger any time. These things have a way of bursting open once they get started."

"Not much time." Start with the problem. The hull is leaking. So patch it. Frixel had shown me exactly how to weld a leaking hatch shut on a research centre voyage. What did they use? "I can fix it as long as you have some supplies." I outlined what I'd need.

"Sure, but all that is in the workshop. If it bursts with you inside…"

"You and Pauli could take the lifeboat and get Fiona to pick you up."

"Abandon my baby? Are you out of your ever-loving mind?"

"Then tell me where that equipment is, and I'll get the hatch fixed."

"Respirators are behind you. Hurry up."

I snatched a respirator from the locker and bounded down the stairs while pulling it over my head. I cracked the hatch sealing off the workshop and slipped inside, the air pressure difference pulling at my hair.

The lights flickered on. Sparks could see me through his cameras, the same ones that made sure I'd never touch his workbench. But now I was going to. I needed a few things that he had stored there, and he had to know it wasn't the time to be precious about his belongings.

I grabbed his mini laser saw and slipped back into the main cabin. Every time I opened the hatch, the chances of exploding the ship multiplied. Just once more. I hacked a piece off the nearest bulkhead with the saw and made my last foray into the workshop.

I sprinkled glow dust around the hatch's seam and found the leak immediately, where the dust got sucked away and disappeared. I'd have to strip away the seal to get good adhesion with the patch; when I was done, this hatch wouldn't open again.

I fired up the laser saw, pulled the trigger, and cut into the hard rubber around the leak. The small pieces got sucked out until the chunk of rubber gave way and the pressure was more equal between out there and in here. Lucky that this section of the ship was effectively bolted on the side of *Conquest* and could be sealed off. Now the chances of the thing bursting like a balloon were much lower, which meant I had a little more time.

The patch itself went really well, but my arm ached by the time it was fully in place, sealed to both sides. Now to fill in the gaps between the metal plate and the rubber on either side. This was the ingenious part of Frixel's lesson. Usually, a hatch would be welded all the way around, because there was no other way to make the seal perfect. That's probably why Sparks immediately ruled it out. The polymer that fancy new ships are moulded out of will reliquefy when it's mixed with…Aha! Sparks had the solvent I needed, neatly marked and everything. I could melt the sides together, and it would form an airtight seal. I hefted the chunk of polymer I'd hacked off the wall and grabbed the labelled bottle from the locker below Sparks's workbench.

I sawed small pieces off the chunk, letting the melty bits fall into the imperfect seal and get stuck there, then laid half the polymer on one side, and squirted it with solvent. Next, I squished it with the heels of my shoes until it more then covered the gap, then tended to the other side. I didn't dare take off my respirator; one, because there was probably still no ventilation in here; and two, because I'd just performed a reaction with the potential to form dangerous vapours—with no ventilation. Once the fans were back on, the ship would be able to scrub the place. If the seal held.

I counted to thirty to let the reaction finish and let the solvent evaporate, then I sprinkled the glow dust on the area again. It twinkled up at me, lying still on the deck, no sign of a persistent leak. Sparks would be watching too, and if there was no sign, hopefully, he'd turn on the fans and get this air exchanged. The lights flashed on and off, as if I were in a theatre lobby at the end of intermission, and the whir of the fans cut through the silence of the workshop. I let out a shaky breath and waved to the camera.

Chapter 14

From then on, every time I walked by the desk where I'd hacked off a piece of the polymer to patch the sabotaged hatch seal, cold fingers crept up my spine. Was there somewhere else on the ship that had been tampered with that we hadn't found yet? That leak had been delayed until we were well out of range of anywhere to safely land.

Sparks had, of course, run about thirty diagnostic checks since, and they'd all come up empty, but there was no guarantee. I also couldn't shake the memory of that panicked moment when the warning lights had flicked on and I'd assumed we were going to be disappeared. It was not only possible but likely that they would come for us eventually. And it didn't help that "they" were still a mystery. Had it been the AVDO who had taken *Lepton*? Had it been HGNT messing with their technology?

That's why I was in the cockpit with Sparks. I tried to look out the viewscreen, but my eye kept flicking back to the warning lights on the dashboard.

"Ready for dinner?" said Sparks. Fiona's gang had offered to cook for us again, and Sparks had accepted on my behalf without asking me.

"I guess," I said. They had been nothing but friendly to Sparks and me this entire trip, but that wouldn't last. We were taking them to the site of Fiona's husband's death, no doubt opening old wounds that they would have preferred remain closed.

Sparks and Janella had a quick conversation over the radio. Would they expect that we have them over here for dinner in reciprocation? All we had were crappy reconstitutor packs, definitely not good enough to feed guests.

"Hold on a minute," said Sparks into the radio and tapped the dashboard. "I'll get back to you. Hang tight."

"What's up?" I said.

Sparks ignored me. "Please identify yourself." He was speaking into his headset, not into the radio we'd been using to keep in touch with *Gracious*. "I can't confirm that." He glanced at me, furrowed his brow, and motioned for me to put on the headset at my elbow.

My stomach fluttered, but I put it on. Who would be reaching out to us? Who even knew where we were?

"She's listening," said Sparks's voice through the headphones.

"Carolina?"

My stomach tightened so suddenly that I swallowed to keep from puking on the dash. "Yarrow?"

"Permission to dock with your ship?"

I tried to answer, but my throat was too tight, and I nodded, which obviously Yarrow couldn't see.

"Permission granted," said Sparks. He was watching me with a little smile on his face.

I tried to grimace at him, but I likely just looked sick. Yarrow had chased me all the way out here? How had he even known where here was? Was Yarrow going to stay with me? Did I want him to?

I pulled off the headset and went down to tidy the galley and clear my head.

Pauli came out of her cabin as the clunk and hiss of Yarrow's ship docking made the deck shudder. Great, an audience.

When the hatch rolled aside, Yarrow was silhouetted in the doorway between our ships. If his could be called a ship. His shoulders brushed the bulkheads on either side, and his head was inches from the ceiling, his antennae flattened as far down as they would go. The dashboard lights wreathed his body. One of the Tachyon ships from Oort?

I held my breath to keep it from shaking as he stepped through into the wider space of *Conquest*. He'd followed me. All the way out here. The deck vibrated, and the stars out the viewport streaked as *Conquest* got under way again. I looked up into Yarrow's impassive alien face, his antennae dancing nonstop.

"You came after me," I said. Utterly inadequate words, but they seemed to tumble from me.

"Yes. You requested that I not follow you to HGNT, but you're no longer—"

I stepped into his arms and buried my face in his soft jumpsuit. He could obviously sense my emotions without seeing the tears streaming down my face, but hiding them was safer somehow.

He wrapped his arms slowly around me. "My ship is still stocked. I can easily return."

I jerked away from him. "Return?" Was he threatening to leave again?

"If you are unhappy with my presence."

I shook my head. "I'm not..." The lights were too bright here; it was too open. There was too much Pauli watching us, clearly about to make a snide comment. I took Yarrow's hand and led him toward my cabin, but I hesitated outside the door. "I just want some privacy. It's not...a sexual overture."

"I understand," said Yarrow and gestured for me to proceed.

My cabin was bigger than Yarrow's entire ship, but still, we sat side by side on the bed, two of his arms wrapped around me. I leaned my head on his shoulder and watched the stars sweep by outside. The wall lights glowed softly, letting me pretend my face and my emotions were hidden, even though Yarrow could sense them in complete darkness.

"I'm glad you're here," I said.

"But part of you is not?"

"Part of me is...confused. I don't know why you'd chase me halfway across human-dominated space."

"Carolina..."

I'd told him once that he needed to express his emotions to me verbally, since I couldn't read them as he could, but maybe I'd been wrong. A gesture like this, coming after me—finding me—way out here when he could have gone anywhere in the Galaxy...I kissed him.

The block of ice in my chest melted, and I threw my leg over his. His arms gripped me everywhere, pulling me close, steadying me, and running down my body. I wrapped one hand around the back of his head, and the other over his shoulder, and held his body pressed against the length of mine.

I traced a finger across the base of one of his antennae, and he took a ragged breath and pulled back, loosening his hold but not letting me go.

"I didn't seek you out for sexual gratification."

The warm bubble in my chest deflated. "You don't want to?"

"I very much do want to." He stroked a hand up my side under my shirt, and his hardness pulsed beneath me. "I want to ensure you are aware that I have no expectation of intimate relations with you. You are under no obligation—"

I kissed him again, and his words turned to a rumble in his chest as I traced a finger up his antenna. He clasped my hips tighter to his body, and I ground into him.

Sparks banged on my door. "If you lovebirds are coming to dinner, now's the time."

"Dinner?" said Yarrow.

"With Fiona's crew."

Sparks banged on the door again. "Either way, your guy will have to move his ship."

"Crap, the port." We'd need our only port to raft with *Gracious*, and right now, Yarrow's ship was blocking it. I scrambled off him. "*Gracious* has five, so you can leave your ship with them." And, what? Share my room? Take another room on *Conquest*? "You can move your stuff aboard here. I'm sure Sparks won't mind."

Yarrow straightened his clothes and stood beside the door, watching me do the same.

"That's if you're staying, of course," I finished as I slid open the door.

"I'm staying." His hand stroking down my back seemed to leach all the tension from my body. "I'll transfer my things to the adjacent cabin before I move my ship."

Or you could just move them in here. No, that was too fast. Keeping our own space for a while would be better. There was no rush. Yarrow wasn't going anywhere. Yarrow ducked his head for a quick kiss before I slipped out the door and he followed me out. Sparks wasn't there, probably having gone back up to the cockpit.

Pauli was planted at the table in the galley, staring at her screen, but she raised her eyebrows at me as I slid in across from her.

Gracious loomed out the upper ports, between Yarrow's ship and the edge of the cockpit. Yarrow popped into his ship and came back aboard *Conquest* trailing a hovercar.

"How did that even fit in your nail-scratcher?"

"Collapsible," said Yarrow. He stowed it in the cabin next to mine and brushed my hair back from my face before heading onto his ship and sealing the airlock. As I got up and closed my side, my chest was tight. Even being apart from Yarrow again for the few minutes until we docked with *Gracious* made my breath shallow.

Yarrow detached and floated away from *Conquest*, passing over *Gracious* and out of sight. Sparks moved us in, and we docked in our usual spot, on one of *Gracious*'s huge mining wings.

It was still strange to open the airlock and have a completely different view from when I'd closed it, despite having watched the docking dance happen out the viewports. At least Yarrow showing up had distracted me from my nerves about dinner. They came back full force, and my stomach twisted. Now not only was I horning in on essentially a family dinner, but I was also bringing my boyfriend along to meet everyone.

Sparks pattered down the stairs and slung an arm over my shoulders. "Ready to have something other than ration packs?"

"I'm having trouble focussing on that part."

"Because of all the awesome sex she just had," Pauli chimed in.

Sparks quirked an eyebrow.

"Um, no."

"It wasn't awesome?" he said.

"What is with you two? We were only in there for five minutes. Because of the...family dinner vibes."

"And you find that troubling?" said Sparks.

Maybe I shouldn't. After all, weren't most people's family dinners comfortable? Loving? Shouldn't I have found the idea appealing instead of nerve-racking?

"Who wouldn't?" said Pauli and finally tucked her screen away and joined us.

Sparks looked askance from Pauli to me when I didn't answer, probably still able to feel the steely tension in my shoulders. "I won't ask. Just focus on the food."

"I'll try," I said.

"No problem at all," said Pauli.

When we came through from *Conquest*, Yarrow had already been pressed into service fetching dishes from the galley to the dining room. I couldn't exactly blame them, considering he had twice the carrying capacity of the rest of us.

The scent of real food hit me, and my mouth watered painfully.

"Grab a seat," said Bez as she set the table.

Fiona was in the midst of rearranging the chairs and place settings to make room for Yarrow. "The head of the table is my seat," she said, "but maybe Yarrow can take the foot so he doesn't have to worry about elbowing anyone."

"I appreciate it," said Yarrow, laying four platters on the table.

Frall came through from the galley with serving utensils, and Sparks chose a seat in the middle of the table, within arm's reach of all the food, Pauli across from him. The rest of us settled as she and Sparks stacked their plates.

Once everyone was served, I picked at my food. The quiet of everyone eating made me want to push my chair back and fly out of the room. In a second, someone would start quizzing me about Yarrow or comment on the flaws of the food...

"This is wonderful," said Bez. "Thanks, Frall."

"No problem, Fiona helped."

"I just did what you told me to."

"Hey, Carolina," said Bez.

I stared at my plate, fork frozen in mid-air.

"I found something that will work for that probe body you need."

I looked up. What? Oh, yeah, the probe. "Um, that's great."

"You'll have to assemble the electronics yourself, but— Frall, did you ever find that open-source firmware to install on the thing?"

Frall chewed and swallowed, nodding. "Oh, yeah, I forgot to tell you. I'll get it loaded as soon as you take a look, Carolina. Just to make sure it's what you need."

"You still need it, right?" Bez watched me quizzically.

"Yes, absolutely!" My voice was too loud.

"You needed firmware, and you didn't even ask me?" said Pauli.

I bit back my retort. How many times had I knocked on her door and she'd ignored me?

Yarrow's hand landed heavily on my leg under the table, and he squeezed it gently. I put down my fork and looked from Bez, who was still watching me, to Frall, who was placidly eating, to Pauli, who had gone back to wolfing down her food.

"Did you manage to get the instruments you need together?" said Fiona from the other end of the table. But she wasn't waiting to pounce; she wasn't even just making conversation. Was she...genuinely interested?

The last of the tension flowed out of my body. "Yes, all that I could have hoped for. A gravitational wave detector would have been too much to ask, since one that small would be in prototype phase, even on research vessels."

"Research vessels have those now?" said Bez.

"Most don't, but there is a prototype version on the Oort Research Centre's vessel. That's where I used to work." I glanced at Yarrow. I almost included him, but did he used to work there, or did he still technically work there?

"I hope they come out broadly soon," said Frall. "There are other ways to determine the density of an object, of course, but as the object increases in size, it becomes more and more difficult to determine the—"

"Yikes, is this really dinner conversation?" said Janella.

"I think we're all interested except for you," said Bez.

"Not true," said Sparks. "I'm not a mining nerd, either."

"Being a mining nerd is not a prerequisite. I find the topic interesting," said Yarrow.

"Okay then, a nerd, period," said Sparks.

"Maybe this will be more up your alley," said Frall. "Where did you go to school, Yarrow, before Oort? There, Janella, is small talk more your thing?"

"You know it isn't."

"My home system of Yrk'uth only has one advanced education centre. The educational system's structure is not like that of human-dominated space."

"Fascinating," said Janella, stabbing a bean.

"That actually is fascinating," said Fiona. "Do you have one-on-one classes like in Bez's system?"

"That varies from student to student. I was selected for a special program that...did not."

This was all news to me. Yarrow had always insisted that his past was irrelevant whenever it came up between us. Maybe I'd just been approaching it wrong all this time? Or maybe he was making an effort to be more open about himself?

"The human system doesn't have time for one-on-one teaching, either," said Fiona. "It's really a shame. Some students can benefit from it."

"Learning in a group setting can also be beneficial," said Bez. "I could have used a more social atmosphere during my formative years."

"We're back to the nerd topics," said Janella. "Can I go?"

"No one is pinning you to your chair," said Frall. "Admit it, you're interested."

"In the finer points of intragalactic education systems? I was more interested in the gravitational wave thing."

"Me too," said Sparks around a mouthful of food. "You should have let them keep babbling about that."

"I don't know much about Yrk'uth," said Fiona to Yarrow. "I guess you don't have many human visitors?"

Yarrow's hand tensed on my leg, but his voice was mild. "None, actually. It's a closed system."

"Doesn't that mean no one leaves? How did you get out?" said Pauli, around a mouthful of food.

Yarrow must have been an exception. He'd mentioned before that he had left under tense circumstances. This probably wasn't the time to talk about it.

"Yarrow from Yrk'uth," said Frall and then snapped his mouth shut. Except he didn't say Yarrow. He said it the way the librarian had, the proper way, even though Yarrow had presumably introduced himself over the translator.

Yarrow had left under such tense circumstances that Frall recognized his name? Definitely not the time to talk about it. Yarrow still looked perfectly calm, but his hand on my leg was just short of painfully tense.

I opened my mouth to ask what the heck everyone else seemed to know—

"Did you all check your ship over?" said Sparks between bites. "I don't know if Carolina filled you in, but we had a little sabotage problem the other day."

"How do you know it was sabotage?" said Janella.

"The hatch interfaced with a junk basket assigned to our ship specifically. Then waited until we were well out of aid range to pop on us."

"She didn't tell us that," said Fiona. "We'll check *Gracious* over as soon as possible."

"Especially since those fuckers at the depot held us up for no reason," said Janella. "I ran a couple quick checks, but I'll do a more in-depth assessment, especially of the ore ports they used. Thanks, Sparks."

"No problem, we're in this together." He glanced at Yarrow as he said it. Sparks liked to pretend that he was an outspoken jerk, but he had clearly just saved Yarrow from having to talk about his personal history in front of six complete strangers; the others were off on a discussion of exactly what diagnostics to run and mechanical parts to check over.

We would talk about his personal history later. I'd let it lie for now despite the curiosity eating away at me.

Bex fetched the probe body she'd machined for me before we said our goodnights and headed back to *Conquest*. I wouldn't be able to sleep without trying the thing out, so I took it straight to my pathetic workbench and got it assembled.

The probe body was a miracle. The firmware was not. That Bex had found hardware that would work with all of the disparate sensors I'd unearthed in the junkyard was amazing, but it wouldn't be enough.

My screen showed utter gibberish where it lay on the scratched workbench next to my Frankenstein's monster of a probe. I could look for something else, but we were getting so close to the site, and I barely even knew where to start. The probes that we usually used were plug and play right out of the box. I was confident in the sensor apparatus; I'd messed with that enough times, and most of the hardware was designed to be replaceable, but the software side was a total mystery to me. If I couldn't get this sorted out, we would have come all this way for nothing. Sensors were great, but if I couldn't tell them what to sense, they might as well be metal bricks for all the good launching the thing would do.

A tap on the doorframe broke my thought spiral. Yarrow stepped into the workshop.

"Is there something I can help with?"

"My frustration carried all the way out to the rest of the ship, eh?"

He ignored my question and approached the workbench. "Is the probe malfunctioning?"

"More like not functioning. I'm grateful to Frall for the firmware, but it's absolute shit."

Yarrow glanced at my screen populated with seemingly random symbols. "Good thing we have a software expert on board."

Was he teasing me? "I've told you before, I don't want to get other folks involved."

He sighed. "Carolina, not only are they already involved, they wish to participate. They have all chosen to do so."

"But they don't know exactly what I'm doing—"

"Nor is it necessary to tell them. Launching a probe is hardly an uncommon activity." He rested a hand on the small of my back. "Would you prefer to fail alone than succeed as a team member?"

What a fucking question. Kind of, yes? But it wasn't just about me. Come to think of it, it wasn't about me at all. This was about Fiona and Graham, about Jasper and Trix. This was about Frall's friend Sadiq and all the people on Pardus Station who had disappeared with no one to remember them.

I shook my head, unplugged my screen from the probe-in-progress, and trudged into the main cabin. I knocked on Pauli's door. Again.

"I know you're in there. I need your help."

"That's a shitty way to ask." Her voice was muffled through the door.

I sighed. Was she going to make me grovel and beg? "Can you just come out, please?" Shouting through the door wasn't doing this conversation any favours.

The door slid aside, and Pauli's face was inches from mine.

"Do you mind?" she snapped.

I stepped back, and she slouched to the galley table, and her screen clicked as she set it flat on the tabletop. I slid in across from her.

"Want to tell me why you're so pissed at me?" Now that I had her here, finally, maybe we could sort this out.

"Besides when you physically assaulted me and forced your way into my private device?"

That was a gross exaggeration. "You were hiding *my* data from me that you stole!"

"Whatever. I guess you don't want my help." She picked up her screen.

Shit. This wasn't how this was supposed to go. I was the adult in this situation. "Wait. I'm sorry I grabbed you, okay?" *But you deserved— No. Calm.* "I should have asked your permission instead of forcing you." *Even though you stole what was obviously my data stick.*

"Yeah, you should have." She got up and slouched back toward her cabin.

"Where are you going? I apologized!" How else was I going to get my firmware?

"You're just trying to get me to help you. I know a fake apology when I hear one. I'll get your fucking firmware, but I'm not doing it for you. I want to take down HGNT, and that's all. Give me an hour." Her door slammed.

Yarrow was watching me from the doorway to the workshop.

"Looks like we have an hour to kill." I scrubbed my hands over my face. He'd witnessed that mid-air collision?

"I also find myself at loose ends. Sparks refused to assign me a shift piloting *Conquest*."

"I'm not surprised," I said and gestured to his workbench. "He doesn't let people touch his stuff. I can only imagine that extends to his custom-ship baby."

"It's just as well. I have a few things to tell you about."

Was this going to finally be an explanation of his exile? I just nodded as he slid in across from me.

"I have been working on the simulation data you uploaded to our shared document."

What? He wanted to talk research? Now? "Oh, good. Have you found anything?"

"I have. Dr. Morbit provided the parameters for the pinch in the simulation. If those parameters were taken from a real pinch in space, I believe that an opening still exists, that the pocket of space beyond the pinch is not entirely shut."

"An opening big enough for a ship to pass through?"

He shrugged. "We would need more experimental measurements to determine that."

Good, since we were on our way to gather them.

Sparks's voice crackled over the comms. "Captain, up to the bridge ASAP."

I sighed and nodded to Yarrow, hauling myself out of my seat. What could be the problem *now*?

Chapter 15

"We have a problem, Captain." Sparks hadn't even given me time to sit down.

I dropped into the co-pilot's chair. "What's our problem now?"

"We're not alone out here."

"You mean the AVDO?"

"I do not. How would we even know if they were following us? I've picked up some chatter from more traceable forms of communication. Seems your boyfriend was less discreet than we might have hoped."

"HGNT?"

"I'm going to assume you don't want them to catch up with us. So what do we do, Captain?"

What the hell was Sparks asking me for? He probably knew a hundred times better how to lose a ship that was following him. But it was a good question. They were tracking us somehow, using either Yarrow's ship or his screen. The Oort ship would be easy to track, since he'd have signed it out, so it was probably the ship they were tracking. But ruling out the screen would be foolish. The longer they followed our trail, the more likely they would be to deduce our destination, and then we wouldn't be able to lose them at all.

We could dump the ship and screen and carry on. If we did that, they'd just project our trajectory out and discover where we'd been headed, and even if they didn't, as soon as we stopped, they'd be on top of us. Drawing them away somehow would be the way to go. We could send Yarrow's ship on autopilot in a different direction, but a very obvious velocity change would be a dead giveaway. No, the best course of action would be to detach Yarrow's ship and send it off, perhaps only slightly faster than our current speed and just a few degrees off from our current course. Make it look like a slight course correction, perhaps program in a few more corrections for later in the flight path. Have it end up somewhere completely different using distance instead of trajectory.

"That's great," said Sparks, when I relayed my plan, "but that ship doesn't have an autopilot. Small, fast, single person? It probably won't even run without someone on board."

"That makes no sense. A single person can't pilot a ship for days on their own." Except for Yarrow, with his ability to pilot in his sleep.

"It's fast enough to hop from way station to way station. It's not a long-hauler."

"You're saying that in order to draw them away, we have to send Yarrow with the ship."

That was totally out. No way was I going to hand him over to HGNT, even if it would slow them down. We had to get rid of that ship another way. Maybe we could outrun them? Get our readings in before they caught up with us? Even if we could get there first, which was doubtful, they would just do exactly what Miller did to us when we had the Pardus readings. Besides, the likelihood of our clunkers outrunning their fancy expensive ships was pretty much zero.

Throwing them off our trail would be the only way. We needed another way to get rid of that ship. If it couldn't fly under its own direction, and we weren't going to send a pilot along, then it would need to piggyback on another ship, one unrelated to the folks I'd dragged into this mess with me.

"Who exactly is it that's after us?" Were we dealing with folks who could make us disappear or just confiscate our stuff?

Sparks tapped on the dashboard's screen. "Hmm...it's a big ship, big enough to carry us back with them if they wanted to. Registered to—fuck me—registered to CHUSI. Dammit, Harlan."

He'd chased us. After our talk, I'd thought he really wanted to help. Apparently not.

We used Yarrow's screen to make the call, since HGNT was probably already tracking it. Yarrow and Sparks sat behind me, just in frame. Miller was in a similar position, flanked by his security guards.

"Ms. Dawn. I see you're aware that we're pursuing your ship."

"Yes, we're aware of that. Do you mind telling me why? Are you so loyal to HGNT that you're doing their dirty work without even a pretext of working for CHUSI now?"

One of Miller's guards fidgeted, but Miller was impassive. "I see you solved your ship rental red flag problem."

"Hi, Harlan!" Sparks waved cheerfully from behind me, but his over-the-top smile didn't reach his eyes.

"Your antics are all very entertaining, but I'm afraid your merry chase is over. You must have noticed that we'll catch you within a day."

So he was back to being HGNT's lackey, was he? The Miller I met with on Luna had made it clear that he didn't support HGNT's methods or goals, but had that been an act to draw me in?

"What happens? You catch up, grab our ship, and haul us back to HGNT holding cells?"

"Now, now. HGNT is not legally allowed to detain anyone. CHUSI can confiscate anything that belongs to them. I understand you have some materials that were acquired without proper permission on board your—"

"*You* gave us permission."

"—and I will be boarding to investigate and confiscate any stolen material."

What the hell? Had he "helped" me get my probe parts from the junkyard just so that he would have an excuse to chase us down and board our ship? If he did board and confiscate my frankenprobe, how would I get the readings I needed to find the pinch in space and prove that it matched Dr. Morbit's simulation parameters?

"I can't believe you set us up like this." Maybe my glare could make him drop dead, even through the screen.

"Yes, well. One would think you would know my true nature by now."

True nature as a spineless, backstabbing weasel? One would think. I ground my teeth.

"Whelp! See you soon then, Harlan." Sparks waved with one hand and gave Miller the finger with the other. Very classy.

The screen went dark.

Sparks dropped his fake grin. "He's got something else going on."

"What do you mean?"

He didn't bother to answer. He must have known better than I ever could that Miller always had something going on behind the scenes.

"Do you think he'll just take the probe? Let us go?"

"Do we have any other option?" said Yarrow.

Yes. Our other option was to try to run and then get caught and have running count as a strike against us...No. We'd have to just sit here and let him take it. I'd made a probe from practically nothing once, maybe I could find a way to do it again? I would have to.

Miller caught up with us just before dinner, as he'd predicted. His ship was twice the size of *Gracious* and could easily swallow *Conquest* and drag us back with him. We rafted with it, and Miller came aboard alone. He didn't even respect us enough to bring his security guards along; he was that sure we'd give up without a fight.

I had to concentrate to keep from tapping my foot as I moved aside to let him aboard. The storm clouds swirling around Sparks's head would probably have been striking Miller with lightning if he'd been any closer.

"What do you want with this ship?" I said.

"Not speaking for yourself today, Sparks?"

"She's the Captain. I'm just the cabbie."

"Understood. Ms. Dawn, I think it behooves you to use a slightly more respectful tone, since I'm saving your ass at the moment. I wanted to have a talk in person, on your ship, since mine is currently being very carefully monitored."

What? Was he trying to play me again? We had no options, and we all knew it. "Fine, let's sit."

Sparks didn't move, but Miller joined me and Yarrow at the galley table.

"Where are you headed?" said Miller.

There was really no sense in lying at this point. "A mining ship disappeared a while back, and we're trying to figure out why."

"Likely an accident."

"Likely." No way was I volunteering information to this HGNT puppet.

"But you think the ship suffered the same fate as Pardus Station."

"We have reason to believe there's more to the disappearance than HGNT let on."

"Does your ship have sensors on it now, Sparks? How do you plan to gather observations once you reach the site?"

He was *not* getting away with playing clueless about the probe. About the sabotage. "We have a probe. You helped us get the parts from the junkyard. Where our hatch got tampered with and nearly caused us to lose a chunk of our ship? Remember?"

"Remember?" His innocent-confusion face was almost convincing. He must practice in the mirror. "I didn't know."

"Okay, that's about enough conversation. Are we done here?" said Sparks.

"No, really. I didn't know. Is that really what you think of me, Clark?"

"Pretty sure we all think that of you," I muttered as Miller rose, reaching a tentative hand toward Sparks, who looked ready to tear it off. If there had been any doubt that these two had history, it evaporated.

Miller shook his head. "I need to give them something."

My probe. "You can't have it. It's not my fault you gave me fake permission to access the junkyard."

"You keep bringing up the junkyard. I assure you, the permit I provided was legit."

"And yet, here you are, ready to revoke it."

"I'm not talking about the probe, Ms. Dawn. I'm talking about Mr. Yarrow's ship."

Yarrow's antennae were jumping. He'd stolen a ship?

"I was slated to return to the research centre, and I took a slight detour." Yarrow didn't have permission to be here? He'd commandeered a ship to chase after me? A warm bubble of...love floated in my chest.

So of course, Miller had to pop it. "Now that we've sorted that out, can we possibly try to be civil?"

Here we were, trying to get rid of the ship, and Miller was just going to take it off our hands? What was the catch?

Miller's screen pinged. He closed his eyes and ran a hand through his hair, his shoulders relaxing.

"What?" Sparks bit out.

"Good news, I'm along for the ride."

"Along for what ride?" I said.

The clunk of a ship detaching made me jump. Miller's ship was leaving. With Miller still on this side of the hatch. No way.

Miller didn't resist as Sparks escorted him to an empty cabin and shut him inside, and the three of us convened on the bridge.

"What is he even doing here?" I picked at my thumbnail.

"You'll have to ask him that," said Sparks.

"I believe that he has told us partial truths. It is possible that this is his attempt to escape from HGNT's control," said Yarrow, far too reasonably.

"Are you sure you're fine with him staying here?" I said. I didn't put my hand on Sparks's arm, but it was close.

"Not even a bit."

"He could stay on *Gracious*."

"No, he couldn't. If he wants to play his little games with us, that's one thing, but the folks over there didn't ask for Harlan to show up and ruin their day."

"Then it's decided. Miller will remain here, under our observation," said Yarrow.

"And once HGNT realizes they've lost their CHUSI pet?" said Sparks.

"If HGNT isn't breathing down their necks already, they will be very soon. We can at least put Miller to work while he's here. He knows more about the AVDO than we do. We should have him look through our notes and fill in the gaps." I pulled out my screen and swiped it on. The battered old thing was getting downright lovable. The shortcut to the "Question Marks" document had moved or something. It wasn't where I'd left it. I hopped over to my documents list, opened the ones shared with me and...nothing.

Okay, this was okay. Maybe it had just been moved. I did a search through my history and found the entry for Question Marks. The change log was still there. I'd made the thing, shared it with Yarrow, and then shared it with this new screen.

> "Question Marks" created by Carolina
> Shared with Yarrow
> Shared with P4U1337

I shouldn't be shocked that Pauli had weaseled her way in here as well.

> Shared with Guest
> "Question Marks" deleted by Carolina

Or our notes had become just one giant gap. Whatever.

◈

When Yarrow came back from tai chi with Fiona's crew the next morning, I was practically vibrating, possibly ready to smash the probe I'd so painstakingly constructed into a thousand pieces. Pauli's firmware was better. It would definitely work *somehow*, if only I could figure out *how*.

"You are extremely tense. I think you could have benefitted from joining us."

"We're only a day away from the site of the accident, and I still don't have a working probe. You're saying I shouldn't be tense?"

"It has no discernible benefit."

I yanked the cord from the probe's port and slammed the access door closed. "Thanks for that. I didn't realize. I guess I'll just relax now that I know being tense has no discernible benefit."

"Carolina, I'm referring to the opportunity to participate in a relaxing group activity."

"I'm sure they'd love having such a tense person there messing up the ambiance."

"The purpose of the activity is to dissipate tension."

Whatever Fiona had said, it was obvious to anyone with a brain that she wouldn't want some beginner horning in on what was essentially a meditation session, and the person who had dredged up her husband's death would be the last person she'd want there.

"I'd be happy to take a look at the probe while you rest."

"Absolutely. Knock yourself out." Hopefully, that idiom translated well.

I stalked past Yarrow out to the galley, where Miller was studying his screen with a frown.

"They're not tracking you too, are they?" I snapped.

"Please, give me some credit, Ms. Dawn." He didn't look up.

"Don't you think you can give that a rest? If you're forcing us to live together, you don't need to be a prick about it." I slammed a ration pack into the reconstitutor. I could practically feel Yarrow and Miller having a silent conversation about me behind my back. Miller would be asking why I was being such a bitch, and Yarrow would just shrug.

"I apologize," said Miller, and I stiffened. "Please, let me know if I can help in any way."

For fuck's sake. Now Miller was so tired of my bullshit he was trying to placate me. "Sure," I said and took the steps to the bridge two at a time.

"Aren't you just a ray of sunshine," said Sparks before I even sat down.

"Can't you let me stew in peace?"

"If you wanted to stew in peace, you'd be in your cabin, Captain."

Goddamn it. "Maybe I'll just head down there."

"Maybe you should," said Sparks, an infuriating smile playing across his features. "You know I'm a captive audience while I'm piloting *Conquest*."

"What does that mean?"

"Just that I have to sit here and take whatever you say."

That was utter bullshit. He could flick on autopilot and leave whenever he wanted. But he didn't. "This whole voyage has been a shitshow. The sabotage, Pauli's attitude, the weird too-nice vibe from Fiona's crew, Yarrow showing up and giving away our position, now fucking Miller hanging around. Can nothing go right? Can nothing go smoothly? I wish I hadn't even approached Fiona. I just wanted to rent a ship and go investigate all on my own, and people keep hanging around and making my life difficult." None of that was true. Well, maybe some of it was true. Some of it felt true, at least.

"I'm sure my piloting the ship makes your life very difficult." How was he still smiling?

"If it hadn't been for HGNT's meddling, I would have been able to get my own ship. They're the ones who made damned *Lepton* disappear in the first place."

"Are they?"

"Indirectly, by doing all that shit with the AVDO. What did they think was going to happen? These super powerful people who can make an entire planet or some shit blink out of existence were just going to let themselves be wiped out?"

"You think the AVDO would retaliate?"

"Wouldn't you?"

Sparks stared out at the stars, his head cocked to the side. "Power is a strange thing. When you don't have it, it's so easy to think you'd wield it a certain way." It sounded like he was going to continue, but he just sighed.

I found myself sighing as well. The fight had drained out of me somewhere along the line, and I slumped in my chair.

"Remind me again why we don't just stay rafted together with *Gracious*?" I propped my feet on the dashboard. Maybe not the best position for a touchy conversation with Sparks, but my dash was always inactivated anyway.

"Because I pilot my own ship, period. I don't get dragged around by some huge mining ship that could shoot off in the wrong direction before you can say disengage." He messed with a couple switches.

"I'm just saying there would be more space for you to get away from Miller—Harlan—if we had the run of the bigger ship."

"Are you disparaging the size of my ship? I'm hurt."

"*Conquest* is great. But with the five of us, it's at max capacity. And I think it would be max capacity even if Yarrow, Pauli, and I weren't here."

"I'm not abandoning my ship because some government official on a power trip is breathing down my neck. Conversation closed, Carolina."

He must really be upset if he was calling me by my actual name. He and Miller had history. Harlan. I was never going to get used to that.

They weren't the type of people to let that history interfere with their jobs, but it did interfere with the atmosphere on the ship.

"Don't you have a probe to get up and running?"

My feet thunked off the dashboard. "Yarrow's taking a poke around it." I fidgeted.

"I'm sure Harlan could help you," said Sparks. He smirked at the look on my face. "Still not over all the projects that he stole from your team, eh? See? Not so easy to forgive and forget when it's you."

"No one's asking you to forgive and forget." There was nothing overt about the awkward tension that filled the ship whenever Sparks and Miller were in the same room, but nonetheless, it wasn't comfortable. "Maybe you could tone down your...glowering?"

"Glowering, eh? I don't think I've heard it called that before."

"You've heard it called something?"

He waved me away with another little smirk.

Whatever he wanted to call his glower, it seemed to bother Miller as well. This morning, Miller and I had been the first ones up, awkwardly sharing a silent breakfast, when Sparks had loomed in his bedroom doorway and turned his glower our way. Miller had dropped his screen and had to scramble under the table for it, then beat a hasty retreat to his cabin.

Whatever it was, it was not my business. If they were fine avoiding each other, then far be it from me to order them around.

The reconstitutor beeped down below. Crap. I'd have to face Miller and Yarrow after the way I'd acted. But when I slunk back down the companionway, only Pauli sat in the galley. Yarrow must still be tinkering with the probe, and lord only knew where Miller was.

I extracted my food from the reconstitutor. Pauli's firmware would work. She'd done what she said and helped me.

"Thanks for the firmware."

"My pleasure. I could hear you cursing from my cabin this morning."

Vindictive. Did she intentionally make it hard for me to install? "You could help instead of—"

Pauli shot to her feet. "I could help? Gee, I wonder what that's like, helping someone out with everything they ever asked me for? I hope I don't get nothing but condescension and abuse in return. That would be so shitty." She stomped to her cabin and slammed back inside.

She was wrong. She'd been nothing but a mouthy brat to me since we'd met. She never listened, made unreasonable demands, and gave me nothing but snark in return. Without me, she'd be disappeared on Exodus right now. She could try showing a little appreciation.

Speaking of showing appreciation, it was Miller's turn to come through. We'd helped him slip HGNT's leash, so he owed us info. I banged on his door.

"Time to tell me about the AVDO," I called through it.

Miller stepped out. "Still in a lovely mood, I see."

"No thanks to you." I stalked back to my food and sat down with it. "Start talking."

"What do you want me to say, now that you have me here?"

"Just tell me everything you know." Why was he being so difficult about this?

"Everything I know. How about we keep it feasible, Ms. Dawn. The AVDO are a sentient species that live in vacuum and inhabit many star systems across the Galaxy. They communicate via EM patterns, as you know, and are able to teleport themselves and objects—even living objects—at will."

He really was determined to make this as painstaking as he could. "No need to start at the preschool level. Get to the point. Where's Pardus? Why wasn't Exodus trapped like them?"

"As you've obviously already ascertained, Pardus Station is trapped in a pocket of space. Exodus Labs was teleported by a free AVDO, thus they made it to their destination."

"Meaning that Pardus wasn't teleported by a free AVDO. Can you just say that next time?"

Miller glared. "As you can guess from Starblink's last words—you're welcome for the translation, by the way—HGNT has been kidnapping and murdering their people for a century. Their attempts to replicate the teleportation ability through less than savoury means have only been thwarted by folks refusing to go along with HGNT's orders. You think you have some right to know everything I know because you burst in here a couple months ago and started fumbling around, making a mess of all my work? How many times did I tell you to back off? How much energy did I waste saving your skin over and over? Don't bother answering because you don't have a clue. You've helped me some. I won't deny that, but don't for one second think that gives you the right to order me around and treat me like shit, Carolina."

That was not what I was doing. I was *trying* to get answers, and everyone else was being so damned difficult. He'd mostly told me what I wanted to know. He could translate for the AVDO; he knew about Dr. Morbit's research, and he had been helping them from the start.

And he wasn't leaving. Was he expecting some kind of apology? I finished my food and cleared my place. Maybe Yarrow had made some progress with the probe. I left Miller there, arms crossed, shooting undeserved daggers into my back with his glare as I walked away.

Chapter 16

Unfortunately, Yarrow had not solved the probe problem while I was cooling off. I gave it another try before dinner, but we were going to reach our spot soon, and with no probe, we might as well not have come at all. But both Pauli and Miller had made it very clear that they were not going to help me, and I'd be damned if I was going to give them another chance to berate me.

Dinnertime rolled around, and Yarrow dragged me away from my probe and over to *Gracious*, even though I had zero desire to interact with another sentient being. We took our places around the dinner table, everyone else chatting. Miller's screen chimed. He furrowed his brow and pulled it out.

"Tsk, no screens at the table," said Frall.

Miller ignored him and picked up, pushing back his chair. He didn't leave the room, so everyone heard him say, "She's right here, actually."

My stomach dropped. Who was he telling about my location? Unless he was talking about Fiona, but that didn't seem likely.

"We're a fairly large group at the moment. I'm not sure that's wise." He glanced around the table. "One moment." He tapped his screen and turned to us. "I have someone on the line who wants to speak to you, Carolina. My screen is secure, but the conversation may be monitored from the other end."

Someone asking to speak to me? "Our location?"

He shook his head. "They won't be able to trace it."

I didn't ask who they were in this case. "Should we go somewhere more private?"

"If you want to."

Did I want to? Yarrow had every right to listen in on this conversation, and Sparks had more than proven himself trustworthy. Either way, they were all in this with me now and deserved to know what we were up against.

"No, that's okay."

"You can put them on the big screen, if you want," said Bez.

Miller nodded and got it set up. Frall, Janella, and Yarrow moved around the table so that they could see the screen, and it glowed to life. I scootched over so that Yarrow could put his chair next to mine.

HGNT's enforcer appeared, complete with background fishtank, looking bored out of her mind.

"When we came to our arrangement, I underestimated quite how foolish you could be. Ruining another researcher's experiment, releasing a libelous video, resisting our security officers' attempts to question you. If you intended your little teleporting stunt to shield you from the consequences of breaking our agreement, I'm afraid you've failed."

My teleporting stunt? She was accusing me of teleporting a space station halfway across the Galaxy? Was she trying to pin their mistake on me, or did HGNT genuinely not have anything to do with the teleportation? If not, then they might still not have cracked it.

"Contrary to my advice, corporate is willing to give you a chance to return yourself to their custody. If you do so, they will overlook the involvement of these other parties."

If they thought I was going to give up when I was so close, they'd never met a researcher before.

"You don't have to waste your breath. You won't get me like that again."

"Very well." She hung up.

"That went super well," said Frall.

"Perhaps next time we can discuss—"

I cut Yarrow off. "Discuss handing me over to my mysterious death so the rest of you can get off scot-free?"

Yarrow put a hand on my shoulder, but I shook him off.

"Big words from the one who dragged us all into this," said Janella. "Some of us didn't even want to come."

"*Some of us* were given the choice to stay behind," said Fiona.

"Some of us weren't," Pauli muttered into her food. She was around the end of the table and had seemed totally uninterested in the call.

"Hey! You'd still be stranded on Exodus if I hadn't—"

Yarrow squeezed my leg firmly and turned to Miller. "They weren't able to access our location, correct?"

Miller shrugged.

I took a deep breath. "Right. So. Miller, contact the AVDO, tell them we want to help, see if they know anything about Pardus."

Miller leaned back in his chair. "Even if I wanted to lead you to the AVDO, I don't have a direct line to them as you seem to think. It's time to wrap this conversation up. If they want your help, they'll be in touch."

What gave him the right to just call an end to the conversation? "What the fuck, Miller?"

Yarrow squeezed my leg again.

Miller squared his shoulders. "I have a few things to take care of." One of which had better be getting in touch with the AVDO. He whistled a jaunty tune and headed back to *Conquest*.

"Shit," said Sparks. "He still does that whistling thing when he's losing it."

They talked among themselves for the rest of our mercifully brief dinner, and I left after the third time Janella glared lasers at me.

I needed to figure out my probe anyway. The useless thing still wouldn't boot properly. It just kept beeping at me, and I had no beepy-code thing for my parts. I picked at my thumb until it bled, but all that did was get blood on my bench. Probably not the first time this piece of crap workbench got bled on.

I jumped as Sparks's voice echoed across the bay.

"We're coming up on the location of the mining colony ship now."

Shit, already? "How do you know?

"I'm picking up a signal from the black box."

Even the fact that there was a black box meant that these people had not been disappeared, which meant that...I scrubbed my face with my hands. This was probably a completely unrelated dead fucking end. No pinch in space, no readings, no evidence against HGNT. At least Fiona could get closure on her husband's mundane, accidental disappearance.

I scrambled up to the cockpit.

The arc of the mangled Dyson ring stretched away, its star's glare shining off the jagged remains of the far end. Debris orbited the pock-marked surface in an unstable halo. Something shadowed the closer end. An AVDO? As it turned toward us, a honeycomb of impressions sparkled against the smooth grey surface. Not an AVDO.

Maybe the black box would tell me what the hell I was looking at. "Might as well play the recording."

"Your wish is my command, Captain," said Sparks.

A series of clicks preceded crackling over the cabin speakers, then a smooth automated voice:

> "That remains information with no relevance to your current role, thus I deemed it unnecessary to impart it."

> "I deem it relevant, and I think the rest of my crew would also."

The second voice was gruff, someone who had spent a lot of time breathing through a respirator.

> "You do realize that I am capable of carrying out the mission without your intervention."

> "Yeah, uh-huh. I realize that. But even you can't kill anyone without a weapon."

> "Desist tampering with my external hardware immediately."

> "Nope, I don't think we will."

"Loosening the bolts will result in an erratic fire pattern that could—"

"Oh, we're not just loosening them, lithium brain."

Grinding. Thump.

"What do you intend to do with my dismembered—"

The recording was fainter now.

"Wilson, open the airlock. That's right."

"You have removed my primary means of carrying out my orders. Secondary elimination systems engaged."

"SELF-DESTRUCT INITIATED... DECLINE WINDOW NOW BEGINNING... DECLINE WINDOW OVERRIDE COMPLETE... SELF-DESTRUCT IMMINENT—"

Static.

What did I just listen to? I turned to Sparks, who shrugged.

"Sounds like a bit of a fight, doesn't it? Raft with Fiona?"

"Good idea," I said. "Share the data from the black box with me as well. Maybe there's something we can use." Sparks would be more likely to be able to parse a ship's black box data than I would, but maybe something would jump out at me.

"Conquest?" Fiona's voice was distorted over the radio, but she sounded strangely hesitant.

"Conquest, Sparks here."

"Raft confirmed. I...haven't listened to the whole recording. That's Graham talking to the ship."

Fiona joined us on *Conquest*, for once. The bridge's viewport was the biggest we had. The three of us silently surveyed the debris. Why had they needed weapons? What had they been ordered to destroy? What *had* the ship destroyed? The Dyson ring?

"I know that shape."

I jumped. When had Miller joined us? "Yeah, it's part of a Dyson ring."

"Not that, Ms. Dawn. The satellite. The orbiting body."

The pitted rock?

"I believe this is—was—an AVDO nesting ground. A nursery."

"Why would they make a nursery in a construction site?"

"They didn't," said Fiona. "HGNT wanted Graham to blow up that...cradle."

But he'd refused. The mining crew had ripped apart their ship rather than follow that order. But the ship had done it anyway, self-destructed and taken the nursery out. Had there been baby AVDO in there?

I shuddered, and retreated to the alley. Any more staring at babies' graves would render me catatonic, and that wouldn't help anyone.

❖

I spent pretty much the entire night listening to the recording again and again, after I'd already extracted every possible detail from Fiona until she walked away and slammed her door in my face, which was after I'd already combed every single obit and news report I could find from the "accident" and come up empty.

I think I fell asleep at some point and dreamt it all.

Graham talking to the computer, an image I found from his obit of him grinning at the helm of a little planet hopper coming to life, the planet hopper morphing into a huge mining ship, the grin morphing into a scowl as he growled at the stubborn AI that it couldn't kill anyone without a weapon. But it had. It had killed a whole nursery full of AVDO along with everyone on the ship.

My brain filled in all the details: miners detaching some hulking piece of machinery I couldn't quite place from the deck; Graham's grim face as they tossed it, spinning, into the black of space. Flesh searing, peeling back from his cheekbones as the ship's AI vapourized them all, leaving nothing but the black box behind.

I woke up panting, Yarrow's hands stroking up and down my back. I uncurled from my fetal position and sat on the edge of our bunk, staring at the floor. Why would HGNT explode the ship? Why not override human control and grab their no-doubt expensive equipment? Because they just wanted the AVDO dead to make way for their construction project. A ship like Graham's was a drop in the bucket to them.

"Carolina."

Once the AVDO were out of the way, why hadn't they completed their project? When was the Dyson ring abandoned? They killed so many people to make way for it.

Yarrow's hand stroked down my spine again, and I flinched away.

"I believe we've exhausted our information. There is nothing more to find here."

"We've been at dead ends before." I swatted away his hand when he tried to stroke my arm, like soothing a pet. I paced the three steps across the cabin and back, making myself dizzy more than anything. "There has to be something more. Why did HGNT give up?"

"Perhaps the monetary cost was prohibitive, as you previously surmised."

"Maybe. I just mean, it's too similar. A whole ship of people go missing—"

"They are dead, not missing."

"Whatever. They're too similar, is what I'm saying."

Yarrow's fucking antennae twitched.

"Don't fucking do that! Don't emotionally analyze me."

"It's an autonomic response—"

I stalked into the bathroom and locked the door. When I came out after my shower, feeling a little more human, Yarrow wasn't in our room.

I trudged out to the galley. Maybe Fiona would talk to me again this morning? Miller sat hunched over a steaming cup, looking how I felt. Great.

"What's wrong with you?" I probably should have kept my scathing remarks inside, but that was energy better spent on figuring this shit out.

"We aren't quite as under the radar as we had hoped. Someone realized who Fiona is and made the connection. My pal at HGNT gave me the heads up this morning—"

The intercom cut him off. "Captain, come on up to the bridge."

Miller didn't even have the grace to look guilty, he just deflated a little more.

"The heads up that what?"

"They were planning to intercept us here."

Fuck, we shouldn't have stayed. We should have taken the black box and run. But without a destination, what was the point? Whatever.

We were here now, and we'd have to deal with it. I spared one longing glance for whatever wake-up juice Miller had in his mug and scrambled up the companionway.

Damn. They'd sent a big one. The ship loomed over us, twice the size of *Gracious*, easy, all dark metal and gleaming lights. They'd parked her here on purpose, but I'd be damned if I was going to be intimidated by a big ship.

"They know it's you, Captain." Sparks's mouth was a thin line.

I gestured for Sparks to put them through. He'd take my shit, but that didn't mean that I wanted to dump it on him.

I slid on the headset and braced my shaking hands on the dash. "Carolina Dawn here."

"Nice to finally be speaking with you, Ms. Dawn." An unctuous voice oozed through the earpiece.

"It's doctor, actually." Whoever this was, all this "Ms. Dawn" shit needed to end. Now.

"Of course. It must have slipped my mind, considering how desperately stupid you behave."

Did he actually just say that out loud? Kronenberg. It had to be.

"Now. I'm giving you one last chance to be smart. Either you hand over the black box and the research you stole from us, or we get rid of it ourselves."

Disappear it to an impregnable space pocket, he meant.

"You have to understand it's all the same to HGNT. If it's all the same to you, I for one would love a chance to give our tech another test run."

So we would be trapped in a pocket of space. So what? Here, there, what did it matter? If this guy thought I was just going to hand back my only chance at proving they did this, he'd realize his error in short order.

"The answer is no."

All the lights on Sparks's console blinked on.

Getting teleported wasn't at all what I thought it would be like. It didn't hurt, to start with, not to mention it seemed instantaneous. Maybe that was the blackout. Something dug into my back. I peeled myself off the floor and into a seat. My head throbbed, but I pried my eyes open. Where had we ended up?

Stars shimmered, an unbroken, infinite depth of twinkling lights laid out before us, nothing I recognized. Were we really in a pocket of space? How could so many stars be here?

Sparks groaned and straightened across from me, swiping at the blood leaking down his forehead.

"Shit." I turned to the first aid kit stowed in the bulkhead at my elbow, and my head spun, making me lean back in my seat. No point in trying to patch up Sparks if I was going to be the next one to face-plant into the dashboard.

Pardus Station hovered above us, a dozen smaller ships docked to it.

A string of very eloquent curses floated up from the lower cabin, and Miller's head popped up the companionway.

"Clark!" He batted my hands away and popped the first aid kit out of the bulkhead.

Sparks actually smiled at him as he rummaged in the kit for bandages and antiseptic, muttering under his breath about fool-hardy missions and the price of knowledge. Hopefully, Pauli and Yarrow had fared okay.

I gripped the handrail tightly as I descended into the lower cabin, my feet still feeling a bit disconnected from my brain. Where was Yarrow? Was he all right? We humans might be able to survive this trip, but had it ever been tested on a Yrk'uthian? A vision of Yarrow, emotion sensors overloaded by the teleport, stretched on the floor of our cabin, bleeding out from the ears, popped into my head, and I smacked the Door Open pad, my hand stinging at my fervour.

Yarrow sat on the floor, his knees drawn up, one set of hands dangling between them, one set flat on the floor, bracing himself.

I stumbled to my knees next to him, and he let me crawl into his lap, wrapping his upper set of arms around me. He could have died. We all could have, though presumably HGNT knew the effects of teleportation on humans. But when they had offered me that choice, I hadn't even thought of Yarrow, and I should've.

"You are concerned. Tell me what transpired." His voice was a mere breath in my ear, his heartbeat a steady thump in the other one.

"They wanted everything. I told them to go to hell." I swallowed hard and sighed. "They threatened to make us disappear if I declined."

"And you hoped to call their bluff?"

"I'm not sure what I hoped for." It wasn't that I thought they were bluffing. I had known that they were capable of carrying out their threat. I just...hadn't cared. And I'd dragged all these folks here with me, Sparks and Miller, Pauli and Yarrow, and— "Fiona! Did their ship come through as well?" I tried to spring to my feet, and Yarrow released me, only to grab my arm again as I saw spots and wavered.

"It would be prudent us to take our time, Carolina. I believe that we are currently in a stable state, as is Fiona's ship. There is no call to rush taking stock of our position."

He was right, and yet, I couldn't wait. I wobbled to the cabin door and trailed a hand on the wall as I crossed to Pauli's door and banged on it, practically hanging off the frame.

A muffled *fuck off* drifted through the door.

"You okay in there?"

"I'm fine. I said fuck off!"

I smacked the Door Open pad, but she'd locked it, of course. Fine. If she said she was fine, then fine. But Sparks hadn't been fine.

Please, please, don't let Sparks be bleeding out on the floor or concussed or in a coma...

Yarrow followed me and braced me as I stumbled up the steps to the bridge. Miller murmured something, and Sparks responded. Sparks's head rested in Miller's lap as Miller stroked a bandage smooth over the gash on his forehead. I collapsed into the co-pilot's chair and buried my face in my hands, pressing my eye sockets until sparkles scattered across my vision.

"You could've at least pretended to play nice with the big corpos, Captain." Sparks's white bandage stood out against his brown forehead. He was right. I should have pretended and then escaped later on and saved these folks from having to deal with the consequences of my selfish actions. I hadn't even asked them before I dragged them down with me. Not that I could change that now.

Okay, time to figure out what exactly I had dragged them into. The best way to do that would be to send out my probe.

"Miller, I'll need you to get the probe up and running. Sparks, can this ship take any readings?"

"I guess that's one way to get over yourself and ask for help," said Sparks.

"Who says I'm asking?" We needed to get out of this pocket, and we needed to do it sooner rather than later.

"Oh yeah, you're the Captain. That means we all have to always do everything you say, I forgot." Sparks rolled his eyes and winced as his bandage wrinkled.

"It's okay, Clark," said Miller in a soft voice I'd never heard from him. "I'll get the probe ready, Captain." He extracted himself from Sparks and ducked down the companionway, not looking at me.

"And I would be happy to run any readings that are possible with the ship's instruments," said Yarrow.

"No way. I'm right here and perfectly capable."

The intercom crackled. "New ships, please identify yourselves."

Sparks gestured to my abandoned headset. Right, this was all on me. I slid it back on. "Pardus Station, this is Dr. Carolina Dawn on *Conquest*. How have you been?" Finally, I was talking to Pardus Station, the folks that I had been looking for for months, the people I'd sacrificed my career for.

"Pretty shit, actually. You one of those academics who's all interested in teleportation and blob aliens and doesn't give half a shit about the rest of us?"

"Um, no. I care very much about—"

"So, yes, then. Fine. Check in with me before you do anything stupid."

Twice in one day, strangers decided to call me stupid. "Absolutely." I guess I'd be cranky too after being trapped in a pocket of space for months. Still, I was here to help. There was no need for them to attack me before even meeting me.

Sparks and Yarrow chattered about what readings to take in the silence that meant the Pardus person had hung up. We would respect their wishes. We'd take some readings, come up with a plan, and then take it to them as a courtesy before we tried anything. As long as Miller was able to get the probe actually running.

I joined him in the workshop, where he had his screen plugged into the probe.

"You know, Carolina, I don't know shit about these things."

What? Sparks had said that he could help. Why did I even bother asking him if—

"But someone on board does. Just get help from Pauli already."

"She doesn't want to help me. I believe her words were *fuck off*."

"You could start by apologizing." He tapped at his screen. He seemed to be doing a lot of work on the probe for someone who knew nothing about them.

"I tried that! Don't you think I tried apologizing? I'm not a total monster, you know."

Miller looked up from his screen. His stare pierced right through me. He didn't have to ask *Did you really?* It was all right there.

We were supposed to be working together on this project. Why was Pauli the one who got to be all immature and hide in her room and reject my apology and avoid helping with any of the work? Did she want me to beg forgiveness on my knees? Absolutely not. She could get over it, or she could stay shut in her room forever.

"There we go," said Miller.

"What?"

"Got your probe working."

"I thought you said you knew nothing about this shit!"

"I don't. But I asked someone who does."

"You got a message out of the pocket?"

"Sure didn't."

He'd asked Pauli for help, and she'd helped him. After she'd refused to so much as talk to me, thrown my apology in my face. Yeah, she so deserved to be cooped up in her tiny cabin all alone. "Great. Thanks. You can go."

Miller bowed—the jerk—and left the workshop. We wouldn't be able to use the sealed floor hatch to launch the probe, but maybe *Gracious* had a hatch we could use.

When I got back to the bridge, Yarrow and Sparks were still at it.

"It is logical that it would be here, after all. Still, it's surprising," said Yarrow.

"I can take you over there if you want. Seems like she's abandoned."

"Who?" I said.

"*Lepton*," said Yarrow.

"She's here?" Of course she was. She'd been disappeared right out from under us. And into this pocket. "Yes, take us over." She had the perfect hatch to launch my probe.

We docked with *Lepton*, and Yarrow helped me haul my probe across. Then we detached from *Conquest*, and Yarrow and I took *Lepton* into a good position, away from Pardus and her docked ships, just past *Conquest* and *Gracious*.

While I waited for Yarrow to launch the probe, I connected to *Lepton*'s server. Holy crap. All our research from the librarian! It was all still here. I collapsed on the seat in front of the desk. Would this be enough to get us out of here?

Lepton shuddered and rocked. *Shit.* What was that? I took the stairs up to the bridge two at a time.

"It appears that the pocket is finite."

"What the hell does that mean?"

"It seems that the probe collided with the boundary of the pocket, and the boundary snapped back into place."

The shockwaves of which had been enough to rock the ship.

The intercom crackled. "What the hell are you doing, Dr. Carolina Dawn? I told you not to do anything without checking with me first!

Is firing off god-knows-what right into the membrane your idea of doing nothing?"

"It's my idea of helping," I fired back. "I'm trying to collect some data to find a way out of this pocket. If you're happy staying in here for the rest of your life then fine, but I'm not going to do that!"

"Carolina," said Yarrow.

"What!"

"Sparks and Fiona are seeking assistance."

"What?"

"The shockwave damaged their ships. They are currently evacuating to Pardus Station."

Chapter 17

S o I damaged their ships. Fiona's home and Sparks's baby. I would fix them, just as soon as we got out of this pocket. I stomped back down to the desk and scoured the information from the librarian. Yarrow came twice to tell me that Pardus's captain wanted to talk to me, and I would go talk to her, once I had a solution for her. There was no point in going to talk to her now.

I'd forgotten about this weird manual that the librarian had given me. I hunched over the desk, peering at my little screen. It was still weird, the diagrams of parts not adding up to anything I recognized. But this chamber was for holding something, and the hatch was to let it out. There was no sign of scale on the diagram.

Yarrow's hand squeezed my shoulder, and I jumped. How long had he been there? "Don't scare me like that."

"I called your name several times."

He was lying. I hadn't heard anything.

"The captain of Pardus wishes to speak with you."

"I know."

"Do you intend to speak with her?"

"Not yet. I can figure this out—"

"I don't believe you can."

"What?" Yarrow didn't think I could do this?

"Carolina, I believe you will need to collaborate with others—with me."

"I will! Just as soon as I can add something useful." What would be the point of attending a meeting if I couldn't bring something to show off? I might as well not attend at all.

Yarrow sighed. "I would appreciate if you would come with me."

"You're going without me?"

"Not if you accompany me, Carolina."

Tag along after my boyfriend and sit there like a lump while everyone else shares their ideas? No. Not in this lifetime. I shook my head.

"We're docked with Pardus Station. If you change your mind, come and find us." Yarrow left me.

I'd be damned if I was going to be sitting here quietly waiting for him when he got back. I scarfed down a reconstituted butter chicken pack from *Lepton*'s galley and wandered out into Pardus Station. The maze of narrow corridors stretched before me. How would I know where Yarrow had gone, even to avoid him? I poked down a few until my corridor opened into an atrium, not unlike a star liner. Waiting there for me was a lavender-skinned figure wearing a robe...

"Trix?"

"Yes! I'm Pardus's Trix! My cards told me to meet you here. Now, who are you?"

Wouldn't she know who I am if all of her beings were part of one consciousness? Except that this one was cut off from the rest of her. "I'm Carolina. I met...you...at Exodus Labs. You're all looking for...you." Too much of this kind of talk and the tension in my neck would turn into a pounding headache.

"So! What do you need me for?"

"Um, you're the one who came to meet me."

She waved my comment away. "I know, but I came to find you because I knew that you're going to need me."

"Can you break us out of this pocket?" I said with a grimace.

"No, of course not."

"Then your guess is as good as mine. Why do I need you?"

"No, I mean, there's no need to break out of the pocket. I've been telling Captain Rylka that over and over. It's more like a bottle than a pocket. It has a neck that we can just...zoom!"

"Zoom?"

"We can fly through."

"No offence, but if you know this, and you've told the captain this, then why are you all still here?"

"We can't find the neck."

The neck. The pinch. Our simulation. Sure, it showed what to look for from the outside of the pinch, but surely it would be enough to identify the pinch from the inside, too.

"I might have an idea about that. Where are the captain and the rest right now?"

"Captain Rylka is in a conference meeting with the newcomers...which includes you, doesn't it?"

"Yes. Can you take me there?" I'd wanted an idea of my own, and now I had one.

Trix led the way to the conference room and followed me inside. Everyone looked up, about ten people, including Yarrow, Fiona, Sparks, Miller, Pauli, and a handful of others.

A tall woman with tightly braided hair glared at me. "You are?" She could only be Rylka.

"This is Carolina," said Trix.

"Finally decided to grace us with your presence, did you? We're not going over everything again."

"It doesn't matter. I think I've solved your problem."

"Excuse me? Everything that we've been talking about doesn't matter?"

Oops. I guess getting along with Rylka would have been a good idea. Whatever, this was too important for politicking.

"I know how we can find the bottleneck."

"Do you, now?"

"Yes, I have a simulation of the pinch or bottleneck that would let us identify the signature of a ship's wake reflecting off it."

Rylka's face didn't light up with hope. She just kept glaring at me. "You really are one of them, aren't you?"

"One of—"

"Fine. You got us into this mess, you get us out. Speaking of which, everyone, get out."

Lepton was one of the few ships with the sensors we needed to find the pinch in space, so Yarrow and I took her out and just started taking readings willy-nilly. The server was beefy enough to compare in real time to the simulation Frodli had stolen for me, so all we had to do was sit back, have dinner, and wait for the thing to tell us where the pinch was.

And once we found it? To fly out through the bottleneck, we'd have to be very sure where it was. Hitting the pocket's wall would shatter our ship, and the reverberations would probably shatter every other ship in here with us. The probe had been small, but *Lepton* was big.

"You didn't stay to speak with your friends."

It was true. I'd made for *Lepton* as soon as the meeting had conclud-ed. I didn't need to see how much they all hated me now, how much

I'd hurt them by damaging their ships—maybe beyond repair, based on what they'd said in the meeting. For that matter, were they even my friends? I'd dragged them all off to be teleported, then wrecked their ships. No, if they'd ever really been my friends, they weren't anymore. All I could do now was try to get them back out of here in one piece.

"We need to get this done. I didn't have time to chat."

"They are concerned about you."

Yeah, right. Concerned about how I was going to pay them back for their wrecked ships, their wrecked homes. I grunted.

"Carolina, *I'm* concerned about you." He faced me, antennae twitching wildly, two hands gripping the arms of his chair, two on his knees.

I pushed my food around on my tray. "What are you concerned about?" Why should anyone be concerned about me? I was the culprit here, the one causing all the problems.

"You are taking responsibility for things that are not your fault."

"Like what?" What exactly hadn't been my fault?

"Everything that has happened to us. You've been trying your best—"

"And look where that's got us. I shouldn't have antagonized HGNT. I knew what they were capable of. I should have talked to Rylka before I launched that probe. I shouldn't even have asked all of you to come with me. I knew what I was dragging you into."

"You did not drag us, Carolina! I followed you! We are all grown adults who make choices about our own lives."

"Okay, yeah, but you all didn't really understand the risks you were taking."

"I don't believe that you understand how condescending that sounds."

Jerk. He could try to comfort me all he wanted, but the truth was, I had to get this figured out. I had brought all these folks into danger, and I needed to get them out again.

Lepton's musical little chime went off.

"Is that it?"

"I will display it on the galley screen." He tapped his screen and gestured to the galley wall screen.

The visualization was a definite match. *Lepton*'s fast server had proven its worth by spitting this thing out in mere minutes. We'd have to go slowly, carefully. Any impact of the walls could cause a reverberation that would amplify and shake any ships inside apart, but it was unquestionably an exit.

Yarrow grumbled behind me.

"What's wrong? It looks perfect!"

He tapped on his screen, and a scale image of *Lepton* popped into existence next to the pinch. It would fit, but it would be tight. An image of Pardus Station appeared next to it. No way was that going to make it without touching, especially because stations flew like bricks; no manoeuvrability whatsoever.

"So we can get out, but they will still be trapped." And we'd be right back at fucking square one.

"I suggest we bring this observation to Rylka and the *Kepler 6* crew and see what they make of it. Perhaps we can ferry people out a few at a time—"

"That's not good enough! The second we come through, HGNT will be there. You think they'll just sit back and let us ferry everyone out? The evidence of the research they're trying to hide?"

"Or perhaps someone will have another idea. This is not a failure, Carolina."

"Sure feels like one to me." I flumped onto the bench seat and glared at the table while Yarrow sighed and retreated back to the bridge, no doubt to pilot *Lepton* back to the station. We would have to open this pocket all at once, before HGNT could realize what we were doing. But how? What was keeping the pocket shut—what was keeping it stable in the first place?

Yarrow went to the meeting without me again. He was perfectly capable of relaying what we'd found. Listening to a bunch of people who didn't know what they were talking about bicker incessantly wasn't my idea of a good time.

I headed for a café in Pardus's atrium, but it was closed, so I settled at one of the tables outside.

"If you're waiting for it to open, you'll be waiting a long time."

"I didn't ask for your opinion on my seating choices."

Miller ignored me and took the seat opposite, spinning the chair and sitting backwards on it. Damn, he'd loosened up since leaving CHUSI. "There's no food left for them to sell."

"Why aren't you at the big meeting?" I asked.

"Why aren't you?"

I shrugged and kept my eyes on my screen. Maybe that would make him screw off.

"I've had enough boring meetings at CHUSI to last me a lifetime. I know how these things always go. You've never asked me what my research is about."

"That would be because I don't care."

"You do so. Feigning indifference doesn't suit you, Dawn."

"Fine, will you leave me alone if I ask you about your goddamned research?"

"Probably not. I'll pretend you just asked me nicely so that I can get on with what I wanted to tell you. I've finished a translator for the AVDO language. It won't let you speak to them, but it will let you understand what they're saying. Their sparkles, I think you called them."

"How did you get that original video, anyway?" He'd mentioned that he was the one to translate Starblink's last words, but I'd never asked him how.

"My handler at HGNT sent it along for me to translate."

"And are you going to give me this translator, or are you just gloating?"

He tapped a few times on his screen, and a notification popped up on mine that I had a new download. How did folks keep doing that to my screen?

"This is where you say *Thanks, Harlan! That will really help me out!*"

"You never told me to call you Harlan."

"And you never told me to call you Carolina."

"You don't call me Carolina."

"Exactly." He got up, pushed the chair back in, and sauntered away, whistling his annoying out-of-tune melody.

I installed his program and ran my video through it. Captions appeared at the bottom of the screen: exactly what had been in that comment on the video that HGNT had posted. Great. If I ever ran into an AVDO again, I could at least understand what they were saying to me.

Yarrow met me on *Lepton* after the totally pointless meeting and confirmed that it had been, in fact, totally pointless. Folks had spent an hour bickering about what to do next until Rylka cut the meeting off.

"They must decide soon, though. The supplies on Pardus are dwindling. It was never intended to be a closed system."

Shit. I had been afraid of this. They'd been trapped here for months, after all.

"They are already under severe rationing."

"That means we can't wait for them to come to a consensus, Yarrow. We can't do anything from inside this pocket. At the very least, we can go get a boatload of supplies and bring them back."

"And if HGNT is waiting for us outside the pocket?"

"I guess we run and hope for the best?"

"That plan leaves something to be desired, but bringing supplies back while we wrestle with this problem is a logical stopgap measure."

"Great. Let's head for the pinch."

"You don't intend to inform the others of what we're planning?"

I didn't. They would try to talk me out of it or ask to come along. If HGNT was waiting on the other side of the pinch to blow us out of the sky, the fewer people we had on board, the better. They'd be safer in here, at least for now. I needed Yarrow to pilot *Lepton*, but that was it.

"We can let them know when we're back with the food."

Yarrow's antennae twitched, but he didn't argue with me. He just sighed and left for the bridge.

I couldn't stay down below for the trip through the pinch. Of course, the walls that we were trying to avoid on pain of death were invisible, so it wasn't as if being up there would give me a better view, but pacing around down below while Yarrow handled the piloting was horribly unappealing.

Yarrow punched the course in on his screen and got his heading, and we unlatched from Pardus Station. Yarrow kept our pace steady as we approached what was presumably the pinch.

The intercom popped. "*Lepton*, you're heading right for the boundary. Return to Pardus immediately."

Yarrow was concentrating, so I took care of responding.

"Pardus, we know what we're doing. Don't worry about it."

"*Lepton*, do not ram the membrane. I repeat, do not attempt to ram the membrane!"

"We're not ramming anything, Pardus. We're heading out through the bottleneck—look, we know what we're doing."

"*Lepton*! Change course! You're going to get us all killed—"

The intercom cut out as we presumably entered the pinch, since we didn't bounce off the invisible boundary of the pocket. The visualization had been clear that *Lepton* could fit through with some room to spare, but still, how could Yarrow tell where it was? If the heading was a little off, by the time we so much as brushed the boundary with a fin, it would reverberate until our ship fell apart. My nails dug into my palms, and the hangnail by my thumb started to bleed. I pressed my finger into it, but I didn't move. Distracting Yarrow right now was a terrible idea.

The first thing I saw when we came out the other side was the ship. The one that had disappeared us, twice the size of *Conquest*, dull grey, but somehow still sleek. Made for travelling fast, but sturdy. The next thing I saw was a big black sparkly blob, coming right at us. I gasped and lurched back in my chair, but it somehow managed to stop just before crashing into our viewscreen. I shakily held up my screen and turned on the translator app that Miller had given me. Had he known that the AVDO were out here? He had said something about contacting them, back on *Gracious*.

I require your assistance to take down the [dull ones/rigid ones] in their [rigid object]. Their technology is [breaking/broken].

I read it out to Yarrow. The AVDO repeated themselves a few times. They had some kind of tech on that ship that had made us disappear. Had they used it to create the pocket? To teleport ships inside it? That had not been Dr. Morbit's intention. He wanted to use teleportation for travel purposes; getting ships trapped in pinched space pockets didn't help him.

Of course, I would help in any way that I could. But how was I supposed to get onto their ship? How was I even supposed to respond to this desperate AVDO?

If you are willing, exit your [rigid object].

"Exit the ship? What is it planning to do?" I tapped my lip.

"You cannot, Carolina. Our lifeboat is gone, and we have no space suits on board."

"We have emergency respirators."

"Which will last you only a handful of minutes in vacuum. No, Carolina, you have no idea what this being plans."

"They need our help, Yarrow. You stay with the ship, and I'll just grab a respirator and go out through the hatch." I made for the stairs, but Yarrow stopped me with a gentle hand on my arm.

"How will endangering your own life help the AVDO? The people of Pardus?"

"After everything I've done that's screwed things up, let me do something to help."

"Carolina, you've done nothing but help since this whole thing started."

"And you've been there for me the whole time." I kissed him, wrapping my arms around his neck and clinging on. If this did actually kill me, then at least I'd have these last moments. Yarrow might not want me to do this, but he wasn't actually going to stop me. "Take *Lepton* back to Lancaster for me?"

"The idea of you risking your life in this way terrifies me," he breathed into my ear.

"Me too."

"Perhaps the AVDO are not aware that humans require air."

"It's possible."

"Someone else can—"

"Look around, Yarrow. There's no one else." I turned away before he could see the tears in my eyes, though of course he knew without having to see them.

Before I could talk myself out of it, I rattled down the stairs, popped open the hatch in the floor, grabbed a respirator from next to the main hatch, and strapped it over my face. I curled into the little airlock and pulled it shut. The emergency release was right next to my foot, and I kicked out, popping the outside hatch open. The ship's gravity let me go, and I floated away, quickly out of reach of *Lepton*. My stomach turned over, but I looked out at the stars to steady myself.

The AVDO loomed under me, like a monster from the deep, and I gasped. I only had a few breaths in this respirator until it was able to get some outside air to filter. The AVDO circled below me, sharklike. Had I made a huge mistake? Was I about to be an AVDO snack? I kept my arms wrapped around my knees, the AVDO still circling steadily. I squeezed my eyes shut, a pull toward the AVDO the only sign that anything was happening. My heartbeat sped up along with my breathing. The respirator was running out of oxygen.

My stomach lurched as I fell. My eyes flew open. I was in a ship. I gasped in breaths, dots dancing in my vision from lack of oxygen. My feet, knees, and palms hit the metal decking. Where had the AVDO teleported me?

I scrambled up, heading straight for a viewport, and there was *Lepton*. The AVDO had popped me through the hull of the ship that had disappeared us.

Chapter 18

I slid the respirator down my face, and it dangled around my neck as I turned. Footsteps. I needed to find the technology and destroy it. I'd need some kind of demo equipment, and I'd need to find the lab. Hopefully, without getting caught. Could I blend in here? How many people were on board this ship? I tapped the nearest Door Open pad as quietly as I could, but nothing happened. Were they all biosignature locked?

I hurried away from the footsteps, which seemed to be walking rather than trying to chase me down. If I could see *Lepton* out this viewport, then aft would be...that way. Okay, I was probably going the right way. Most ships had repair supplies somewhere aft or near the lifeboats. If I could find a laser saw, that would be ideal for causing maximum destruction in minimum time; plus, I knew how to use one and probably wouldn't accidentally saw my own limbs off.

The corridor curved, following the hull, probably twin to one on the other side of the ship. It emptied into a larger hangar, and I peeked in. The footsteps weren't behind me anymore, but it seemed almost too quiet. Had they seen *Lepton* appear? Did they know the AVDO was there, and had they seen it circling? They must know the circling thing would lead to a teleport if they'd been studying the AVDO to steal their tech.

An emergency locker stuck out, bright red against the dull grey hangar wall, and I hustled to it, my footsteps echoing in the cavernous hangar. I hauled open the locker and shoved aside the respirators, patch kits, and emergency rations. Buried at the bottom, the laser saw didn't budge the first time I tried to lift it. I hauled on it again, and it came free in a shower of emergency ration packs. *Yeah, baby.* Now we were in business. Finding the lab would be the trick. None of the rooms were marked, and they all seemed to be locked.

I crept to the corridor on the other side of the ship and snuck down, tapping each Door Open pad on my way, just in case, but none of them seemed to be activated. I turned away from a pad midway down the corridor. Two security guards gaped back at me. I booked it.

I exploded into the hangar and kept running to the very far end, heavy footsteps right behind me. Was I caught at a dead end? *Shit. There!* An open doorway! I ducked inside and smacked the door control to shut it behind me. The door slid shut as the security guards' pounding footsteps arrived. I activated the laser saw on the door seam, melting the seal to the door. Yeah, that sucker was not opening again.

I panted as the banging started on the outside of the hatch, the laser saw dangling from my limp hands. That door wasn't budging again, but what had I got myself into?

The ceiling was strung with pipes. A hiss of steam gushed from one to my left, and I jumped, the saw clattering to the floor. I was alone. I could come back for it once I figured out what I was dealing with.

Lights flickered from deeper inside the dim, portless cabin, and I edged toward them. Maybe the lighting would turn on when it sensed me in the room? A weight solidified in my gut. The lights wouldn't be from a console. They were like stars, without the flickering quality, glittering and changing.

Shit.

As my eyes adjusted to the gloom, a dim shape came into focus, a dark blob melted on the floor, rammed through with leads in at least three places. I dropped to my knees. This little one was maybe a quarter the size of Starblink. Bile rose in my throat, and I swallowed it back. A child? The AVDO was buckled to the deck with a steel band, cutting into its fragile membrane, matte welts on either side. It had been here a long time.

They'd caught and enslaved a young AVDO. This was their tele-portation tech, the miracle that Dr. Morbit had been working on for a century. They were using this person against their will. Was this the plan to scale their tech up? Were they trying to enslave more AVDO? Had I inadvertently killed their next victim when I landed on Starblink?

The glittering had continued unabated since I'd come in. This little person was trying to tell me something. I pulled out my screen. Maybe Miller's app could translate for me. I held it up, but the sparkles didn't translate. Maybe this AVDO was speaking a different language. Or it was suffering so egregiously that it couldn't even speak a coherent sentence. That or Miller's app was busted. It didn't really matter why; this wasn't helping. I stuffed my screen away. I had to get this little one out right now.

Black fluid oozed around the nearest lead, and when I touched it, the floor vibrated with what I could only assume was the AVDO's scream. Okay, no pulling out the leads. I'd have to cut them. I turned back toward my laser saw, but it was gone.

Someone was in here with me.

I took two steps back before I bumped into the wall, a hanging pipe brushing the top of my head.

Whoever it was had a laser saw. And I was fully aware of what it would do to flesh. I was totally going to end up like Starblink, bleeding out on the floor, only no one would record my last words, and my death wouldn't be an accident.

"It's not as bad as it looks, you know."

Rounding the other side of the confined AVDO was Dr. Grell Morbit, my laser saw slung over his shoulder.

Not as bad as it looks? Good, because it looks pretty bad.

"I'm sorry, Carolina, but I can't let you kill this one, too. You have no idea how long it takes to find one of these things, let alone catch it."

That's what he was worried about? Me killing part of his tech?

"Are you from Geometry? Be honest, now." He brandished the laser saw. He must have seen me turn pale. "Even if you are, I'm not going to use this on you." He chortled as though the idea was ridiculous when he was the one with a tortured and enslaved sentient being in his ship. "I just want to know what I'm dealing with, you know? Why you want to destroy my research so much."

"I'm not from Geometry. I never meant to kill Starblink."

"What's a Starblink? Oh, yes, the cute little name you gave to my new AVDO. You must be one of those people who name their probes. Does this have a name, too?" He waved the saw again, and I recoiled flat against the wall in spite of myself.

"You don't know that the AVDO are sentient?"

"You sound like mt old team. It took them much longer to confront me." He waved his free hand in front of his face, as if he could dispel their personhood. "Some folks think so, I suppose. But HGNT is more than happy to give me all the funding I want for my research as long as I take care of any infestations of the things I find. Since the Dyson ring debacle, they've been quite generous."

Infestations. My stomach threatened to turn itself inside out again, but I swallowed hard and kept my eyes on the genocidal alien with the laser saw. "And they get your teleportation breakthroughs for themselves." Patents on a torture device. That was the manual I'd found: a torture device that would pretty much let them print money. Charge folks for teleportation? Who wouldn't pay for that? As far as they were concerned, no one needed to know about the AVDO suffering for their convenience.

"Our team could crack this, you know. We're almost there."

Our team. He thought I would still have anything to do with this after finding out about... The AVDO before me shuddered, and a tremor shook up from the floor, resonating in my chest before dissipating.

"You know how I got here, Dr. Morbit?"

"Please, tell me. I'm very curious."

"An AVDO teleported me."

"That's wonderful, Carolina! We'll record your methods and see if we can recreate it at scale."

He wanted to know my methods?

"Tell me, how many leads did you use? I find the voltage has to be pumped fairly high before they slip into the transportation state."

I bent and wretched onto the floor. He was forcing this baby AVDO to teleport by pumping them full of electricity. I wiped my mouth with the back of my hand and stepped over my puke toward my mentor. My nails dug into my palms. What the hell was I going to do, punch him? *Fuck, yes.* I was going to punch this piece of shit. I pulled my elbow back, ready to slam my fist into his neck, but searing pain lanced my thigh, and I collapsed to the floor.

"Perhaps not," said Dr. Morbit, lowering the laser saw. "Don't worry, it's cauterized. You won't die, not from that one." He chuckled. "Did you think I was going to let you hit me? Switch on your brain, my dear!"

I gasped, my hand clamped to my burnt side, my jumpsuit sticking to the oozing flesh. It didn't hurt. *Shit.* It should hurt where I was touching it. *That's a fourth-degree burn.* Stars danced in front of my eyes. *I'm going into shock.*

The stars froze and then flickered the same pattern a few times. I probably *was* going into shock, but that was the little AVDO, not my vision. I focused on the pattern, grasped for my screen, but it slid through my burn-juice-covered fingers and cracked on the deck. Whatever. I could imagine: *Get up! You're the only way we're getting out of here!*

I slid to my knees. Fighting someone with a laser saw was not going to get me anywhere. What else could I do? Talk my way out of this?

"You want to know what I did to make an AVDO teleport me? What tech I used? I didn't make them. They asked for my help, Grell, to get their baby away from you."

"And you think I never spoke to them? You think I wasn't wide eyed and full of wonder back when I first discovered these creatures?" His heavy tread came closer. "I asked, I begged. They wouldn't get involved. Said we weren't worthy of teleportation. What was I supposed to do?" He kicked my knees out from under me, toppling me to my face on the steel floor plates. "My practical team thought that way, but I must say I had higher hopes for you. Alas, no. You ended up in that pocket just like them." His footsteps crossed behind me, and the hum of the saw had me flinching before I realized that he was opening the hatch I'd sealed.

Fuck! Fast! The security lackeys were out there. They'd be pissed I sealed them out. Grell might be willing to hurt me, but hurting me was their actual job description, and damned if I wanted to find out how good they were at it. I slid to my knees and crawled around the AVDO. At least back here, they'd have to find me first.

We were at the absolute tail end of the ship, so...that bulkhead was an outside one. My respirator still dangled around my neck. If I could break through it, cut through the AVDO's tethers and the leads skewered into its body, we'd be home free. Well, mostly home free. If it was still capable of teleporting, hopefully, it could get itself home. Especially with the help of the AVDO outside. As for me...

But that would still leave Grell. Still leave this bay, ready to entrap the next unsuspecting AVDO they hunted down. As long as the AVDO were living in secret, someone would try to use them. Teleportation had been humanity's dream since long before we took to the stars.

Not time to figure out what happens next. Just focus on not dying. A dial on the bulkhead behind me was marked with voltage numbers. Probably their torture-meter. The battery sat under it, the wires from the terminals looped over and around the AVDO and connected to six leads spearing into its flesh. I yanked the wires out of the battery. If I could break the metal band holding it down, the AVDO would be able to teleport away. But Grell had the laser cutter, and I wasn't getting through steel with my bare hands.

Grell's ponderous tread came closer. I wasn't getting the saw back without serious burns. I mean, more serious burns. I closed my eyes and took a breath. Steel. What can cut steel? Heat to melt, cold to shatter, acid to eat it away. I opened my eyes. The battery. I scrambled up and lifted the battery over my head as Grell came around the corner. He must have thought I was going to throw it at him, because he ducked back behind the AVDO, giving me the time I needed. I smashed the battery onto the floor next to the band holding the little AVDO, and it cracked, acid running out to pool at the soldering join. Grell popped back out and grinned. He probably thought I'd missed him.

The steel band popped and recoiled, whipping into the ceiling, leaving a dent the size of my head.

"Go!" I shouted to the AVDO. Which made no sense, because there was no way they could understand me. But they must have got the gist, because in a second, they were gone. Leaving me staring at a dumbfounded Grell and clutching my fourth-degree burn.

This place was just going to get another AVDO trapped if I didn't do something to smash it up. I had this moment while Grell was still trying to figure out what had happened. A hiss of steam obscured him, and I lurched up and snagged the hose, hanging all my weight on it until it stretched and snapped, spewing hot steam into the bay. If Grell had had fancy equipment and instruments, electronic devices and a carefully calibrated set-up, that might have wrecked it all beyond repair, but he didn't. This was just a torture chamber where he pumped electricity into a helpless being. I landed on the steel plating where the AVDO had been a moment before.

Now that the steam hose was depressurized, where was that hiss coming from? I looked up to where the belt had dented the ceiling. Except it wasn't a ceiling. It was the bay doors. One of which was now dented and had a ruptured seal. I fixed my respirator in place.

"You think you're getting those doors open, do you?" The steam had cleared, and Grell advanced on me, the laser saw still clutched in his hand. He laughed. "That hose was the pneumatics for the lift there, that opens the doors."

Fuuuuck.

"It won't take much longer until they open the doorway you sealed," he said.

And when they did, I'd lose all chance of escape. Avoiding a sedentary academic type like myself was one thing, trained security? Forget it. I breathed through my respirator. *Doors open. Doors open!*

A crack like that was sometimes enough to make a bay pop. That's why Sparks had been so panicked when our hatch had leaked back on *Conquest*. But these doors were reinforced, and they were holding. If they hadn't burst yet, they probably wouldn't. Not on their own.

But I still had a laser saw. Yes, it was in someone else's hand, and yes, I had already had the entire left half of my skin seared off by it, but it would do the job to pop the bay doors. Asking Grell nicely probably wouldn't do anything. Clearly, he had no shame. I had to hit him where it would hurt. His research.

I pushed aside my respirator. "Seems like HGNT was wasting their money."

His eyes narrowed. I had him hooked.

"You know this place is a glorified torture chamber, right? They gave you all the money you could want, and you built this. No fancy equipment, no technical breakthroughs, just kidnap a kid and make them do the work for you."

"I wouldn't expect you to understand."

"Now, I don't think this will happen, but I'm curious. If they gave out a Nobel Prize for teleportation, do you think they'd give it to you...or to the AVDO you enslaved?"

"You want to be on the side of the AVDO, Carolina? This is what I do to the AVDO."

The laser saw flicked on, and I crashed into Grell, throwing him backwards, his head cracking on a bulkhead, the beam of the laser saw searing into my shoulder, then higher.

Pop!

My ears rang. One of the bay doors banged open, all the air rushing out, sucking with it anything not tied down. The safety on the laser saw cut it off, but the heavy saw crushed my ribs, and I fumbled my respirator into place with numbing fingers as I blacked out.

Chapter 19

I woke up in bed. On *Lepton*. Yarrow held my hand.

"The AVDO teleported you back. I suppose they're aware that humans require protection from the vacuum of space."

I cleared my throat. "Okay, good." Someone had bandaged my burns. The AVDO Dr. Morbit had been using for his experiments was free. But we still needed to get everyone out of the pocket. I struggled to sit up. "Are we on the way to get supplies?"

"Supplies?"

"For Pardus." I swung my legs over the side of the bed, and Yarrow gripped my arm. "Don't tell me you forgot the plan."

"It's no longer necessary."

Shit, had the pocket collapsed? Were they all dead?

"It seems freeing the enslaved AVDO opened the pocket."

"Opened it?"

"For long enough that Pardus Station and everyone aboard emerged unscathed." He gestured to the viewport.

I levered myself up, and he helped me across to look out. Pardus Station was right there. We were docked to her. Smaller ships puttered by us.

"*Gracious* and *Conquest*?"

Yarrow shook his head. "There was no time, and they were too badly damaged."

I hobbled back to the bed, my head spinning much less now.

Yarrow kept on with his update. "Supplies have been ordered from several nearby outposts. The AVDO have disappeared."

I sat back on the bed. Pardus Station. Undisappeared. The AVDO, out of HGNT's clutches, at least for now. Then my work here was done.

Yarrow watched me.

"You don't have to stay here anymore. I'm really fine."

"We're all waiting for you so we can celebrate. Come find us in the atrium when you're ready."

I nodded. No way was I going to sit there with everyone talking behind their hands and pretending to thank me, when it was researchers like me who had done this in the first place. Rylka had made it very clear that she was not a fan, and Fiona and Sparks wouldn't thank me for destroying their ships.

Yarrow gave me a soft kiss and left me alone. As soon as the door closed, I pulled out my duffle and packed in whatever shit I could find lying around. Lancaster wouldn't want my toothbrush and stuff when Yarrow returned *Lepton* to him.

I hauled it all out to the galley and grabbed some butter chicken packs for the road. The stairs to the bridge were a little harder to manage, so I left my duffle on the floor and clutched the handrail as I went up one step at a time. I made my call, and within minutes, I'd been granted the use of a little hopper that would get me back to Earth in one piece.

I had enough food for the trip, and the hopper would have everything else I needed. I thumped back down the stairs. I wouldn't be able to stop in case HGNT still had it out for me—

"Where are you going?" Fiona leaned against the frame of the airlock.

I rummaged in my bag. "Just getting out of your hair. Pardus Station is back where it belongs, which means we're not trapped here anymore."

"That doesn't answer my question."

"What?"

"Where are you going, Carolina? Away from here is not a destination."

"I'm sure that, after what I pulled, no one wants me around. I'll figure out where I'm going once I'm off. I can always go crash at my parents' place." I zipped my bag and slung it on my good shoulder. Only one problem.

Fiona was blocking the doorway.

She stared me down, arms crossed and jaw set. "You're just going to disappear? That's your plan?"

I nodded. Everyone would be glad to get back to their normal lives after I'd barrelled through and fucked everything up.

Fiona's screen chimed, and I used her distraction to duck by her. She might think that everyone loved me, but that was just the high from our success talking. Once everything had a chance to sink in, everyone would realize that I was more of an annoyance than anything.

The ship I'd been assigned was sitting at the gate, as promised. But it was already occupied by someone big. And blue.

"Yarrow…" I breathed, but he was already turning.

"You thought to abandon me?" As usual, it was impossible to read his expression. "I'm finding it exceedingly difficult to express my anguish at the thought, Carolina."

"You have other people now, Yarrow. You don't have to cling to me like a lifeboat."

"I am aware that we have found a community that has embraced us."

I shook my head, and my throat closed. They'd embraced me because I'd provided a route to get them out of the pocket, that was all. None of them would want me around now that that was done, and I couldn't ask Yarrow to come along with me. Not now that he'd settled in with everyone so well.

Yarrow's screen chimed, and he read something off it and then stepped off my ship. I couldn't bring myself to look at him as I slammed the airlock door in his face. Leaving him would hurt at first, but he'd realize that he could have pretty much whoever he wanted on Pardus. He was a hero.

I slammed my pack into the narrow bunk and threw myself into the pilot's seat, swiping the tears from my eyes.

"Dawn requesting voyage clearance," I croaked into the communicator.

"Denied." I could swear that was...

"Miller, aren't you done playing with me yet? I won't bother you again, I promise."

"I've heard that before, Ms. Dawn. I can't allow you clearance to disappear."

The communicator crackled.

"Come on, Captain. Did you really think we'd just let you take off?"

"Goddamn it, Sparks! Haven't I caused you enough trouble?"

"Damn right, you have. I've never had a Captain so reckless. Getting us chased by annoying, if handsome, government officials, using my workbench without permission—yes, I know about that—getting me stuck in a pocket universe. And destroying my *Conquest*."

So he was keeping me here to chew me out. Perfect. "Yes, I'm sorry. I put you in danger. I'll pay you back for your ship, I swear. Can I go now?"

"Sorry? The fuck should you be sorry? You got me to talk to Harlan after seven years. You let me be part of taking down a corporate genocide campaign. You can shove sorry up your—"

"As Clark said, Ms. Dawn. I can't let you disappear. You're upset, and I think it would behoove you to delay your voyage until you're thinking more clearly. Fiona told us you have nowhere to go. So stay."

Sparks's quiet voice crackled. "I've granted your ship clearance, Carolina. If you want to run, you run. I know how it is. Just...turn around again before you go too far."

"Let me know if you need help with your résumé," said my dad.

They were on their way out, because of course they were. I'd set up in the basement, my old room having long since been turned into an office. By now, my burns were almost healed, with regular treatments. My parents had insisted on taking me to get them treated to prevent scarring. God forbid their daughter have scars.

Yarrow had called so many times, I'd blocked his number, and I guess he told the others I didn't want to be bothered, because I hadn't heard from them in weeks. I wrapped my robe tighter around myself and stepped onto the porch to wave goodbye. Everything in this neighbourhood was designed to be retro, the houses all eerily similar, the yards, each with their single misshapen tree.

And an old beat-up van parked in front of our house? My father was already storming down the driveway toward it, trying to get it to move out of the way. I hugged myself and hung back in the doorway.

The last thing I needed was for strangers to see me in my robe. The far-side sliding door rumbled open, and a couple folks walked around the back of the van. One of whom was blue.

Yarrow had come to my parents' house? *Oh shit.* I was in my robe. I stumbled inside and slammed the front door. A quick dash down the stairs, and I had to decide what to put on my body. Hopefully, something clean...relatively clean, anyway. I scrounged some clothes off the floor and started back up the stairs as the tromping of a dozen shoes echoed overhead.

My parents had invited them in?

"Come out, Carolina! I fucking know you're in here!" Pauli? "If you thought you could just leave us behind, then you're as stupid as Rylka said you were!"

"Great, Pauli. Wonderful. She's extremely likely to come out now that you've insulted her." Miller?

"Yeah, good going, pintsize. Now she'll never come out." Sparks?

"All of you, hush. You're being childish. Mr. and Mrs. Dawn, you have a lovely home. Thanks so much for inviting us in." Fiona.

Janella was muttering something about how she didn't even want to come as I poked my head through the doorway at the top of the stairs.

Bez and Frall were in the hallway with Trix.

"You disappeared before your party, so we've brought it to you." Frall held up a lopsided banner and Bez a case of starshine.

Trix waved. "I brought my cards. Don't worry. You'll get a way better reading this time. Now that I know the whole story, I can see what the cards were trying to say last time."

My parents stood awkwardly in the entryway. "Who are your friends?" said my mum.

"And why are they in my house?" my dad added.

"They're, um, we worked together." I glanced around at them all. "And I don't know why they're here."

Pauli looked my parents up and down, scowled, and retreated to the kitchen, loudly opening and shutting every cupboard in the place, presumably hunting for party snacks she wouldn't find. My parents weren't party snack people.

Frall and Bez retreated to the living room to hang their banner. Yarrow put his arm around me.

"And who is this...person...touching my daughter?" said my dad.

What the actual fuck? Who says something like that? My father, apparently. "This is Yarrow."

"Pleased to meet you." Yarrow waved.

My parents didn't return the gesture.

"You stopped taking my calls. I was very concerned about you."

"I'm sure you've heard that everyone knows Pardus is back." Fiona stood shoulder to shoulder with Yarrow, her arms crossed.

"That backwater station no one had heard of before they started crying victim?" scoffed my dad.

"So all those folks are safe now, Captain. Looking to get a hefty payout from HGNT for negligence as well."

"They probably should have known what they signed on for. Those people never read their contracts." My own father.

"As it turns out, their contract contained a clause assuring them their safety would be prioritized. Risky untried teleportation experiments do not fall under that umbrella." Miller stepped up on my other side, Sparks flanking him.

Yarrow only had eyes for me. "Will you come with us, Carolina? How are your injuries? Can you travel?"

Everyone looked at me.

Pauli sauntered back in, crunching a plain chip—the only kind my parents bought. "If we're doing the dramatic family confrontation thing, can I at least sit the fuck down first?"

We filed silently into the front room, Frall and Bez having hung their banner—*Thank you CarolinNA*—possibly made by the children of Pardus?

My parents sat on the couch, and I took the wingback chair by the window, Yarrow standing beside me. Trix curled on the rug and dealt her cards onto the coffee table. Sparks sat across from me, and Miller sat *on the floor* at his feet? Never in my wildest dream did Miller sit on the floor. Not that there were enough chairs for everyone.

My mom broke the painfully awkward silence. "Are you aware that Carolina is unemployed? Unemployable? After everything all of you dragged her into, she was fired from the job we found for her, offended her supervisor so egregiously that he got rid of her twice, and she went on the run. Oh, yes, you likely do since you all worked with her." She turned to me. "We'll find her a new position. Somewhere nice. Maybe here on Earth."

No one seemed to know what to say to that. They weren't leaping to my defence because there was no defence. It was all true. Except who did the dragging.

Tears overflowed my eyes and dripped down my neck, and I slumped back in my chair. Yarrow knelt before me, wrapping me in all of his arms, pulling me to his chest.

His murmur was just for us. "If you could sense my emotions, you would know that what I feel for you is unlike anyone else. I lost my family, my home. No one can sense my emotions, no one even cares to try. Except for you."

"That's not true," I croaked, rubbing my teary face on Yarrow's soft shirt. "Everyone likes you."

His chuckle reverberated through his chest. "Everyone likes you, too."

"They only like me because they don't really know me..." Was this how Yarrow felt as well? People liked him, but they didn't really know him...except for me?

The tension in my shoulders melted away, and I clung to Yarrow. These people cared enough to ambush me and bring me a party. They really thought that what I'd done was...good? That *I* was good.

Yarrow pulled back, but I kept hold of his hand. "This is Yarrow. My boyfriend."

My mom's mouth opened and closed, and my dad huffed and puffed.

"That's not acceptable, Carolina."

"Now this sounds like Kronenberg family reunion," said Pauli around a mouthful of chips. "I highly recommend leaving forever. It's working at a ten out of ten for me."

Yarrow tried to pull away, but I held on and turned to him. "Can I really come with you? You...don't mind?"

"No, Carolina, I don't mind," he said, smiling softly down at me. "Would I have come here if I minded?"

"Maybe you just wanted to see Earth in the spring?"

"Earth is beautiful in the spring. But I came for something even more beautiful."

Ohmygod, he did not just say that to me! I was so blushing. "I didn't know you flirted."

"I've been learning."

"I like it." I tilted my face up, just for a quick little kiss, and my mum cleared her throat. I pulled back. "Just let me get my stuff."

"Get your stuff for what, Carolina?" said my dad.

I heaved a sigh and stood before my parents. "You don't want me here, which I understand. I'm the daughter who disgraced you, ruined your reputation, lost the job you got me...I get it. Don't worry, I'm going."

"Do you even know who this alien is?" His eyes narrowed on Yarrow.

"She doesn't," said Yarrow.

I twisted to look up at him. *What?*

"Yarrow from Yrk'uth. Ran away and destroyed his planet's future."

That...couldn't be true. Yarrow would never do something like that. He was beyond loyal. But he wasn't denying it. And he had once told me that people had possibly died because of something that he'd done, a choice that he'd made.

Everyone else was watching me. They already knew. And yet here they all were with him. There must be another side to the story. I stood next to Yarrow.

"Why did you leave?"

"They wished for me to join the *raglu-thmal*. The...collective consciousness of the planet. I declined. There was no one to take my place, but still even knowing that, I refused. Without a full complement, the planet could have become unstable." He shrugged helplessly. "I will never know. No communications are allowed in or out of Yrk'uth."

He'd refused to give up his entire being to save his people from a possibly turbulent future. But it sounded as if folks weren't lining up to take on the job, either. He'd made his choice and been exiled, abandoned by his own people, an entire planet.

"You see? You won't be going with him." My dad was still talking.

Yarrow studied the wingback's upholstery.

"Actually, I will be."

Yarrow's gaze snapped to me.

"Nothing you could say would change how I feel about you. I know you, Yarrow."

"My daughter will not be seen with—"

I turned on him. "Finish that sentence and I'll never be seen with *you* again."

He recoiled, and his face hardened. "We'll talk about this another time."

"We absolutely won't."

"I see you've chosen a"—his nostrils flared—"an alien over your family." He checked his watch and looked at my mom. "We're going to be late."

Their daughter was being thrown a hero's party, was introducing them to her friends, her boyfriend, and they were worried that people might talk if they were late to whatever they were going to. It didn't actually matter what I did, did it? They were never going to care about me. They were never going to think I was great, to accept me the way...the way family did. The way all these folks did.

I forced a smile and turned to my parents. "You go ahead. We're leaving anyway."

Yarrow and I finally had our own room after travelling as a mob from Earth.

I sat awkwardly on the bed. "Did you really mean it?"

"Mean what, Carolina?"

"That I'm special to you?" My nails were all bitten off after so long living with my parents. I couldn't even get a corner up to nibble.

"More than anything."

"I'm not just a convenient human who—"

"No." He knelt in front of me and brushed my hair back from my face. When had he started doing that? His people didn't have hair. His kiss stopped my whirling thought spiral. "I missed you very much, Carolina."

"I missed you too," I managed between kisses, finally cracking up.

"You introduced me to your parents as your boyfriend. I understand that has significance in human culture."

"Oh, yeah. I mean, I know we never talked about it. If you don't want—"

"I do. Very much." He sat beside me and pulled me into his lap. "Your injuries?"

I straddled him. "Pretty much healed. They don't hurt, at least."

"I'm glad," he said. "Even when I do this?" He gripped my hips firmly, sending a bolt of pleasure through my belly and lower.

"Definitely doesn't hurt."

Soon, we had each other's clothes off, and Yarrow was kneeling between my thighs. All it took was a playful stroke up his antenna to have his face buried in my pussy, lapping and kissing me as if he were savouring his favourite food after being on rations for a month.

"Both," he gasped.

I shook my head in confusion.

"Both antennae."

He'd told me that both was too overwhelming for him. "Are you sure?"

"Please, give me this."

I swallowed hard and nodded. I carefully brought both hands to the base of his antennae and traced my fingers around them. He groaned against me, and his fingers dug more firmly into my hips. Stroking my fingertips gently up the stalks of both antennae elicited another groan, and Yarrow speared me with two fingers. My back arched, and I instinctively gripped Yarrow's antennae, hard. He let out a growl unlike anything I'd ever heard, human or otherwise.

"Sorry, I didn't mean—"

He sucked my clit firmly, and I spasmed and crested. He gave me one last lick and eased his fingers out before wrapping his arms around me and moving my boneless body fully onto the bed. He settled over me, his hips cradled between my thighs, four elbows pressing into the mattress, caging my entire torso.

"If you wish to modify positions, simply inform me." His cock throbbed rhythmically against my thigh.

"Do you want me to...touch your antennae again? Was that okay?"

He chuckled. "Yes, it was *okay*. It was extremely pleasurable." His cock gave a shudder. "I would very much like it if you gripped my antennae...firmly."

"Both?" I didn't want to overstep. Not now that he was asking for something.

His hips jerked, and our noises twined together at the friction. "Yes, please."

I did as he asked, making him slide against me again. With him pressing me into the bed like this, he could do whatever he liked—that was always true, but it wasn't always quite so obvious. I shivered, and my hips bucked up to meet his.

He froze. "Is this position too...constricting?"

"What? No, it's"—I shivered again—"possessive."

"Which is a positive element?"

"Yes, absolutely."

"For a moment, I sensed an...uncertainty."

"I'm very certain."

"Carolina..."

I could have grabbed his antennae again, made him forget what he'd sensed in me, but Yarrow was going to find out about this feeling sooner or later, it was going to come up again. "You're not ashamed to claim me."

"Ashamed?" Maybe the translation wasn't clear.

"Embarrassed to associate with me."

Yarrow grumbled in his chest. "I understand the concepts, I am baffled by the implications. And yet, there is truth to your words." He slowly slid his length against me. "I want to claim you."

I wriggled in the cage of his arms and slid my hands up to circle his antennae. After that, we were both lost as he slid into me and did as he desired, something I'd never expected or realized I needed from him. He didn't just want me to take my pleasure, he wanted me.

When I gathered my courage and gripped his antennae firmly in both hands, Yarrow let out that feral sound again and snaked a hand down to my clit, and another under my hips. The perfect angle and his circling fingers brought me to the edge, but his words tipped me over:

"I would claim you a thousand times over, Carolina. I would tell the universe you're mine, if you let me."

A fresh wave of pleasure shook my body. All my loneliness, all my insecurity, my carefully constructed walls, all washed away with my orgasm, and when the ripples of pleasure finally subsided, a stillness filled my centre, like glowing sea glass, tossed by the waves, smoothed over and over by the battering sand until it lands safely on the beach to be gathered up and treasured.

Thanks so much for reading *Project Pardus*! If you liked it, please leave a review on your platform of choice. Even a line or two is very helpful for other readers!

If you want to be the first to hear about new releases, consider joining my newsletter at join.elizabethshearly.ca.

Dear Lovely Reader

Project Pardus was hard for me to write in so many ways. It started as a fun break novella between entries in the Weary Warrior Women series. That was in September 2023. By the end of October, I realized I was no longer writing a lighthearted romantic romp. This book had teeth. It was going to be about a genocide, and as you know, it's not a novella.

Sci fi and fantasy have been, since their inception, pathways for the author to explore and excise thoughts and feelings about the state and trajectory of the world. Carolina didn't solve the Galaxy's problems, not even close. She didn't even take down the evil corporation HGNT. But she refused to participate in a system that was kidnapping, torturing, and exterminating sentient beings.

When I started writing *Project Pardus*, I had no plan, no outline, just a vague image of a space station disappearing mysteriously. That's the other reason it took so long to finally wind its way to you. I went off on tangents, had about five different point of view characters, and ended up cutting a quarter of the book and rewriting it. Abandoning the safety net of the outline, of course, meant that I was free of its constraints as well, and I discovered things about my process that I can use to loosen up the rigid parts of my system. And some of the deleted scenes will make their way into the world as bonus scenes one of these days, especially the one between Harlan and Clark, where they discuss Clark's "glowering."

Carolina, like most of my characters, was a mystery to me when I started writing. As I got to know her better, I realized that she was falling for a trap: she thought her worth was determined by the people around her, their attitude toward her, and their approval of her. Not to say that this changes much by the end of the book, but she has learned, at least, to be selective about who she gifts with the power to influence her. Especially as a white woman under patriarchal white supremacy, the voices telling us to fulfill our role and gain status by subsuming our very selves are legion. Those uplifting us and believing in us as full people are few, but drawing close to them so they echo the loudest in our lives is well worth the effort.

As I write this, it's April 2025, and the real-life kidnap, torture, and extermination of humans has not abated; if anything, it has spiked. We are all going to need to refuse to participate in these systems, build something new outside of them, and stop grasping for status within them if we want them to wither and die.

I hope *Project Pardus* meant something to you, as it means so much to me. <3

Looking forward to our next adventure,

E. F. Shearly

Elizabeth F. Shearly

Endless Sea of Stars

The ground shakes under Jeanie's feet, and she staggers across the pristine corridor. Her blowtorch digs into her hip when she collides with the wall. The blaring alarm pounds through her head. We get it, the moon is imploding! She's still far away from the ship that's her only escape from the disintegrating base. Too far away.

Years ago, Jeanie and Liam thought the isolated moon base would be a middle ground between her spacefaring lifestyle and his need for the stability of a space station. It didn't take long to realize that the life they chose was making both of them miserable.

But now it's literally falling apart around them, with no escape in sight. No escape but one slim chance they have no choice but to take. It may not be comfortable or pretty, but it just might keep them alive long enough to save their marriage.

Also By Elizabeth F. Shearly

Endless Sea Of Stars
Dread Spring
Keep the Good Parts
Project Pardus

Second Acts of Weary Warrior Women

The Swordswoman and the Vampire
To Break A Dragon Bond
A Pentagram Of Candles and Spectres
Her Castle, Her Howl, Her Pack
The King's Pixie Seer

About The Author

Elizabeth F. Shearly writes science fiction and fantasy tales, from flash fiction to novels and everything in between. She holds a B.Sc. in physics, and you'll find plenty of science in her science fiction, though the fiction always takes precedence. No matter what she writes about—spaceships or magic, walking cities or medieval castles—romance always finds a way to blossom, whether as the main plot or as a background story.

When she's not watching characters play-act in her head, you can find her relaxing on the couch with her two cats, playing a video game or knitting a sweater.

patreon.com/ElizabethFShearly

instagram.com/ElizabethFShearly

bookbub.com/authors/elizabeth-f-shearly

facebook.com/ElizabethFShearly/

goodreads.com/elizabethfshearly